CHANGES

by

Linda Sawley

Linda Sawley

**Linric Publishing
England**

Published in 2005 by LinRic Publishing
18 Victoria Lodge
READ, Lancs
BB12 7SZ

British Cataloguing in publication data
Sawley, Linda
Changes
I. Title
Classification: Historical Romantic Fiction

ISBN 0 – 9534329 – 6 - 3

Cover design by Nikki Moore, Design Department, Printing Services, University of Central Lancashire

Printed by Printing Services, University of Central Lancashire, Preston, Lancs

Photograph on front cover by kind permission of and © to The National Trust Photographic Library/Andreas Von Einsiedel

Acknowledgements

To Santa Montefiore for her kindness and encouragement.

To my brother-in-law Edward Habiak for proof reading and comments!

To my sister Cynthia I'Anson for pointing something out to me that I hadn't noticed – and I wrote it!

To Jackie Hindle, my local librarian who always supports me and finds me competitions to enter!

To Denise Slights, for providing a peaceful haven for me to write, whilst keeping Jim busy fishing.

To Nikki Moore for the cover design and her advice

To the David St John Thomas Charitable Trust for inspiring me to continue writing.

By the same author

<u>Non-fiction</u>

Everyone Else's Children
(Autobiography)

<u>Fiction</u>

A Ring in Time

The Key

This book is dedicated to
Anne Wareing
who continues to believe in me.

It is also in memory of
Philip Hanson
October 1986 to July 2004

Chapter 1

The night was dark outside but Jenny Marshall sat in her rocking chair looking out, the curtains still wide open. She sighed as she rocked, holding the arms of the chair tightly in her grip.

The house was quiet, the children were in their beds and the servants had retired for the night. The gas lamps in the attractive lounge were burning low in their mantles; Jenny had told the maid to leave them that way.

She sighed again, more deeply this time. I shouldn't be sighing like this, she thought to herself, I have so much to be grateful for.

Tomorrow, March 27th 1895 was her thirtieth birthday. To be more precise, it was the date that she always used as her birthday. The Clitheroe workhouse in Lancashire where she had lived as a child gave her that date as her birthday. Even the year wasn't necessarily the correct one, but the nearest guess to her approximate size when she was unceremoniously dumped on the workhouse step. Only her name and the fact that her mother was unwed was on the scrap of paper fastened to her blanket. The workhouse had also given her the surname of Mitchell, which she had kept until her marriage just before the Christmas of 1886.

So much had happened in her life since the day she was abandoned in the workhouse. Both good and bad. As a teenager she had been taken to a large house, Ormerod Hall, at the top of Manchester Road in nearby Burnley, as a scullery maid.

The biggest change that had happened to her was when she inherited a gown shop at the age of 18. She had no idea who had bequeathed it to her at the time and was not allowed to go on to the fourth floor, which was at the top of the shop, for three years, neither was she allowed to know who her benefactor was.

It had all been overwhelming at the time, but Jenny rose to the challenge. The previous manager, called Mrs Bruce, had run away the night before Jenny took over her shop. Along with her went most of the stock and a great deal of money that should have been in the bank.

In three years, Jenny had managed to turn the shop round from being a failure to being the most successful gown shop in Clitheroe. She had also managed to rescue her friends Susy and Marian from the workhouse and give them jobs in her shop.

Those three years had not been easy. But Jenny and her friends had worked hard. Having lived in a large house as a servant, Jenny understood how the gentry lived and dressed and behaved. They had also insisted that she spoke correctly at Ormerod Hall, so that gave her an advantage when she dealt with the middle and upper classes.

Jenny's eyes strayed to the piano that was in the corner of the room. On top of the piano was a photograph taken in a picture booth at the seaside. Jenny was stood to attention behind her beloved Jonny, who was seated in a chair. The three children were kneeling at his feet, leaning on to his knees.

Her eyes started to fill as she looked at the photograph. Oh how she missed her husband. Only weeks after the photograph had been taken, a horse had killed Jonny. He had been rescuing a child who was about to be trampled by the horse.

It had taken Jenny many weeks to even get out of bed after this but eventually, she had got back into her normal routine. Work and the children had helped to keep her sane.

She sighed again. How she missed Jonny, especially in the evenings. During the day, the children and her work kept her busy. Once the children were all off to school, Jenny would go into her large shop on Castle Street and catch up with her business. She also had her late husband's business to oversee. Jonny had set up his own transport and delivery company. After his death, she had offered to sell the business to his young work colleague, Robert, but he declined. He felt that he was too young and inexperienced to take over the business, but over the last two years, Robert had slowly taken over the reins and Jenny hoped that soon he would ask to buy the concern from her.

Jenny had another interest; she had bought some derelict, slum properties and refurbished them to a much higher standard, but not increased the rent. The property was in the Bawdlands area of the town, down Parson Lane, and she now had a waiting list to rent one of her properties. It brought in a small but steady income.

Yes, she was very busy, but it didn't fill the ache in her heart from the loss of her husband. The evenings were the worst because once the children were in bed, and the staff had retired; she had no adult conversation. No one to tell her hopes and dreams to. No one to discuss whether something was viable. Mind you, Jonny had often laughed at her high-flown ideas and dreams. He couldn't understand the drive that made her want to be even more successful than she already was. She was not short of money: indeed, she was very rich. But something did drive her. She was always looking round for new ideas. Trying to make sure that she was ahead of her competitors and keeping her customers satisfied at all times. Part of the driving force was that she never wanted to be poor and helpless again, nor her friends and relatives.

Despite this, she was still a good employer. She knew the uncertainty that many people had when they lived at the whim of their employer. She had heard tales when she herself had lived in the workhouse. Whole families thrown out of work and out of their houses when a mill closed down, or where the father was a union agitator.

No, she kept her staff in secure employment and was respected for it, both by the staff and also in the town. A lot of her staff had come from the same Clitheroe workhouse where she had lived. She ran a bonus system for the staff similar to the Co-operative movement that had started in Rochdale. They received a percentage of the sales that the shop made, and this was shared equally amongst them.

Jenny looked at the clock. It was almost twelve of the clock. She must get to bed, or she would be tired in the morning. Turning the gaslights down, Jenny took a candle and made her way slowly up to bed. Roger, her manservant had locked the house before he and his wife Maggie had gone to bed. The rest of the house was in darkness.

She went into the twins' bedroom first. They were nearly eight years old but still shared a bedroom, even though there were plenty spare for them to have one each. They fought like cat and dog during the day, but always wanted to share the bed at night. As usual, they were curled around each other, like two spoons. Ben was on the outside, with his arms encircling Rachel, as if protecting her.

Jenny always smiled to see them so peaceful like this, and wished that they could be like this whilst they were awake. Rachel was the dominant twin: always bossing Ben and Ellen around. Rachel would never need protecting, thought Jenny wryly.

Next, Jenny went into Ellen's bedroom. Ellen was flat on her back, her bedclothes kicked off, her head turned to the side and her arm twisted around her head. She always slept this way, as had her father before her. It used to amuse Jenny and Jonny to see her asleep just like him. Now it brought a lump into Jenny's throat as it reminded her again of her loss. It was odd that the twins didn't adapt this posture, but then neither did Susy, Jonny's sister.

Susy had been her best friend in the workhouse; they arrived shortly after each other and their birthdays were only ten days apart. Later, a younger girl called Marian, whom Jenny had befriended, had joined them. The three had been inseparable and all came to work in the shop as soon as Jenny could afford to employ them.

Happy days, thought Jenny, reliving those early times in the shop. Nowadays, there was so many staff that she could hardly remember some of their names. She went into the bathroom and then to her own bedroom. Putting the candle on the bedside table, Jenny climbed into bed, blew out the candle and was soon asleep.

Chapter 2

'Mummy, mummy, wake up, Happy Birthday,' screeched Ellen early next morning, dragging Jenny fully awake within seconds. Ben and Rachel followed Ellen.

'It is not fair, mummy, I am the oldest, I should have been the first to waken you today. Scold Ellen, please,' said Rachel in a whiny voice.

'You are only the oldest by about ten minutes Rachel,' laughed Jenny, 'Ben wasn't far behind you. It doesn't matter who wakes me first, I am now fully awake, thank you. And thank you for your wishes.'

'Come down to breakfast, mummy, Cook has made your favourite breakfast and we are going to help her bring it into the dining room,' urged Ellen.

'Just let me get dressed then, children, and then I will be downstairs quickly.'

The children clattered down the stairs, arguing and shouting as they went. Jenny laughed to herself as she quickly got washed and dressed and followed the children into the dining room. It was obvious that the children were up to mischief as they were suppressing giggles throughout the meal.

'Have you finished mummy?' asked Rachel.

'Yes, thank you,' she replied.

'Then we will bring your birthday present.' More giggles ensued as Rachel left the room, but the other two conspirators said nothing, merely smiling at Jenny. Rachel returned with a large basket, similar to the one that Maggie or Cook took shopping when they went to the market. Her eldest daughter was carrying the basket very carefully and Jenny noticed a large bow had been tied lopsidedly on the handle of the basket.

'Here you are then mummy. Here is your very special present,' said Rachel all full of smiles.

'Why thank you, it is a lovely basket. Just what I need.' The children all collapsed into fits of giggles. Suddenly, something moved inside the basket. Jenny opened the lid of the basket and looked inside. There inside was a small scruffy puppy, looking very frightened.

'Rachel, where have you got this puppy from?' asked Jenny crossly. 'Do you know where it has been? It looks pretty mangy to me.'

'Some big boys were going to drown it and I scared them off,' said Rachel earnestly. 'You have always told us to look after small things that couldn't look after themselves.'

There was a silence in the room, broken only by Ellen beginning to cry. Jenny sighed. This had been a clever bit of chicanery by the children. They had been asking for a puppy for some time, but Jenny had always managed to find a reason not to have one. They had bought a puppy when she and Jonny had first moved to the large newly built house, but it had died soon afterwards. Part of the reason for not having another one was because the children had been so distressed when it died.

Jenny looked at the hopeful faces of her children, and felt a surge of love, even though she was very cross at the way that they had tricked her into getting a puppy. A special birthday present, indeed.

'Who is going to take it for walks and look after it, if we keep it?' Three little voices answered 'me' in unison.

'Alright. We will keep it, but the first sign that you are leaving the care of the puppy to Maggie or Megan and I will give the puppy away. Do you understand me?' Three little heads solemnly nodded their assent. Jenny smiled at the children.

'What are we going to call it then?'

'We thought that we would let you chose the name, mummy,' said Rachel smoothly. Oh the guile of that innocent face, thought Jenny to herself. She was pretty sure that Rachel had planned the whole thing.

'Then we will call it Patch, because he has a patch over his left eye.'

'Thanks mummy,' screamed Ellen, picking Patch up and nearly strangling him.

'Take care, or you won't have a puppy at all. Now put him down. We will have to sort out some bedding for him and find a place for him to sleep.'

'Can we take it in turn to have him in our bedrooms, mummy?' asked Ben.

'That is not fair,' retorted Ellen. 'You two will have more turns than me, 'cos you will keep him two nights in your rooms, 'cos there is two of you.'

Jenny interrupted the argument that she knew would ensue.

'No-one is having Patch in their bedroom. He will sleep in a kennel in the garden or in the washhouse when it is bad weather. Now get ready for school and you can ask Maggie if she will take you into town after school to buy some things for the puppy.'

'Thank you mummy,' chorused the children, in full accord for once, as they ran off upstairs. Jenny shook her head in amusement. But she had to hurry as she had a busy day ahead of her, too. No rest for the shopkeeper, even if it was her 30th birthday.

After the children had left the house, Jenny got herself ready and asked Roger to drive her to the shop in the carriage. Going into the shop, she thought that all the staff were smiling at her broadly, but no one said anything to her, beyond 'good morning', so Jenny thought nothing of it.

She made her way into the kitchens to check that there had been a delivery from Crabtree's the bakery further down the road. Jenny told the staff that there would be a short meeting at the close of the day, but that they would shut the shop a little early for this special meeting.

The busy routine of the shop took over and Jenny made sure that she walked around the shop to talk to each head of department, if not every member of staff.

Around three of the clock, Jenny went into the kitchen to check on the progress of the surprise, which she had prepared for her staff. She had laid on a sumptuous banquet for them all in honour of her birthday.

Half an hour before the usual closing time, she asked the staff to close the shop and gather in the dining room. She got there before them and could see that they were all mystified by the layout in the dining room. The tables had been pushed to one side, and were covered with crisp white tablecloths. It was obvious that there was something under the tablecloths. Jenny smiled at everyone as they came in and then moved to the front of the tables.

'I just wanted to thank you all for your hard work, and although you don't know it, today is my birthday, so I have prepared a little meal for you all to share. Please remove the covers, Mrs Marshall,' she said to her mother-in law, who helped out in the kitchens.

Jenny helped Mrs Marshall remove the covers and was surprised to see her friend Marian standing next to her, in front of all the staff.

'On behalf of all the staff,' said Marian, 'I would like to present you with a small token of appreciation on your birthday, Jenny.' Now it was Jenny who looked amazed. They had turned the tables on her. She wanted to give them a surprise and they had surprised her. It was like the children with the puppy all over again.

'Why thank you,' replied Jenny, 'you shouldn't have bought me a gift. How did you know it was my birthday?'

'That was easy,' replied Sarah, her first member of staff that she had inherited with the shop. 'With your two best friends and your mother-in-law all working here, it was easy to know about it. Do open your gift.'

Jenny looked at the small, neatly wrapped gift. She carefully removed the outer packaging. It was a solid gold bracelet that had delicate scrolling on. Jenny recognised the scrolling; it was the same as that on the locket that she had received from Mr Duxbury, the father of the first bride whose wedding she had arranged.

'Why, it matches my locket. How did you manage to get a bracelet to match?'

'It did take some effort,' laughed Marian Williams. 'First we had to ask Mr Duxbury where he had bought it. Then we discovered that it was from Nettleton's jewellers next door. So it was easier after that. We asked Mr Nettleton if he could find a bracelet to match. But we were surprised when he managed to get the exact match.'

'Thank you. All of you,' said Jenny with a catch in her voice. 'It means so much to me. The locket was a gift from the father of the bride at my first successful wedding. And now my matching bracelet is a present from all my friends. I couldn't have thought of anything better myself. Now please, all get something to eat and enjoy yourselves.'

The staff needed no second invitation, all flocking to the tables laden with food, and exclaiming over their favourite foods. Jenny had heard the door open whilst she was talking, and looked to see that Mr Nettleton, the jeweller himself had come into the room. She thanked him for his work in matching the bracelet to her locket.

Mr Nettleton had become an integral part of her business. As the owner of the shop next door, he was able to come in and advise customers who were planning a wedding. He would bring a selection of rings into Jenny's shop, within an appropriate price range, so that the customer could take their time choosing the wedding or engagement ring plus gifts for their bridesmaids and flower girls.

Indeed, Jenny had a little room set up especially for this purpose. The staff had nicknamed it 'the jewellery room'. It worked perfectly and was mutually convenient for each of them. As brides-to-be came in to purchase a ring, Mr Nettleton would give them a card from Mitchell's Modes to offer their services as wedding planners and vice versa.

Behind the jeweller was Mr Briggs. He had been her advisor and solicitor from the first day of her inheritance. He was an important part of her life and she thought a great deal of him. He too, was bearing a gift, a large posy of flowers, which he presented to Jenny.

Whilst she was thanking him, Mr and Mrs Canning came into the room. They had also been important in helping her start her business. Mr Canning owned the local printers and he and his wife had given her a lot of advice when she needed help with advertising and signage, not to mention a credit arrangement. Indeed, Mr Canning had ordered two gowns for his wife in lieu of payment for his services. In that way, Jenny was able to have all her shop bags, hatboxes, signs and leaflets done in the same colour, without having to make a large hole in her £1000 which came as part of the inheritance, along with the shop.

By making dresses specially made for Mrs Canning, Jenny's name began to be known in the town and many more people from Clitheroe started coming to her shop after seeing Mrs Canning's gown at the local Christmas ball. From there, her success was assured.

Jenny thoroughly enjoyed her party and encouraged the staff to take some food home for their families. Towards the end of the party, her children arrived and were generally petted by the staff, and ate far too much, until Jenny was worried that they would all be sick.

On the way home, they told their mother all about the new bedding, toys and food that they had bought with Maggie, and that Roger had made a nice kennel for Patch in the utility room at the back of the kitchen. The whole family soon fell fast asleep that night, after such an exciting day. Not a bad thirtieth birthday after all, thought Jenny as she placed the bracelet in her jewellery box, along with the locket.

Chapter 3

Next day, it was business as usual. Jenny was holding a meeting with her heads of departments, to discuss the display of the Spring collection and wanted to get some idea of the stock that would be coming in shortly. Marian still kept overall control of the stock but she had a team of people helping her as she only worked very part time since she had had the children.

One of the helpers was her husband Will. Will was now responsible for getting all the orders for goods into the shop, after planning meetings with the head of departments. They would decide what they would like to stock and Will would find it for them. He often travelled all over the country finding bargains or new and unusual stock for the shop.

His real name was Jed Williams, but he was nicknamed Will by most people. Marian had met him when he came to the shop as a traveller in ladies goods. Jenny often wondered if she had called him Will because the name Jed reminded her too much of the father of her first child –young Jeremy Ormerod - who had raped her whilst she was a servant at Ormerod Hall; a job which Jenny had obtained for her.

A knock on the door disturbed Jenny from her reverie.

'Come in,' she called. It was Josephine, the newest girl from the workhouse. She opened the door slightly and whispered a message.

'I can't hear you, come right in please.' The girl crept a little way into the office.

'Janet said ter bring yer this letter, Missus.' Josephine leaned forward, dropped the letter on to Jenny's desk and retreated to the back of the room again, nearer to the safety of the door. Jenny picked up the letter, but paused and looked at the little girl who was the reluctant messenger.

'What is your name?' Jenny asked softly.

'Josephine, Missus.'

'My name is Jenny, or Mrs Marshall, which ever you prefer. But not Missus.'

'Sorry, er, Mrs Marshall. You won't send me back, will yer?'

'Back where? To your department? Do you not like your work here?'

'The workhouse. I 'ates it. Don't send me back Mrs, please.'

'I won't send you back, Josephine. Has someone been frightening you?'

'They sed at t' workhouse that yer'd send me back if I were bad. I 'ave tried ter be good, 'onest.'

Jenny looked at the earnest little face, which was looking beseechingly at her. Her heart melted.

'No-one will send you back to the workhouse. Ever. I promise you that.' Jenny watched the little girl's face slowly relax and a large grin replace the wary, frightened look.

'Do you like working here, then?'

'Yes, Mrs, it's reight grand. And th' food's good an all,' replied Josephine enthusiastically. 'Yer've no idea Mrs,' said Josephine, warming to her theme, 'how bad it is in there.'

'Oh yes I have, Josephine. I used to be there when I was younger than you.' Josephine stared at Jenny incredulously.

'Where Mrs, where was you?'

'In Clitheroe workhouse. But the matron that was in charge when I was there was much harsher than the new managers. The Lofthouses' run a luxurious hotel compared with how it was when I was a girl.'

'Yer wer in th' workhouse, then?'

'Yes. I only left when someone gave me a job as a scullery maid when I was twelve. Then I inherited this shop and since then I have always tried to give positions to girls from the workhouse, because I do know what it is like.'

There was a stunned silence.

'Was there anything else then Josephine?' Josephine jumped to attention.

'No Mrs. Just th' letter.'

'Thank you Josephine. You can go back to your department. Where do you work?'

'Wi' Janet, int' lingerie bit,' replied Josephine, struggling over the unfamiliar word.

'Well, run along then. And Josephine, try and copy the way Janet speaks. Our customers like to hear good English.'

Josephine looked a little sheepish.

'Yer, Mrs, I will try. Janet keeps on abaht it, but I fergets. Er, I mean, I forget. Thanks Mrs.'

With that, she skipped out of the room and away down the staircase.

Jenny laughed to herself, remembering how scared she had been when she had lived in the workhouse and marvelled again at how her life had turned out. Eventually she turned to her letter. It had a Yorkshire postmark and was addressed to

'The Proprietor'

She opened the thick vellum envelope and took out the single sheet of paper. The address read:-

Bradford Workhouse
Bradford
West Riding of Yorkshire
England

How strange, thought Jenny, just when she had been reliving her past as an inmate herself? And now she had got a letter from a workhouse. She read on.

Dear Madam

I trust that this letter finds the person to whom it is relevant. One of our inmates wishes to speak with you. She is in extremis and is very agitated. She wishes to clear her conscience before she meets her maker. I would be very grateful if you could see your way to coming and visiting this pitiful wretch. She is most insistent that she must see you. May I urge your speedy response to this letter, or you may be too late. The woman's name is Bruce.

Jenny dropped the letter as if it had suddenly become hot. Her heart was pounding. Bruce had been the manager of her gown shop whilst she was a scullery maid. She had left the shop the night before Jenny came to claim her inheritance. With her, had gone a large amount of money and almost all her stock. The shop had been running at a loss or barely making money for years before Jenny had inherited it. Or more likely, had been making a huge profit, which was going straight into Bruce's pocket.

It was Bruce who had abandoned her to the workhouse, telling them no details of her family. Even giving the workhouse a false name. No, she wouldn't go and see this woman. She never wanted to see her again. She screwed the paper up and threw it on the floor. Oh the agony that the woman had caused her, and now she wanted her forgiveness. What cheek! thought Jenny.

She tried to carry on with her work but she couldn't settle. Her anger started to dissipate and she became curious about what had happened to Bruce. Why was she in the workhouse? Surely with all the money that she had taken, she could have set up a good business. Besides, who was she not to forgive anyone? Was she setting herself up as God?

Then it dawned on Jenny like a revelation. Bruce had known her mother. She still knew so little about her mother. She bent down and picked up the crumpled piece of paper and straightened it out again.

Bradford workhouse. How far would it be from here? She got up purposefully from her desk and went down the stairs and out to the back forecourt of the shop. Crossing the courtyard, she heard Robert's voice before she saw him. What a wonder this young man was now. In just two short years that he had been managing the delivery business, he seemed to have grown in both confidence and stature.

'Robert, Robert, have you a minute?'

'Why certainly Mrs Marshall, How can I help you?'

'I need a large favour. I need to go to Bradford urgently. Can you take me? It may take a long time and we may have to find lodgings overnight. Will this be alright?'

'Just give me half an hour to sort things out and then I will be ready. Will that be soon enough?'

'Yes, we will go by way of my house first, so that I can pick some overnight things up in case we have to stay. I will see you in half an hour, then.' I will also have to cancel tomorrow's meeting for the Spring collection, she thought, making herself a note to leave a message for her secretary.

'I will be ready with the wagon at your convenience.'

Jenny hurried back to her office and picked up the telephone. She was one of the first shops and houses in Clitheroe to have a telephone, but being a working mother, it had proved a boon on more than one occasion. As she waited for the exchange to connect her, she pictured Maggie or Roger at the other end. They were such an efficient couple in every matter, but when it came to the telephone, they were different all together. Maggie downright refused to answer it and Roger would not lower his voice, but shouted, when speaking into it. Jenny usually had to hold the receiver away from her ear if Roger answered when she rang home.

There was no such problem with her eldest daughter. Although just short of eight years old, Rachel spoke confidently into the receiver, as if she was an employee of the telephone exchange.

It was Rachel that answered this time.

'The Marshall residence.' Rachel said in her best manner.

'Hello Rachel. It's mummy. I have to go to Bradford. Could you tell Maggie and Cook that I may be away for a day or two. I will come home first to see you all.'

'Are we not coming with you, mummy?'

'Not this time my dear. I have to go to see someone who is very ill. It would not be appropriate. Besides, you would miss school.'

'Mm, yes, I would. How long will you be away?'

'Only until tomorrow, I think.'

'And you will call and see us before you go, mummy, won't you?' The children all seemed frightened that they might lose their remaining parent, and often asked where she was going and wanted constant reassurance of the time that she would be back.

'Yes, darling. I'll be there in about half an hour. Now I must go, I have things to do here at the shop before I can come home. The longer I talk to you, the later I will be coming to see you.'

'All right mummy. I will put some things into an overnight bag for you.'

'Thank you. I will be home soon.'

'Bye Mummy.' The telephone disconnected with a loud click. Jenny smiled at the maturity and practicality of her eldest child. Although quite bossy with the little one and even her twin brother Ben, Jenny knew that she could always rely on Rachel. She had a sensible head on her.

Jenny returned to her paperwork and called in Agnes, one of the office girls. Agnes was Susy's assistant. Susy, Jenny's sister-in-law, was now expecting her first baby at long last and had trained Agnes to take over her role as bookkeeper.

'Agnes, I have to go away overnight to see someone in Bradford. Will you be happy to do the final balances of sales today on your own?'

'Yes, Jenny. Susy lets me do them by myself now and just checks them for me occasionally, with her being near her time.'

'Thank you Agnes. I knew that I could rely on you. Susy tells me that you have made great progress since you came here.' Agnes smiled proudly.

'Thanks Jenny. I do love the work. Figures just seem to come so naturally to me and yet lots of the girls struggle.'

'Good. Now, I must get on. I have to go home before I go anywhere.'

Jenny got her coat and hat from off the peg and turning the gaslight out, left the room and went out to the stables to find Robert.

They were soon on their way to Waddington Road in Clitheroe where Jenny had her large house. Her youngest child, Ellen, came rushing towards her as she went in through the door.

'Mummy, mummy, come and look at my painting. I did it for you at school.'

'Why Ellen, you nearly knocked me over. Where is this painting?'

'It is in my bedroom. Come on.' Ellen grabbed hold of Jenny's gown and tried to pull her towards the stairs.

'You bring it down to me Ellen. I have to go and see Maggie and Cook. Perhaps you could tell Robert to go into the kitchen and get a drink. He's outside with the carriage.'

'Oh, has he got Blackie with him?' Ellen cried with delight.

'I'm sorry, I didn't notice which horse it was. You go and find out.' Ellen rushed past her into the garden. Jenny laughed to herself. Ellen's life revolved round horses and painting.

Jenny went into the kitchen to explain the need for her journey to the staff. She knew that the children would be safe in their care whilst she was away. The kitchen soon became crowded as first Robert and Ellen, and then Rachel came in to see her. Rachel brought a large overnight bag down with her.

'Here are some things for you mummy. I have put a black dress in for you, with the person being very ill. Just in case.'

'Thank you Rachel.' Fancy a child of seven years thinking of including black garments at a time like this, thought Jenny. Mind you, the children had seen rather a lot of black garments in their short lives. Rachel especially had begged her mummy to change out of her black clothes far sooner than etiquette would have allowed her to. Sometimes at home, she had worn other colours just to please them, but had always been suitably attired when outside.

Cook cut in at this point. 'I've made you both some sandwiches to eat on your journey.' She handed over a large basket, covered with a crisp white cloth. It felt very heavy and, knowing Cook, would have fed a family of six, not two of them.

'That is so thoughtful of you Cook. Thank you. But now we must get on our way, so that we might get there tonight. By the way, where is Ben?'

'He is across at Aunty Marian's. He is staying for tea with Luke and George, and then Uncle Will is bringing him back afterwards.'

'I don't think that we have time to call back there on our way. Please tell him that my journey was urgent, Rachel.'

'I will. Bye mummy,' she said, giving Jenny a brief hug, unlike Ellen who nearly choked her, hanging on to her. Her eldest daughter was quite cool and collected for her age, but young Ellen was still very affectionate.

The family waved them off at the door. Robert clicked the reins and told the horses to set off. The carriage moved slowly away from the kerb, gathering speed as they went up Waddington Road and turned off towards Chatburn.

The weather was fine and promised to stay so for the rest of the afternoon and evening. Robert drove the horse at a brisk pace, leaving Jenny to her thoughts. What would she find when she got to the workhouse? Would she be too late? Would Bruce have anything to tell her about her mother? What did Bruce want to say to her? All these thoughts were swirling around in her brain.

Her mind then went back to when she had first opened the door to the top floor of her shop. The upstairs contained a sumptuous suite of rooms, which surprised Jenny with their opulence. There were two bedrooms, a kitchen, a large lounge, a bathing room and a workroom and storeroom.

It had been such a shock finding out that her father was Lord Ormerod, whom she had worked for. He had never given a hint of knowing who she was, all the time that she had worked for him, even until his death.

All she knew about her mother was that she had been a servant at Ormerod Hall and had fallen in love with the master. When she was expecting a child, Lord Ormerod had set her up in a shop, so that she wouldn't be abandoned like Marian had been, by his son. From the painting that was in the apartment on the top floor, Jenny realised that she didn't look like her mother or her father, but strangely she looked like the old Lord Ormerod's daughter. Well, that made her a half sister too, she supposed.

The only other thing that Jenny knew was that her mother had died in childbirth. Indeed, Jenny had been worried about that when she was in labour with her first baby. Or babies, as it had turned out to be, having given birth unexpectedly to the twins. She fell to musing about the strange twists of fate in her life as they lurched along the rough roads towards Bradford.

Chapter 4

After several hours driving along bumpy roads, they approached the outside of the workhouse. It was all in darkness. Robert got out of the carriage and hammered on the door. It was quite a long time before anyone came to answer.

Jenny got out of the carriage when she saw a light coming past the window. The door creaked slightly open and an elderly man peeped out.

'What do yer want?' he asked Robert, rather gruffly.

Jenny stepped forward. 'I am here to see someone called Bruce. The matron has written to me.'

The man's demeanour changed instantly when he heard and saw Jenny. This was obviously a person of great wealth and standing.

'Beg pardon, missis, I didn't see yer there.' He opened the door widely and ushered them into the hallway. 'Come this way, I'll tell matron that yer 'ere. What name shall I say?'

'Mrs Marshall, from the gown shop in Clitheroe,' she replied. The man stared up at her in shock, but then remembered himself and set off up the corridor, asking Jenny and Robert to follow him. Robert asked if he could get some accommodation for the horse and the man said that he would see to it shortly.

He led them into a spacious lounge, decorated with elegant furniture and then left them, saying that he would go and find matron. As he walked away, Jenny noticed that he walked with a severe limp and looked to be in pain as he walked.

As they waited for matron, Jenny admired the room and it's furniture and Robert replied that he bet the workhouse inmates didn't get to come in here. Jenny and he laughed together, both having been brought up in the workhouse regime. They were still laughing when matron came into the room.

'Mrs Marshall? How kind of you to come so promptly. I have ordered some tea for you. Ah, here it is,' she said as an elderly woman entered the room carrying a tray, followed by the man who had opened the door. She turned to the man and told him to take Robert down to the stables after his tea.

Matron poured the tea as if it was a vicarage tea party, holding polite conversation with Jenny, but totally ignoring Robert and the two inmates. Jenny tried to include them in the conversation, but eventually gave up. The man took Robert away to stable the horse but matron seemed inclined to talk further.

'Is Mrs Bruce still able to talk? Jenny asked eventually.

'Only just,' replied matron. 'She has periods of lucidness and then drifts off into another world. I will set up a comfortable chair by the bed and you can decide whether you wish to stay or not, once you have seen her. Did you know her well?'

'No. Not at all. But she knew my mother.'

'Ah, a friend of your mother, then.'

'Not exactly. She worked for my mother in a shop and when my mother died in childbirth, Bruce put me in a workhouse. I didn't meet her until I inherited the shop when I was 18 years of age. And then she disappeared.'

There was a look of shock and disbelief on matron's face. Jenny wasn't sure whether it was from disgust at what Bruce had done to her, or that Jenny herself had lived in a workhouse.

'Oh dear, you have had a difficult time. No wonder that Bruce wishes to speak with you. I am sure that it has been weighing heavily on her conscience.'

I doubt it, thought Jenny to herself, but smiling at matron, said nothing. These revelations seemed to galvanise matron into action. She led the way out of the room and across into the main part of the workhouse, which as usual, was far more sparsely furnished.

They walked on to the top floor where the infirmary was. Jenny caught her breath at the smell as she entered the large dormitory room. It was a smell of unwashed bodies and decay. Even matron held a handkerchief against her nose as she walked down the ward.

At the bottom of the ward, they went through some doors into a corridor. On the right hand side was a small doorway, matron opened the door and led Jenny in. The smell in here was far worse than the main dormitory and Jenny gagged as she walked into the room. She felt for the handkerchief out of her pocket and was glad that she had doused it with lavender oil before she had set off from home.

The room contained a small bed and had a tiny candle by its side. An overflowing chamber pot was in the corner. There was no other furniture in the room. In the bed was a tiny shrivelled body, curled up on her side. She looked to be semiconscious as far as Jenny could tell.

'Bruce? Bruce? You have a visitor here,' called the matron harshly, shaking her at the same time.

Slowly, very slowly, Bruce opened her eyes and stared at Jenny.

'This is the proprietor of the gown shop in Clitheroe. Mrs Jenny Marshall,' she said to Bruce. Turning to Jenny, she said that she would leave them together and she would send the man up with a chair. With that she left the room.

Jenny remained motionless, quite a way from the bed. A crooked finger stretched out from the rough blanket and beckoned her nearer. Jenny swallowed, but did as she was bid, even though she felt very frightened.

'Got to say sorry. Did wrong,' Bruce gasped, then as if the effort had exhausted her, she went back to sleep.

Well, thought Jenny, have I come all this way just for those few words? If so, it will be a waste of time. She could have written and saved me the bother. Feelings of anger coursed through her. She prodded Bruce.

'Why did you put me in the workhouse and say you didn't know who I was?' demanded Jenny angrily but there was no reply. The eyes stayed closed.

After a while, with no further communication from the figure in the bed, the door opened and the elderly man came in with a chair.

'Oh thank you. That is kind of you. Where is Robert, my carriage driver?'

'E 'as put 'is horse away and fed 'im and he's down in th' kitchen. Matron said that I 'ave to stay 'ere wi' yer. She said I can get mi pallet and bring it up 'ere and sleep outside th' door, if yer don't mind, Mrs.'

'That is very kind of you. I don't mind at all. Will you be comfortable there?'

'Aye, I'll be fine. I'll be back shortly,' he said and disappeared out of the door. Jenny was glad that he was coming back. It was strangely eerie in this room and she was a little frightened of Bruce, even though she was far too ill to be able to do anything to harm her physically. Bruce's eyes remained closed. Jenny looked down on her. How had she got in to this state and ended up in a workhouse? Perhaps she would never know.

The elderly man came back and positioned his pallet across the doorway, so that Jenny could see him.

'Will there be anything else, Mrs, else I'll get some sleep. I 'ave ter be up early in t' morning,' he asked.

'Thank you, no, there is nothing. By the way, what is your name?'

'Marshall, Miss. Like yourn. Tha'll not ferget it, will yer, beggin' yer pardon?'

Jenny laughed. 'No, that is true.' The man got down on his pallet fully dressed and wrapped himself up in the rough workhouse blanket. He was asleep in seconds. Jenny turned back to look at the woman lying in the bed. She sat down in the chair and must have dozed for a while. She was wakened by a low voice, muttering. She went over to the bed.

'What is it? What are you saying?' Jenny asked.

'Got everything. Not like me,' muttered Bruce, her breath catching in her throat.

'Who? Who got everything?'

'Your mother. Mary Stuck Up Barnes.' Bruce stopped speaking as her breathing became more ragged. Eventually it calmed again. Jenny waited in silence, her heart pounding. After a while, Bruce started rambling again.

'All right for her. The Lord looked after her. Not like me. Got thrown out of my place when I was with child. No money, no reference. Ended up in a place like this.' Bruce stopped speaking again and drifted back into sleep.

Jenny tried to piece together what she had heard. So Bruce had been expecting a child and had been thrown out just like Marian. No wonder she was bitter about Jenny's mother. It would have seemed that her mother got everything. Not only looked after by the lord, but set up with a lovely shop as well. It was becoming obvious why Jenny had been abandoned in the workhouse. With her out of the way, Bruce could make something of herself.

Jenny was startled out of her thoughts when the rasping voice started again.

'Never thought you would come back. Shock when I saw you that day. Knew I had cheated you. Had to go.' She paused for breath. The waiting was agony for Jenny. There was so much she wanted to ask her.

'What was my mother like?' Jenny asked.

'Fortunate,' came the reply. 'Spoilt,' was the next word that she gasped out.

'Tell me about her.'

'Not like you. Dark, taller.'

'Tell me more about her.'

'Kind. Good to me. Showed me how to run business.'

There was another silence whilst Bruce slept again.

'Where is your child now?'

'Don't know. Left in workhouse.'

'Where?'

'Blackburn.'

'Did you never go back?'

'No. No money. No house. Needed a job.'

'What was it? Boy or girl?'

'Girl. Reminded me of master's son who fathered it. Didn't want it. A bastard.'

Silence returned. Jenny sat sadly reflecting on her own illegitimacy. She watched the woman in the bed and wondered again how she had come to this state. A voice broke thorough her reverie. Bruce was trying to sit up.

'Name's Mary, same as your mother. She'll be well into her thirties now.'

'Who?'

'Girl. Left her in Blackburn when I got a position.' Bruce fell back exhausted against the pillow, the long sentence taking its toll.

Jenny waited until she caught her breath.

'How did you come back here, then?'

'Had a shop,' she rasped in short sentences. 'Got a man. Said he loved me. Moved in with me. Robbed me. In debt. Back here.'

'Sorry,' replied Jenny, although secretly she was thinking how strange it was that Bruce had had the tables turned on her. But then she felt guilty. She wouldn't wish anyone to have to die in this place.

Jenny noticed that Bruce's breathing was becoming more ragged and there seemed to be gaps between the breaths. She decided that the end must be fairly near now, and that she would stay. There was no point going at this time. And anyway, she may wake up and give her some more information.

Eventually, the gaps between the breaths got longer and longer and Jenny frequently stood up to see if it was all over. Then there would be a gasp and another breath was dragged in. Slowly, her breathing ceased altogether. Jenny covered Bruce's mouth with her own hand to see if she could feel any breath. There was none. Bruce had finally died. The last link with her mother was gone. Jenny would not get any more information from her now.

Moving slowly, Jenny turned to the doorway to wake the old man up. She looked down at him, feeling sorry that she was going to have to disturb his sleep. As she reached down to waken him, she froze. He was laying on his back, with the blanket kicked off, his head to one side, with his arm wrapped around his head. Just like her own youngest daughter and her husband had done.

As if aware of her nearness, the old man woke up and jumped to his feet.

'Sorry Missus, do yer want me. I were 'ard on fast asleep then.'

'Yes, Bruce has just died. Do you need to get the Matron?'

'No, she won't care,' he replied bitterly, 'I'll just get th' nurse. They'll get th' doctor in t' morning. No point getting 'im at night. Nothing 'e can do.'

The old man limped off down the corridor bringing back a nurse with him. She confirmed the death, and asked the old man to take the lady into the sitting room and get some tea for her. She then returned to her other patients, giving Jenny only a curt nod.

The old man came back and asked Jenny to follow him into the sitting room. Here, a tray of tea was awaiting her.

'What is your first name, Mr Marshall?'

'Mine Missus?' he asked suspiciously, 'It's Ben.'

'Did you have any family?'

'Aye,' Ben said, hanging his head down sadly.

'Where are they now?' Jenny persisted.

'Probably still in t' work'ouse. Or even dead. 'Ad ter leave 'em in t' work'ouse after the troubles in th' cotton mills. We 'ad no money. Said I'd be back fer 'em, but I never did. What sort of man am I?' At this he burst into tears. Jenny felt helpless, seeing this grown man cry. Her own thoughts were racing anyway, at the wonder of who this man could be.

Eventually, he got himself under control.

'Sorry Missus, I don't know what came over me.' He wiped his tears away with his rough shirtsleeve.

'Did you have children?' Jenny persisted.

'Aye, six. But three on 'em died i' childhood. T'other three went in th' work'ouse wit' mother. Oh, I missed 'em. It were alright at first. I tramped round a lot, but then got a good job. ''Elping build new 'ouses all over Bradford. I got a 'ouse and a bit o' money together, and was ready ter send fer th' family. Then I fell off mi ladder. Broke mi leg badly. Never bin reight sin it happened. Lost mi job, and all mi money. 'Ad to come back in 'ere. Fair broke mi 'eart it did.' He looked as if he was going to start crying again, so Jenny distracted him with another question.

'What were your children called?'

'The ones that were left, that went into th' work'ouse were Martin, Susy and Jonny.'

The pain seared through Jenny's chest. Her suspicions were right. This was probably Jonny's father. Her children's grandfather. But she had to be sure. They were common enough names.

'Which workhouse did you leave them in?'

'Clitheroe, over i' Lancashire. I 'ad ter tramp o'er 'ere ter gerra job. Cotton were dead i' Lancashire.' It was now Jenny's turn to burst into tears.

'Ere, Missus, what's ter do? I didn't mean ter upset yer like, but yer did ask.' The old man stood looking embarrassed.

'Mr Marshall, I think that you are my father-in-law.'

He looked at her fine clothes and said disbelievingly 'Nay, lass, 'ow can that be? I think yer mistaken.'

'I was married to Jonny. We have three children. Your grandchildren.'

'Ow come Jonny married yer, yer being a toff? Oh, beggin' yer pardon, Missus, didn't mean ter be rude, like.'

'I'm no toff, Mr Marshall, I was brought up in Clitheroe workhouse, too. But I was lucky and inherited a shop. Your Susy is my best friend.'

'So they are all still alive then?' Mr Marshall asked.

Jenny's face saddened. 'I am afraid not. Jonny was killed in an accident two years ago. And Martin died shortly after they arrived in the workhouse. I think he just faded away. But Susy is still alive and well. She is expecting her first baby shortly. But your wife is very frail now I am afraid.'

'Mi wife? Th' old gel's still alive?'

'Very much so, and she works in my shop.'

Mr Marshall sat staring at Jenny as if he was having a dream. Suddenly he pulled himself together.

'Will tha tek a message to 'em for mi? Tell 'em what 'appened ter mi, and say sorry, like.'

'I'll do better than that. I'll take you with me!' Jenny exclaimed. 'You don't think that I am going to leave you in here? I'll take you home to your wife and child. And grandchildren for that matter.'

'Grandchilder!' said Mr Marshall incredulously, 'Ow many 'ave I got, did yer say?'

'Three. I've got twins at nearly eight years. Ben and Rachel. And then young Ellen at six years. They . .'

Mr Marshall interrupted. 'Ben? Did yer say Ben?' Yer called yer lad Ben?'

'Yes, after you. We thought that you must be dead because we hadn't heard from you.'

'I couldn't tell 'em. I were too ashamed. Besides, I can't write proper.'

'Well you can see them soon. Can you get the Matron up? I want to arrange papers to take you out of here.'

'Will she let yer?'

'Oh, I think so. I have got a lot of people out of Clitheroe workhouse in my time. They are usually very grateful to have one less inmate.'

'She won't be pleased ter be woken up at this time in t' morning.'

'Just try please.'

To Mr Marshall's amazement, matron agreed to him leaving the workhouse, but looked very disbelieving when Jenny said that he was her father-in-law.

Two hours later, they were on their way home: Robert being as surprised as Mr Marshall at the development. On the way home, Jenny explained to Ben Marshall how she had come to inherit the shop, and a little of her own parentage.

Eventually, they got back home. Jenny decided that she would take him to her house first. Here, Ben could clean up and get used to being out of the workhouse, before he met the family.

Chapter 5

The children were at school when they arrived home. The staff were all amazed at seeing Jenny's companion and even more so at who he was. Jenny sent a message to ask old Mrs Marshall to come down for tea that night at four of the clock promptly, as she had a surprise for her, but gave no more details.

Next she rang Cosgrove's tailors and asked them to come to the house with complete sets of new clothing for Ben. She also asked the barber to call round to trim his hair properly.

Then she rang Marian and asked her if she could pick the children up from school and keep them for tea. That arranged, she then rang Susy and asked her to come down with her husband at six of the clock, again promising a surprise, but giving no details. He could meet the grandchildren last! She didn't want to overwhelm him at first.

Old Ben Marshall was newly spruced up and sitting in Jenny's lounge by four of the clock. He was rather nervous, not having seen his family for so many years. When Mrs Marshall arrived, Jenny led her into the lounge. Mr Marshall slowly got to his feet, staring at this well dressed woman who entered the room.

'Look, I've brought someone to see you,' said Jenny to Mrs Marshall. Mrs Marshall stared at the man in front of her.

'Ello, lass, it's bin a long time,' said Mr Marshall.

'Ben,' cried a delighted Mrs Marshall, as she rushed across the floor to meet him.

Jenny left them there together. She heard cries of surprise and delight as she closed the door. Smiling to herself as she left the room, she was startled by Maggie coming down the corridor.

'Shall I take tea into them, Mrs Marshall?'

'No, I think they will want to be alone for a while. I'll come and have a cup of tea with you though, Maggie.'

'Yes, Madam,' replied Maggie with a tight little smile. She never could get used to her boss calling her by her first name, and coming into the kitchen for a cup of tea with the staff. They walked back to the kitchen together, Maggie continually trying to let Mrs Marshall go before her at doorways. Cook looked up in astonishment when Jenny sat down at the kitchen table, but she too, was used to their boss arriving in the kitchen.

They sat companionably for a while, talking about the journey that Jenny had undertaken with Robert and the wonderment when she found her father-in-law. Eventually Maggie apologised, and said that she must help Cook get on with the meal. They started bustling round the kitchen, but Jenny carried on sitting by the table, watching Maggie and Cook at work.

After a while, the bell from the lounge rang. Maggie wiped her hands on her pinny and rushed to the door.

'No Maggie, you carry on here. I'll go and see what they want.' Jenny left the room and went into the lounge. The old couple were sat together holding hands on the settee. For a moment, Jenny was envious of this couple. She could no longer be reunited with Jonny, but at least she had ensured that his parents were reunited in their old age.

Mr Marshall rose as Jenny entered the room. Mrs Marshall looked embarrassed.

'Jenny, sorry to ring the bell, but we couldn't see where you were.'

Jenny laughed. 'I was in the kitchen, getting in Cook's way. I think that she was glad when you rang the bell, to get rid of me. Now, what did you want?'

'Nothing in particular. I just wanted you to come back in; so that I could say how grateful I am that you brought Ben back. I am so happy. I never thought that I would see him alive again.' She beamed at Ben, looking almost girlish and Jenny smiled at the picture that they made.

'She doesn't 'alf sound ladylike, now. Can't believe it's mi old woman,' replied Ben.

'Oh, that's Jenny. She makes us all talk proper at the shop. It's become a habit now.'

'Would you both like a cup of tea now? The evening meal won't be until half past six,' asked Jenny.

'Please,' said Mrs Marshall. Jenny went back down to the kitchen to ask Maggie for a tray of tea. Roger had come in from the garden, bringing some homegrown vegetables for Cook.

'Afternoon, Madam, young Rachel has just rung from Mrs Williams, wanting to know what the surprise was. I told her that she would have to wait. Is that correct?'

Jenny laughed.

'Perfectly correct, Roger. What a minx she is, trying to find out from you. Wait until she comes home.'

As Maggie was taking the tray of tea to the lounge, the front doorknocker sounded. Jenny took the tray off Maggie, who went to answer the door.

'Good evening Miss Susy, er I mean Mrs Butler, Mr Butler.' She curtsied as she spoke to them. 'They are in the lounge, if you would like to follow me.'

Susy was in the final stage of her pregnancy and waddled slowly behind Maggie, grumbling to her husband about having to come out in such an advanced stage. Maggie opened the door and announced them. 'Mr and Mrs Butler, Madam.'

Susy waddled into the room, staring at her mother who was sat on the settee, holding hands with a strange man. Mr Marshall stood up, looked at Susy and limped over to her.

'Susy, Susy, mi own little girl.'

'Dad,' gasped Susy disbelievingly, 'we thought you were dead!'

'Aye, and I did an all. Thought yer were all dead bi now. Eeh, it's reight grand ter see yer again, Susy. Mi little girl.'

'Not so little now dad!' laughed Susy holding her tummy, 'but hopefully it will not be for much longer now. I only have another week or two to go before my confinement. Oh, by the way this is my husband, Arthur Butler.'

'Pleased to meet you, Sir,' replied Arthur politely.

'Aye, same 'ere,' replied Mr Marshall, obviously embarrassed at meeting someone new, who also spoke well. He felt a little out of his depth.

'Arthur is a bank manager now dad. He has just been promoted.' Mr Marshall just smiled, quite overwhelmed by his son in law, who was a bank manager, his wife and daughter who now spoke very grand, and his rich daughter in law who owned a large shop and house. He squeezed his wife's hand very hard.

'Eh, tha's done well by 'um, love, I'll say that fer yer. I'm reight proud of yer.' Everyone seemed to be a little close to tears, so Jenny was relieved when Maggie announced that the meal was ready.

They all moved into the dining room. After a sumptuous meal, they got up and went back into the lounge and Maggie brought drinks of tea on a small trolley. Arthur was fussing around Susy, who was finding it difficult to get comfortable, being so near her time. Mrs Marshall and Jenny got up and served everyone with a cup of tea.

Everyone had just got a drink and was relaxed when the door flew open and in ran Rachel and Ben, closely followed by Ellen.

'What's the surprise, what's the surprise?' bellowed Rachel, running up to her mother.

'Rachel, do not be so rude. Can't you see that we have guests?' Rachel coolly looked round the room, taking in who was present. On her second glance she noticed her grandfather.

'Sorry mummy, sorry Sir,' she bowed her head politely towards her grandfather, who was a stranger to her.

'Rachel, this is your surprise. This gentleman is your grandfather. Granny's husband. Your daddy's father.'

For once the children were silent.

'But I thought he was dead,' piped up Ben eventually.

'Ben, don't be so rude,' said Jenny. 'So did we all, but he was in a workhouse in Bradford, because he hurt his leg and couldn't work.'

'Well why didn't he write to Granny then?' demanded Ben.

'It doesn't matter why, Ben. Just go and say hello to your grandfather.' Jenny was becoming increasingly worried, not to mention embarrassed. Perhaps she had dealt with this badly and should have told the children what was happening before they met him.

All three children dutifully walked across the room and bowed their heads slightly to their grandfather and said hello.

'Now who's who, like?' said Mr Marshall. Rachel's head shot up when she heard her grandfather speak with a common accent, but a look from her mother silenced her. Sometimes, Rachel reminded Jenny of her autocratic ancestors far too much. She had a way of looking down her nose at people, which was so reminiscent of Lord Jeremy Ormerod, Jenny's half-brother, although she would never acknowledge him as such.

'This is Ben, this is Rachel, they are nearly eight years old, and this is Ellen, who is six,' replied Jenny

'I'm called Ben Marshall, an all,' said Mr Marshall. 'I think they named yer after me.'

After a short silence, Jenny replied. 'That's right Grandfather, we named Ben after you. Now children, you are a little late tonight. I think that you should all be going to bed. Go down to the kitchen and tell Megan that it is time for bed.'

'Who is Megan?' whispered Mr Marshall to his wife.

'The nursery maid,' she replied.

Mr Marshall chuckled. 'Eh, fancy our Jonny's childer 'aving a nursemaid. I can't get o'er it,' he continued chuckling. 'Who'd 'ave thought it?'

'It was all down to Jenny,' replied Mrs Marshall. 'She saw us all right. I was near death when she rescued me and Susy from the workhouse. Now are you coming home with me tonight, or have you got a taste for this high living at Jenny's?'

'Home? Where's home? D'yer live wi' our Susy?'

'No. I have my own house. Susy and I shared it before she got married, but it is just mine now. Susy lives in a big house just up the road from here, under the railway bridge. Handy for the bank for Arthur.'

'Well love, I'd like ter go 'ome wi' yer. By, that sounds grand. 'Ome. Not said that word in a long time.' He grinned broadly at his wife.

'I'll get the coach brought round to the front of the house,' said Jenny.

'I think that we will go as well, Jenny,' added Susy. 'I have the most awful backache. It must be the way that I have been sitting.' Susy stood up, helped by her husband, but let out a loud gasp. 'Oh, my back, such pain,' she cried. 'Oh no, something has happened. Jenny, I need to visit your bathroom.' Susy tried to hurry out of the door, but stopped as a wave of pain overtook her.

Arthur clung to his wife, looking worried. 'What is the matter, Susy? Can I help? Shall we hurry home?'

'I think that it is too late to go home,' said Mrs Marshall, 'I think that the baby is on its way.' She took her coat off again and hurried over to Susy. 'Can we use one of the spare rooms, Jenny?'

'Certainly. I'll just get help.' She jangled the bell pull. Maggie came hurrying into the room, so savagely had Jenny pulled at the bell.

'Maggie, Mrs Butler's time has come. Could Roger ring for the doctor, and could you and Cook come and help us get Mrs Butler into bed?' Everyone scurried off on their errands and Mrs Marshall and Jenny helped Susy upstairs to the spare bedroom. When they started to undress her, they realised that her underclothes were all wet.

'Looks like you are on your way, love,' said Mrs Marshall. 'Your waters have gone, so we had better get you into bed.'

'It was awful, mum, I could feel the water trickling but I couldn't say anything in front of the men.'

'Eh lass,' said Mrs Marshall reverting to her local accent, 'tha dad were there when you were born. He won't be bothered, you came so quick, he had to help me. Mighty proud he was that he had brought a bairn into the world.'

But Susy wasn't listening. The pain had returned and was more severe this time. She stood gripping the bedstead as if her life depended on it.

'Come and get yourself into bed, Mrs Susy,' said Maggie soothingly, 'I've put sheets of newspaper in the bed to protect it.' Maggie gently helped Susy climb on to the big bed just in time as another pain seared through her body leaving her gasping.

'Mum, the pain's so strong, I can't bear it,' Susy gasped when it subsided. Mrs Marshall laughed.

'Too late for that, Susy. You'll have to bear it now. Looks like you are going to be quick in childbirth like I was. Usually it's hours and hours with your first one.'

'Thanks mum. That's really cheered me up. I don't think I can stand this for much longer. Ooh, here it comes again.'

The women looked on, as Susy writhed about the bed in agony. Jenny tried to soothe her and wiped her forehead when the pain subsided. A knock at the door revealed Arthur looking extremely worried, bringing the doctor in tow.

'Are you all right Susy. It's been a long time. Here's the doctor now.' Arthur hovered in the doorway.

'Thank you Mr Butler,' said the doctor, 'I will attend your wife now. Please wait downstairs.' Reluctantly, Arthur left the room after giving Susy a weak smile of encouragement. The doctor carried out his examination and asked how long the pains had lasted.

'Well, Mrs Butler, you are quite advanced. A very quick labour for a first child. You are lucky. It is nearly time for you to push and yet you say the pains only started two hours ago?'

'I was quick when I had her,' said Mrs Marshall to no one in particular.

'Well, I've had backache all day,' said Susy to the doctor, 'but then my waters went. It must have been all the excitement.'

The doctor looked quizzically at Jenny.

'We found her father, my father-in-law, in the Bradford workhouse yesterday and they have all been reunited after twenty years and more,' explained Jenny. 'It was quite emotional for us all.' The doctor nodded but before he could say anything Susy gasped again.

'Doctor, I feel like I am splitting inside. Help me, help me,' wailed Susy. The doctor looked again at Susy and told her that she could start pushing the baby out. After a few minutes of sustained pushing during the contractions, the small body slithered out and immediately started wailing.

'Oh let me see my baby,' cried Susy.

The doctor laughed. 'Don't you want to know what it is, Mrs Butler?'

'I know it is healthy, and it is crying, so it doesn't matter what it is.'

'It is a boy,' said the doctor, 'and he seems to be perfect in every way. I'll check him over later when I've finished here. And now here comes the afterbirth. Just lie back and let nature take its course, and then you can hold your baby.' Susy flopped back on to the pillow, exhausted.

There was a loud knocking on the door. 'Is everything all right,' shouted Arthur. Jenny went to the door to reassure him, with the baby in her arms.

'Here, look at your son,' smiled Jenny.

'A son, a son,' gasped Arthur. 'Oh Susy, I'm so pleased. Was it very bad?'

'Now then Mr Butler, just go back downstairs whilst we finish sorting your wife out, and then you can come back and talk to her,' said the doctor firmly.

'Sorry Sir, I'll go and tell his grandfather.' Arthur ran happily back downstairs to tell Mr Marshall the good news.

Upstairs the doctor completed his work and left instructions with Grandmother Marshall until a nurse could be found.

'Can Mrs Butler stay here until she recovers, Mrs Marshall?' the doctor asked Jenny as he came downstairs. 'I wouldn't like her to go out in the cold night air.'

'Certainly, that would be the best plan. We could manage her care with my staff, so that we wouldn't need a nurse.'

'I'll be on my way then. There must be something in the air tonight, there are two other ladies having confinements tonight, but she has beaten them all. Tell that young lady well done.'

Maggie showed the doctor out, and brought Arthur up to see his wife and new son, who was now laid in Ellen's old cot hastily retrieved from one of the attic rooms. He peered at the baby from the end of the cot, but refused to hold him.

'What do you want to call him, Arthur,' asked a sleepy Susy.

'I would like to call him after your brother Jonny, if Jenny wouldn't mind,' replied Arthur. A delighted Jenny replied in the affirmative.

'Jonny Butler. That sounds fine. Will he have a middle name as well?' asked Grandmother Marshall.

'I would like his middle name to be Arthur, after his father,' replied the new mother.

'That is good, Jonny Arthur Butler it shall be then,' said the proud father.

'And now it is time for Susy to rest. So downstairs all of you,' shooed Mrs Marshall.

'Could the children come and have a peek at their new cousin before you go to sleep, Susy?' asked Jenny.

Susy didn't get a chance to reply.

'Only for a few moments, then,' replied Mrs Marshall.

Jenny went and got the excited children, urging them to be quiet as they bounded along the corridor to the spare room. They crept into the bedroom and looked in awe at the baby.

'What is he called?' asked Rachel, the first to recover her voice.

'Jonny Arthur Butler, after your daddy,' replied Susy.

'My daddy was called Jonny Marshall, not Butler,' piped up Ellen. They all laughed.

'Yes, but they are calling him Jonny after your daddy,' replied Jenny, glad of something to laugh at, as she had been close to tears again. Ellen seemed satisfied at this explanation. Then Mrs Marshall hurried them out of the room to allow Susy to rest.

After all the excitement, the house soon settled down for the night, old Mr and Mrs Marshall deciding to stay the night rather than going home.

Jenny went up the stairs, completely exhausted after the day's events. On going into the twins' bedroom, she found that Rachel was still awake.

'Rachel, are you still awake? Is anything the matter?'

'No mummy. There is nothing wrong. I was just thinking.'

'What about? Just general thinking or about something specific?'

'About Granddad Marshall. He talks like common people and yet Grandma and Susy don't.'

'Rachel, that is very rude of you. He can't help the way he talks. We all talked like that until we learned to speak more correctly. He is not common at all. He has just not had the advantages that you have had, young lady. If I had not inherited the shop, you would probably have been born in the workhouse and would have spoken exactly like Granddad Marshall.'

Rachel pulled a face. 'I don't think that I would have liked to have been born in the workhouse. It sounds awful. That is where you were born, wasn't it, mummy?'

'No, Rachel, I wasn't born there.'

'Well, how did you get there if you weren't born there?'

'I was taken there after my mother died.'

'How old were you?'

'About three or four years of age.'

'What was your mummy like? You never talk about your parents.'

Jenny swallowed. This line of conversation was getting difficult. 'I can't remember my mummy,' she said quietly.

Rachel remained silent for a few minutes, trying to work out this new concept.

'And did your daddy go into the workhouse to find you and take you home?'

'No.'

'Why not?'

'He wasn't there when my mummy died and couldn't find me afterwards.'

Another silence.

'Then how did you get to the workhouse?'

'A lady took me to the workhouse and left me there, saying that she only knew my first name and that my mother had died. They gave me the name of Jenny Mitchell, but it was not my real name.'

'What was your real name then?'

'Genevieve Barnes.'

'Genevieve? Why that is a lovely name, mummy. Why don't you use it?'

'I was used to being just plain Jenny. I didn't know my real name until I was twenty one years old.'

'Why?'

'Oh Rachel, that is enough for now. It is time that you were asleep.'

'Just one more question, mummy, please?'

'What is it, Rachel?'

'What happened to the lady who left you in the workhouse?'

'She died earlier in the week. That was the lady I went to see in the Bradford workhouse and I am so glad that I did, because that is where I found your Granddad Marshall. Now, go to sleep young lady, or you will be too tired to take Patch a walk before school.'

Jenny kissed Rachel on the nose and tucked her into the blankets, kissed Ben who was sleeping peacefully, and left the room. Rachel had disturbed Jenny with all her questions. It had been an emotional week, and some day Rachel and the other children would have to be told the full story of their ancestors. She did not relish the telling of the full story at all and would leave the rest of the story for as long as she could.

Chapter 6

Two weeks later, Jenny was surprised to get a visit from her father-in-law at the shop.

'Hello, father. What a delight. Come in and sit down. I'll get us some tea. Have you come in to see your wife?'

'No lass, I've come ter see you,' said old Ben purposefully.

The door opened in response to Jenny having rung the bell for her secretary.

'Ah Janey, could you bring some tea for myself and my father-in-law, please?'

'Certainly Jenny,' replied the young woman, another survivor from the workhouse.

'Now what is it, father? Are you happy? Do you have enough money? Can I do anything for you?'

'Nay lass, I'm happy enough, but I can't be beholden to you. I need something to do. Time hangs heavy on a man when he has allus bin busy.'

'But you deserve to have nothing to do. You have worked all your life.'

'I know, but it's 'abit. I can't bide 'aving nothing ter do. Please give us some work,' he said beseechingly.

Jenny thought for a moment. 'Do you remember that Jonny had a carters business? A young man called Robert has looked after it and I thought that by now he would have asked me to buy the business, but he is not interested in being a boss. He likes to be out doing the deliveries. Could you run this business for him and me?'

'Nay lass, I'm no boss either. I can 'ardly just read and write. I'm good at sums though.'

'So is your Susy. That must be whom she gets it from. If you could do the day-to-day organisation of the deliveries and keep the books, Susy could show you how to go about doing the books properly. What about it?'

Old Ben Marshall was nodding his head. 'Yes, I would like that, if you will help me.'

'I will do better than that. I will get Robert to help you.' She rang the bell again and asked Janey to get Robert to come into the office as soon as was convenient.

'I will ask Robert to contact you if he is happy with the arrangements. Why don't you stay for lunch with your wife in the staff canteen and discuss this with her?'

'I will Jenny and thanks. I am grateful for all what you 'ave done, like, but I'll be much 'appier if I can do something back.'

Jenny smiled and escorted old Ben out of the office. How like Jonny his father was. If only Jonny could have lived long enough to see his father restored to the family. Jenny shook her head as sad memories threatened to engulf her and picked up a report, which was waiting to be read.

A short time later, a knock on the door heralded the arrival of Robert.

'Robert, thank you for coming to see me. Do sit down.'

'Is there a problem, Jenny?'

'Not at all. I just wanted to ask you something. Are you still interested in buying the carters business from me?' Robert looked downcast and started twisting his hat around in his hands.

'What is the matter, Robert? You look positively worried?'

'Well, Jenny, if you don't mind, I would not like to buy the business. I am getting married in two months, and I need all the money that I can get now. Not that I am not grateful, but you understand, don't you?'

'I do understand Robert. You have never been interested in buying the business if I am honest with myself, but I wanted to give you every opportunity to have your own concern. Well, I have a proposition to put to you. My father-in-law is a little at a loss for something to do. He has been working all his life and finds it very hard to stop now. How would you feel about him running the business with you as his manager?'

Robert began smiling. 'I would love that Jenny. I don't like doing the business side of it all. As you know, I love going out with the horses over the hills and away with the deliveries.'

'Well that is settled, then. I will get Ben to come and talk to you. But there are two conditions to this arrangement.'

Robert looked worried.

'You will be called delivery manager and of course there will be a raise in salary, especially as you are going to be married. And the other condition is that I will plan, arrange and pay for your wedding as a thank you for all the hard work that you have done for me. That is, if your bride-to-be's parents don't object.'

Robert beamed broadly. 'They'll not object, Jenny, she hasn't got any parents. We were worried about how we would pay for everything. It is so kind of you.'

'Who is she, Robert? Do I know her?'

'No. She is a scullery maid called Emily at Lady Jolley's place in Waddington. I met her when I was doing deliveries there for you. She will have to leave once we are married. They don't allow married servants living out.'

'What will she do? Will she work or will she stay at home?'

'We would prefer her to work at first, 'til the bairns come along.' Robert stopped abruptly and started blushing.

'Would she like to work here Robert?'

'Yes,' came the short and very quick reply.

'Then bring her in on her afternoon off and we can see where she will fit in.'

'Thank you Jenny. I must admit you have taken a lot of worry off my mind. She will be delighted about the wedding offer. She was just going to wear her best dress and re-trim her newest bonnet. And she saw the weddings that you planned for three of Lady Jolley's girls, so she knows how good you are.'

'Well, make an appointment for Emily with Janey, so that I can set some time aside to plan her wedding.'

'Thank you again.' Jenny smiled as Robert left the office. That was easy, she thought to herself. Three happy people and a problem solved. She didn't get as much time to plan weddings now as she had done previously, but she always set aside time for staff and old customers.

Also, she would not have the worry of overseeing the carters business once old Ben got used to the ropes. She would contact Mr Briggs, her solicitor, to ask him to help old Ben. It would be better coming from another man, rather than a woman, although his daughter Susy would help him as much as she could.

She wrote herself a note to ask Janey to contact Mr Briggs as soon as possible. Yes, she reflected, a good days work.

A week later, a very nervous Emily came for her wedding appointment with Jenny. Robert had brought her into the shop and up to Jenny's office.

'I'll leave her with you, Jenny. Weddings are women's talk,' he grinned. 'Just tell me what to wear and where to turn up and I'll be there.'

'Thank you Robert. I am sure Emily will give you instructions as to how you should behave, won't you?' Jenny asked. Emily nervously nodded a reply.

'Now what style of dress are you thinking about Emily?' asked Jenny after Robert had left.

'Anything Mrs Marshall. I'm sure that you will know best.'

'But I would prefer to make what you would like. It is your special day. What were you going to wear if I hadn't interfered?'

'My best dress is a navy serge, very plain as befitting my station.'

'Oh dear, that wouldn't look very good if you wore that when I planned the wedding would it? Not a very good advertisement,' laughed Jenny. 'Do you like blue?'

'Yes, and Robert likes me to wear blue, too.'

'What about a pale blue dress, not too fancy so that you can wear it as your best dress for Sundays, high days and holidays afterwards?'

'I would like that. I really like pale blue, but I wouldn't have chosen it, as it is not practical enough.'

'Where are you getting married?'

'In Waddington church. Mr Greenwood, the butler is giving me away, my having no family left.'

'Good, and how many bridesmaids are you having?'

'Er, none. It would just be extra expense.'

'No expense to be spared now. Do you have anyone in mind for bridesmaids?'

'My close friend. She is a maid with me, her name is Helen. I could ask her.'

'Nobody else? It is usual to have a little flower girl as well.'

'Not really. Helen and I are so close. We started work together on the same day and we are friendly with the other girls, but none are as special.'

'I could think of someone who would love to be a flower girl,' said Jenny.

'Who?' asked Emily.

'My youngest daughter. She is very aggrieved that she was too young to be a flower girl for her aunty, when her older sister performed that duty. She mentions it every time I plan a wedding.'

'Oh yes, let her be my flower girl. If you don't mind,' Emily asked nervously.

'Mind? I would be delighted. It would keep her happy for many a day. Now when is the wedding booked for?'

'The first of August.'

'We will have to get on with the arrangements then. What colouring is your other bridesmaid, Helen?'

'Dark haired like me. And blue eyes like me as well. That was one of the things that we noticed about each other when we first met.'

'Yes, I noticed your blue eyes, that is why I suggested pale blue. My daughter has blue eyes, too. What about a dark blue for Helen and a floral print for Ellen? I could trim Helen's dress with the floral print from Ellen's dress and vice versa.'

'Yes, that sounds lovely. What style will the dresses be?'

'I am not sure what yours will be like yet, but I will do the other two dresses with a high waist and full skirt. Helen's will have leg of mutton sleeves, but Ellen's will be plainer, as befits her age. Now, your accessories, let me see.' Jenny sat pensively as she sketched her ideas on the paper. A knock at the door interrupted her thoughts.

'Yes, come in,' she called. It was Janey.

'Sorry to disturb you Jenny, but Lady Morag Martin has been on the telephone. They have had a bereavement. Could you go to their house?'

Jenny's heart missed a beat. This was her distant family. Lady Morag was her half-sister, although it had never been acknowledged as such. Who could have died?

'Did she say who had died Janey?'

'No Jenny. It wasn't actually Lady Martin. It was her housekeeper. Do you want me to find out?'

'No, no, I just wondered. Yes, I will ring and arrange to go immediately. Thank you Janey. Emily, it looks like we will have to postpone the rest of our planning session. Come again on your next day off and we will carry on with our plans. But on your way out, go into the ladies gown department and get them to measure you up for your dress. Also, could you ask your friend to come in at her convenience and be measured?'

'I will Jenny, and thank you for everything. It is so kind of you.'

Jenny interrupted her. 'Think nothing of it. Your Robert has been such a help to me since my husband died, that I could never repay him. It is a small measure of my thanks.'

'Thank you anyway. Goodbye,'

'Goodbye. Thanks for coming.' As Emily left, Jenny opened her book to find the telephone number she needed. She waited for the exchange and asked to be connected to the Martin's home in the nearby village of Gisburn.

An hour later, Robert was taking Jenny and Catherine to Gisburn, with a large stock of black ready-made clothes for both the family and servants. Catherine was fairly new to the shop, but had been trained by Marian to help with the wedding planning and all other dressmaking. She was fast proving her worth.

They were taken into the drawing room. After a short wait, Lady Morag herself came into the room. Jenny and Catherine rose respectfully.

'Lady Martin, I am sorry to hear about your bereavement,' said Jenny.

'Thank you Jenny. It is Lady Hortense, my sister-in-law who has passed away, my brother Jeremy's wife.' Jenny was shocked. Hortense could only be in her early twenties.

'I am sorry. She was so young, whatever happened?'

'Died in childbirth. Child with her, too. A boy as well. Jeremy is besides himself.' Floods of memories came back to Jenny of the young Lady Hortense losing babies or having girls, which Lord Jeremy didn't want. He wanted an heir. She remembered the bruises and the crying girl, too. Poor Lady Hortense. Not much of a life married to Lord Jeremy, Jenny's own half-brother.

'Yes,' continued Lady Morag, 'that is why we need full mourning, with it being such a close relative. We will all need black outfits, servants as well.'

'I took the liberty of bringing some servants' gowns with me, also some sketches for your own requirements. Will the men be needing outfits as well, or are you going to ask Cosgroves to undertake there?'

'Yes, just the women. Cosgrove himself is coming this evening. Shall I send your girl to measure up the servants?'

'Yes please. I think that I have your measurements and your daughters, so I will just show you some ideas that I have had.' Catherine left the room accompanied by a maid who had been in attendance throughout. Jenny showed the pictures to Lady Morag, who seemed distracted.

'You seemed shocked when I told you who had passed away, Jenny.'

'Yes, I remember Lady Hortense from when I worked at Ormerod Hall. She is so young and has had such a sad life. It is upsetting to hear sad news like this.'

'And you know more than you are saying about what happened to her with my brother. He was not a good husband, by any means.'

Jenny remained silent, unable to voice her true opinions to this lady.

'Jenny, I know who you are. I will never talk about it before others, but I know that you are my father's daughter.' Very shocked, Jenny still remained silent, not daring to look at Lady Morag.

'I think that I guessed it years ago, but I didn't like to think about it too much, especially when Mama was still alive.'

'I . .er.. had . .er. . no idea,' stuttered Jenny. 'I didn't find out until I came of age. It was a great shock to me too, and I have never told anyone except my husband. I couldn't believe that Lord Ormerod had let me live there in front of everyone without telling me who I was. He never let me know whilst he was alive. He even made me look after your mother, knowing that I was his mistress's daughter.'

'I think I knew whilst your mother was still working there, before I was married. I once watched them together, your mother and my father. They didn't know I was watching. But she left shortly after that, so I thought nothing of it. But you and I are so alike. Not just the hair, but also our slim build and some of our mannerisms. When you stand up, you smooth your clothes down just as I do.'

Jenny smiled ruefully. 'That is true. I always do that. I hate to think that my clothes may be ruffled.'

'I'm surprised that no one else noticed it, the likeness. It was a strange thing that my father did in having you brought to the house. We thought it was someone who had asked my father for help, as he didn't usually involve himself in hiring and firing the servants. Do you know why he brought you there?'

'No. I have thought about that a lot. Perhaps he felt guilty that I had been abandoned in the workhouse after my mother died.'

'Is that what happened? What happened to your mother?'

'She died in childbirth as well, and the woman whom your father had employed to help my mother with the shop took me to the workhouse and said that I had no relatives. She ran the shop to her own benefit, then ran away the day before I took up my inheritance, leaving debts and no stock in the shop. At least your father provided for me and has enabled me to radically change my life. And I have rescued many other people from the workhouse who would never have had the chance to get away otherwise. Yes, I am a wealthy woman now, all thanks to your father.'

'Our father,' Lady Morag gently reminded her.

'Yes, I suppose so, but I never think of him as my father, I still think of him as Lord Ormerod, as I still think about Jeremy as Master Jeremy, rather than Lord.'

'Talking of whom, we must get back to planning the clothes. But can I say Jenny, that I will never mention it to anyone, but would like to acknowledge it privately when we are together. I feel quite a bond between us.'

'Thank you Lady Morag.'

'Morag, when we are alone.'

'Morag, then. And thank you for being so kind. Now here are the sketches. I can have these made up for you by tomorrow evening. Will that be early enough?'

The door opened and Catherine returned to the room.

'Yes, tomorrow evening will be fine. Thank you,' replied Lady Morag, fully an autocrat again, with no hint of the intimacy that had just taken place. Jenny and Catherine gathered their things together and left the room. As Jenny went through the door, she turned back and smiled gently at Lady Morag and received a similar reply.

Jenny was very thoughtful on the way home, reflecting on all that Lady Morag, or should that be Morag now, had said to her. Truly, she had been astonished at all that had taken place. Although on reflection, she had always thought that Lady Morag was the nicest person in the family when she had worked there. At least there was now a person with whom she could talk freely about her parentage.

Jenny was pleased. She now had a sister, something which she had long since regretted not having – even though it was not a relationship that would be acknowledged in public. Yes, sisters were precious things, a joy to have. But there was one thing for sure. She would never acknowledge Jeremy as her brother. Not after what he had done to Marian, nor after what he had tried to do to her as well, when she was a scullery maid.

And then the awful truth dawned on her. If he had done the same to her as he did to Marian, it would have been incest. And who knows what the child would have turned out like. Thank goodness that I managed to fight him off, thought Jenny. No, she would never acknowledge him.

Chapter 7

Susy Butler had asked Jenny if she could borrow her children's christening robes and Jenny had agreed. Secretly though, Jenny had arranged for Marian to make a new set especially for Susy and her new family. Marian was an exquisite embroiderer and had made Jenny's own robes for her children as a gift when the twins were born – indeed she had had to hurriedly make another robe when the second twin arrived, totally unexpectedly.

Jenny's robes were in ivory satin, with short sleeves and little overdresses, as their christening had been in the late summer. As this christening was taking place earlier in the year, the little dress for Jonny was to have long sleeves. It had a short bodice, which was covered in lace and pin tucks, flowing out to a full skirt. The lace was repeated in row after row around the hemline and around the wrists. The sleeves were covered in tiny embroidery patterns all the way down to the lace at the wrists. There was also a row of embroidery above the lace frills around the hem. The matching satin bonnet also had the same embroidery and lace to match.

It was truly exquisite and Jenny was pleased that Marian had managed to make another beautiful gown for her family's children. Her nephew, her Jonny's namesake, would look impressive for his christening.

It has been a special moment when Jenny was asked to be little Jonny's godmother and she eagerly awaited the day. Her own children all had new outfits for the event and were as excited as Jenny was.

The day dawned and they set off to the church together, having arranged to meet Susy and her family at the parish church. Jonny looked resplendent in his robes. Susy had been thrilled by Marian's thoughtfulness in suggesting that she make the new robes. It also helped Jenny in deciding what to buy for her nephew, as she had provided all the necessary materials and trimmings for the gown.

Little Jonny behaved beautifully throughout his christening service and they went back to Susy's house for a light repast. Jenny held him for long periods during the day and found herself wishing that she could again hold a newborn baby of her own in her arms. This thought shocked her, as she had tried to suggest to Jonny that they try to limit their own family. The risk of another set of twins had always been in the back of her mind, but four children in six years had seemed a lot at the time. Sadly her fourth child had been born prematurely and not lived, shortly after Jonny's death.

Now, holding this little boy in her arms, she grieved all over again for the little boy that she had lost. His loss had been subsumed in the overall loss of losing her husband. It didn't matter that she had three other healthy children; she still wanted that other little boy and missed him sorely. She had been luckier than most women of her generation. In the poorer houses in Clitheroe, there were women who had lost all or most of their children and were worn down with years of childbearing and grief. Indeed, her mother-in-law had lost three of her six children.

Perhaps it was because Susy had had a boy. She would not have felt this way if it had been a girl. Or would she? Was her body telling her that it was time to have another baby? Too late, she thought, no more babies for me without Jonny. Unless, she pondered, unless I marry again, but no, she put that thought from her mind. Nobody could take the place of her beloved Jonny. Ever.

Jenny was startled from her reverie by Marian's oldest boy, George.

'Are you all right, Aunty Jenny? You look quite sad.' He placed his hand on hers and gave a little squeeze.

'I am fine, George. I was just thinking about your Uncle Jonny. That is why I must have looked a little sad. Come, let us go and take a stroll round the garden together. That will make me feel better.' They took little Jonny back to his mother and set off into the garden, admiring the rich blooms of the apple blossom, which was flowering all down the side of the garden.

George and Jenny had a special relationship. It had been there right from his birth. Jenny thought that it was because she felt somewhat responsible for his birth. If she hadn't got Marian a job at Ormerod Hall, Marian wouldn't have been raped by Master Jeremy, she had told herself on many occasions. But afterwards, when she knew the truth about her own parentage, she realised that there was a blood tie. This child's father was her half-brother, so that made the child a kind of nephew. Whatever, they had always had a special relationship. George would often come and tell Jenny things that she was sure he wouldn't tell his mother.

After their walk, Jenny did indeed feel better. She entered into the rest of the party with no further sad thoughts and joined in the games which her own and Marian's children organised. The children chattered as they went home in the coach, saying how much they had enjoyed this special day. Jenny could only agree. Her Jonny would live on through his little namesake.

Chapter 8

Jenny was excited. This was the first time that she would actually attend the Clitheroe Christmas ball. Ever since she had inherited the shop, she had hoped to go to the ball, but she had either been too nervous, getting married, expecting babies or in mourning, so one way and another, she had missed them all. Her gowns had gone to many a ball, but always on other people: not on her. She had listened vicariously to the tales of the balls many times and yearned to go. Nothing was going to stand in her way this year.

Each year, the Clitheroe ball was a challenge to the gown shop. So many local ladies came for a ball gown every year, and there never had to be a duplicate. Last year there had been twenty-seven orders for gowns and this year, there were thirty-three orders, well, thirty-four if she counted her own gown. A great challenge indeed.

Her own gown for the ball presented a difficult decision. It was over two years since Jonny had died, and so she was out of full mourning, but she didn't want to shock the worthy burghers of Clitheroe. In the end, she chose a rich lilac satin for the ball. That would satisfy the strictest observers of mourning etiquette, although the rules were relaxing somewhat nowadays. The dedicated mourning observers still cited their dear Queen as being the role model for mourning, but Jenny privately thought that over thirty years of strict mourning was a trifle excessive.

She had chosen a simple style for her dress. It was in the new fashion of a fussy top and sleeves, but a fairly plain skirt. Bustles were very small nowadays and the fashion books said that they were becoming unfashionable and not practical for the modern young woman.

The attention to detail was on the sleeves of her gown. They were of the highest fashion. The full leg of mutton sleeves ended just half way down the upper arm, with the rest of the sleeves being very tight, all the way to her wrist. There were tiny pearl buttons all the way down the side of the sleeves. The shoe department had made her some cream coloured slippers, trimmed with pearls. They had also made her a handbag and shawl to match the outfit in cream satin trimmed with tiny seed pearls. The neckline was modest, befitting a widow and Jenny wore a string of pearls, which she had found in her mother's bedroom many years ago. They looked perfect and completed the outfit.

Jenny often wondered if her father, Lord Ormerod, had bought the pearls for her mother. They looked as if they were of a very high quality, being very milky-white in colour.

Mr Briggs, the solicitor, had agreed to escort her to the ball. He was to pick her up at eight of the clock. It was almost that time before she was ready, as the children kept coming into her bedroom to see how she was getting on with her preparations. In the end, she had to shoo them all away, or she would never have been ready. She told them to wait downstairs.

As she walked down the stairs, the children clapped their hands in delight. It was a long time since they had seen their mum all dressed up ready to go out. Rachel fussed around her mother as if she was the mother and Jenny was the daughter.

'Rachel, I will be all right,' said Jenny. 'Now leave me alone. I am a grown woman and Mr Briggs will escort me, so I will be quite safe.'

'I just want you to have a good time at the ball, mummy.'

'I will, I promise you. I have waited a long time for this occasion.'

A knock at the door heralded the arrival of Mr Briggs. Ben ran to the door and got there before Maggie had even got out of the kitchen.

'Hello Mr Briggs, she is ready. Rachel says that you have to take good care of her,' Ben hurriedly said to Mr Briggs, who laughed.

'Oh I will take great care of your mother, Ben. Very great care. I know that as the man of the household you are concerned about your mother's safety and that is a good thing.'

Ben visibly puffed up when he was referred to as the man of the house. Jenny, having come into the hall at that point, smiled at Mr Briggs, grateful that he was so sensitive to her child's needs.

'May I say how lovely you look, Jenny?'

'Thank you, you may,' replied Jenny just a trifle coquettishly.

'Shall we be going, then?'

Mr Briggs offered his arm to Jenny and they went to the waiting coach. The children waved them off from the doorstep, almost as excited as Jenny was.

'Your children are a credit to you, Jenny.'

'Thank you. It is not easy at times, working and being on my own.'

'Would you like to give up having to work?'

'Oh no, I love my shop. I would hate not to have a business.'

'Do you never get tired of it?'

'Sometimes, when there are difficulties with deliveries or supplies. Or if one of the children are ill. Then it is difficult. But I couldn't bear to think that I would never have a business to run. Do you not get tired of being a solicitor, Mr Briggs?'

'Very frequently,' Mr Briggs laughed, 'and I thought you were using my forename now?'

'I am sorry, Joshua, it is because we were with the children. I never want them to become familiar with people's first names, so I tend to use everyone's surname. What makes you get fed up with your job?'

'People who change their last will and testament on a regular basis! That really makes me weary of the job.'

'Are there many people like that?'

Thankfully, no. I have one old man with no children. He regularly changes his will, depending on which nephew or niece has done him a favour, or upset him. It is quite difficult keeping up with him. One of these days I won't bother preparing a new will but knowing my misfortune, he would probably go and pass away that day and his affairs would not be in order. I would never forgive myself,' Joshua chuckled.

'How often does he send for you then?'

About once a fortnight. Occasionally weekly; and on a rare occasion he manages to go for a month.'

'Once a fortnight? That is absurd. I don't think that I could remember what I had said on the last occasion if I was changing it so frequently.'

'Precisely. I made mine many years ago. After my partner Mr Shoesmith died suddenly, as it happens. It made me realise how fragile life is. But I have never changed it since that date.'

'Yes, life is fragile, isn't it? I never thought that I would not see Jonny again that fateful day.'

'I am sorry Jenny. I didn't mean to remind you of your sad loss. Come, we must talk of brighter things, or we will become quite morbid. Tonight is Clitheroe's premier event of the year. We must not be glum.'

'No indeed,' replied Jenny, visibly cheering. 'Ah, here we are.'

The carriage stopped outside the ballroom and Jenny was instantly aware of bright lights and other coaches dropping people off. They walked into the foyer, were announced by the Master of the Ceremony and walked down into the main ballroom.

Jenny looked around her. She saw all the ball gowns on display, noting her own shop's creations, and those of other establishments. Even at this lovely ball, she could not quite forget her work and the need to be aware of the latest fashions. The colours of the ball gowns were a riot of differing shades. Bounces, flounces, frills and furbelows seemed to be the order of the day. But bustles were definitely going smaller and some ladies were not wearing any bustle at all.

Jenny could see that the next fashion would be for very straight skirts. She would have to have a word with her design team in the morning, she thought to herself.

A hand shook her from her designing schemes.

'Jenny, what are you thinking about? You are in a trance.' It was Mr Nettleton, the jeweller from the next-door shop.

'The shop, would you believe?'

'Yes, I would believe it with you. Come, have a dance with me. Captain Parker of Browsholme has just taken my wife on to the dance floor.'

'Oh, yes I can see her. She does suit that pale blue colour.'

'Are you trying to attract compliments for your creation?'

'Of course not. I am just saying that she suits pale blue. We advised her well.'

'And cost me a lot of money.'

'Surely you don't begrudge your wife a new gown for a ball.'

'Oh no. The gown was very reasonable. It was the sapphire necklace and earrings that she just had to have to go with it,' he laughed, 'was that your idea as well?'

Jenny blushed. 'Not exactly, although I did mention that it would look well with sapphire jewellery. Oh dear, have I caused you a problem?'

Mr Nettleton laughed again. 'Certainly not. It helped me decide what to buy her for a joint birthday and Christmas present this year. Besides, I like the idea that you tell your customers which jewels they need to compliment your gowns. Especially if you send them next door to me,' he laughed uproariously at this.

'I try my best,' replied Jenny smugly, and they both laughed.

The dance had finished by this time and Mrs Nettleton and Captain Parker were heading over to them.

'Mr Nettleton, I return your dear lady wife.'

'Thank you Captain Parker. May I present Mrs Jenny Marshall of Mitchell Modes?'

'Good evening, Mrs Marshall. I am pleased to meet you at long last. I seem to hear quite a lot about you in the town.'

'You do?' asked Jenny curiously.

'Yes, I am on the Board of Governors at the workhouse and your name is always being mentioned. You seem to be offering us a one-woman rescue service for young women with no foreseeable means. Almost every time we sanction an inmate leaving the house, they seem to be coming to you. It is very commendable, my dear.'

'I am happy to perform that function.'

'Why do you like to take all your staff from the workhouse? Is there any particular reason? Or are you just a great philanthropist?'

'No, replied Jenny quietly. 'I came from the workhouse myself.' Captain Parker was aghast.

'Surely not, I mean, er, I, er, I know that you are a successful businesswoman in the town. I just assumed that you were a person of wealth.'

'Indeed not, Captain Parker,' said Jenny becoming a trifle haughty in her manner. 'I was an inmate in Clitheroe workhouse from being a small child until I went to work in Ormerod Hall at Burnley as a scullery maid. I only inherited my shop when I was eighteen years of age,' she said proudly.

'Well, that is very commendable. You deserve success. That explains a lot.'

'What do you mean, it explains a lot?' Jenny said sharply.

'Why, just that you are so keen so take inmates from the workhouse into your establishment, I meant nothing more.'

'I would like to help more than I do already, if that were possible.'

'In what way? What else could you do that would exceed all your good work already?'

'I would like to be on the Board of Governors of the workhouse.'

There was a stunned silence. Jenny looked down, worrying that she had come out with this idea too suddenly, and that Captain Parker would think her too forward. Eventually he broke the silence.

'Well my dear, the governors are usually male. It is a man's world in business and commerce.'

'But I am a business woman and Mrs Lofthouse is allowed to attend the meetings, is she not?'

'Er, well, yes,' Captain Parker blustered, 'but she is the matron. 'She is the only lady who attends these meetings and is only there because she is the matron, not because she has any power. Ladies do not usually take office in local government.'

'Some ladies do. I was reading only recently about a lady with a famous son, Samuel Crompton, who invented the Spinning Jenny in Bolton. She was the overseer of the poor in Bolton.'

'Yes, well I suppose that there are some exceptions, but it is not the normal pattern.'

'Are there any vacancies coming up on the Board of Governors?' persisted Jenny.

'Yes, there is one. Reverend Wilkinson has just passed away and he will need to be replaced. But I am afraid that there is little chance of you being given a place on the Board of Governors.'

'Why?'

'Probably Reverend Wilkinson's successor will be given a place.'

'Is that always the case? Is that place tied to the reverend gentleman who is the incumbent of the parish?'

'By no means. The place has to be filled by a voting procedure.'

'So I could apply for a place?'

'I suppose so, but it would mean . .'

'Could I or couldn't I?' Jenny interrupted.

Captain Parker sighed.

'Yes, you could apply. But there may be little chance of being voted on to the Board because you are . .'

'A lady,' Jenny finished the sentence for him.

'Yes,' said Captain Parker, bowing his head in embarrassment.

'I see,' replied Jenny with dignity, belying the anger that had arisen in her. 'You do not wish any woman to interfere with local government, even though she pays the same taxes and has taken on many of the workhouse inmates over the last 12 years. Thank you Captain Parker, I understand. Good night, I will leave you to your lady wife.' She turned away from him, towards the Nettletons. 'Mrs Nettleton, Mr Nettleton, I bid you goodnight, too.'

Jenny marched off quickly, muttering to herself. She was relieved when she saw Joshua Briggs coming towards her.

'What on earth is the matter Jenny? You look positively murderous,' said Joshua.

'This town and all the men in it,' Jenny replied forcibly.

'Oh dear, am I included in that sweeping gesture?'

'No, you are excluded. But all the other men. Especially the ones connected with the workhouse.'

'What has brought this on, Jenny? You were quite happy when I left you with Mr Nettleton.'

'I was. But he introduced me to Captain Parker of Browsholme.'

'A fine gentleman, one who is very generous with both his time and money.'

'Humph,' snorted Jenny. 'Not very generous in his opinion of women.'

'I don't understand your attitude, Jenny. He is a perfect gentleman in every sense of the word.'

'I asked him if I could be on the workhouse Board of Governors now that Reverend Wilkinson has passed away. He said that ladies were not encouraged to be on the Board of Governors.'

'Oh Jenny,' said Joshua aghast. 'Why do you want to be on the Board of Governors?'

'Because I want to help people in the workhouse even more than I do already. I want to make conditions better for them. And also I can find out when there are suitable people who could come and work for me.' Jenny replied forcefully.

'So you want to make sure that you get the best workforce, then?'

'No,' shouted Jenny. 'I want to help people. Not just get the best for myself. I find that attitude offensive.'

Joshua took her arm and led her out into the conservatory.

'Now my dear, let's just sit in here for a while, whilst you calm down,' soothed Joshua.

Jenny pulled her arm away from him and sat down near the large tropical plant. Joshua continued to talk soothingly to her, but Jenny ignored him. Eventually, when all else seemed to be failing, Joshua suggested that he would recommend her for a place on the Board at the next meeting. Instantly, Jenny smiled and suggested that they go back into the dance hall. Joshua followed her, shaking his head behind her back. No sooner had they got back into the ballroom than supper was announced.

They both partook of a lovely meal and then returned to the ballroom, having several dances with different partners.

It was soon time to go home. Jenny was very tired, after all the strenuous dancing. As they got into the coach, Joshua asked Jenny if she had enjoyed herself.

'Oh yes, thank you. I have had a lovely time,' she replied, 'well, most of the time,' she managed to laugh, remembering her fit of pique.

On arriving home, Joshua led Jenny into her house and Jenny offered him some light refreshment before he returned home to Sabden village where he lived, some four miles from Clitheroe. He accepted gratefully but seemed a little distracted. Jenny thought that it was probably due to her outburst earlier, and decided to be more amenable to him for the rest of the night.

Maggie welcomed them into the house and said that she would bring refreshments into the lounge. They went into the lounge where the lights were sparkling in their mantles, casting a glow on all her beautiful furniture.

After Maggie had left the tray, Jenny poured them both a cup of tea and they settled companionably by the fire. Joshua was still quiet and Jenny tried to keep the conversation flowing. When it continued to flag, Jenny started to yawn and made suggestions that perhaps it was time for Joshua to go.

'Actually Jenny, before I go, there is something I would like to ask you.'

'Yes?' said Jenny expectantly, hoping it was about the Board of Governors at the workhouse.

'Well, I . . er I was wondering if you would do me the honour of becoming my wife.'

There was a stunned silence.

'I have loved you from afar ever since you arrived in our office at eighteen years of age,' stuttered Joshua. 'It would make me so happy to be your husband, if you would consider it. You have been a widow for more than two years now and I have waited this long so there didn't seem any indecent haste.' There was a further silence.

'I realise by the look on your face that I have startled you. I do not push you for an answer tonight. I know you will need to think about this. Take all the time that you need. There, I have said enough. I will go now. I will see myself out. Goodnight and thank you for a wonderful evening, Jenny.' He stood up, made a small bow and left the room quickly.

Jenny was so stunned by his proposal that she didn't even follow him to the door, her good manners deserting her in her state of shock. Marriage, to Joshua? She could hardly believe it. She sat sipping her tea, desperately unhappy. She couldn't marry Joshua; she knew she couldn't. It would feel like a betrayal to Jonny.

Besides, she thought of Joshua as an elder brother, not a potential husband. He was so much older than her, she mused, but then age wouldn't matter if she cared for him in that way. Perhaps I have been too familiar in my dealings with him, Jenny reflected. But then I have behaved no differently lately than I always have. And do I want to marry again? Not really. I am happy as I am with the children and my work.

She laughed to herself; she couldn't see Joshua letting her carry on with the shop if she was his wife. No, she did not want to marry again. Well not yet certainly, perhaps never. But definitely she did not want to marry Joshua Oh dear, how was she going to tell him? She knew that it would hurt him dreadfully and probably ruin their good business relationship. She had relied on him for so much ever since she had inherited the shop.

Jenny went up to her bedroom, but sleep was a long time in coming as she worried over the results of her refusal. She even considered marrying him after all and looked at the possibility from all angles. But after much consideration, she decided that she couldn't marry him. It would not be fair. But how would she tell him? Eventually sleep overtook her, but she had a restless night and awoke feeling far from refreshed.

Chapter 9

Jenny wasn't allowed any extra sleep after her late night. Her bedroom door was thrown open and her three lively children bounced into her room at an unearthly hour, or so it felt to Jenny.

'Mummy, mummy, tell us about the ball,' shrieked Ellen.

'Here is your morning tea,' said Rachel. 'Cook said that I may bring it up for you, as I am the eldest.'

'And I opened all the doors for her,' Ben chipped in.

'Thank you children, thank you all,' replied Jenny. 'I had a lovely time and danced all night, so please give me a moment to recover and then I will tell you all about it at breakfast time.'

'Did you dance with any princes?' Ellen wanted to know.

Jenny laughed. 'Now go downstairs, all of you and I will be with you shortly.' Washing and dressing quickly, she was soon downstairs in the dining room. The children all started talking at once as she came into the room.

'Quiet,' she shouted, 'or I shall send you all up to your bedrooms at once.' It worked instantly. She then proceeded to tell the children all the details of the ball, disappointing Ellen that there had not been any princes in attendance.

'Not even the Prince of Wales?' she asked earnestly.

'Not even the Prince of Wales,' Jenny replied mournfully.

'Why not? Did nobody invite him?'

'Perhaps not,' replied Jenny. 'I don't know really. I don't know anyone in Clitheroe who knows him well enough to invite him to our ball.'

'Well, when I am old enough to go to the ball I shall write to Buckingham Palace and invite him to the ball. I am sure he will come.'

'Don't be a goose, Ellen,' said her older sister. 'Princes don't come to little market towns like this. And anyway, it will be years before you go to the ball. But I will be going very soon, won't I mummy?'

'Not very soon, Rachel. You have a few years of growing to do yet.'

'Oh it is not fair. I would love to be grown up now. Then I could stop going to that ridiculous school you send us to.'

'Are you not happy at school, Rachel?'

'No. I know all I need to know now. Most children leave school at nine or ten years of age. I just want to leave school and start working in the shop.'

'Which shop?' asked a surprised Jenny.

'Ours of course,' replied Rachel, a tone of disdain in her voice.

'Do you mean my shop?' asked Jenny, with just a hint of emphasis on the word 'my'.

'Yours, ours, it means the same. It will be ours after you are gone, mummy, and I would like to work in it as soon as I may. When can I leave school? I can do writing and sums now, enough for what I need in the shop. I don't need to learn about history to run a shop.'

Jenny was stunned. She had no idea that Rachel had any interest in the shop – yet alone wishing to work in it. She had not thought about the future of the business beyond making an income for her children and keeping them out of the workhouse. Passing the shop on to the next generation was something that had not occurred to her.

And Rachel was the last of her children whom she thought would be interested in the shop. Rachel was often quite aristocratic in her demeanour: hardly a subservient person who waited on other people's pleasure. This was indeed a turn up for the books. But it was something that Jenny must put away for the time being. Today was more important. She had a shop to run; children to sort out; a home to supervise. Yes, she would think about this new idea another day. Rachel was only eight years old. Time enough another day. She recovered herself quickly.

'And what makes you think I won't be here to run my shop? I intend to be around for a very long time yet, so don't start making plans for after I have gone. It will be a long time before you inherit the shop, young lady.'

'Well, as the eldest, I think that I should be allowed to work in the shop first.'

'If that is the case then Ben can start working in the shop ten minutes after you,' Jenny teased.

'I don't want to work in the shop. I don't want to sell gowns; that's women's work. I want to be an engineer and see how things work,' replied Ben.

'You do, Ben? Where have you got this idea to be an engineer?' said Jenny

'We have been learning about Mr Stevenson at school in history. He made railways. And now they are making horseless carriages, which can sort of have engines like railways and won't need horses. Won't that be grand?'

'Very grand,' replied Jenny, surprised at her son's desire to be an engineer.

'Well, I wouldn't like a horseless carriage,' piped up Ellen, 'because I would miss seeing the horses. I love the horses. Can I have a pony, please mummy? You said that I could when I was older and I am older now. Oh please mummy.'

'But Ellen, you only asked last week. You are not much older yet. I meant several years. And before you go out rescuing any stray ponies, I do not want a pony for my birthday, Christmas or any other time, thank you,' said Jenny with a stern face. Deciding it was time to change the subject, Jenny asked Ellen what she would like to do when she was older.

'I don't want to do anything, mummy. I just want to stay at home with you and look after you. And look after my pony as well, as I will be much older then.'

So much for changing the subject, thought Jenny. 'Come along children, time for piano lessons. Wash your hands and faces and comb your hair. Mr Marsden will be here very soon. I hope you have all done your practice pieces.'

The children groaned in unison.

'Do we have to have piano lessons, mummy?' wheedled Ben. 'I would much rather be reading about Mr Stevenson. I have brought a book home from the Public Lending Library.'

'Piano lessons first,' said Jenny firmly, 'then you can do whatever you want for the rest of the day. I am only going into the shop this morning and will be with you this afternoon. You can decide what we will do between you.' Slightly mollified, the children went off to prepare for their lessons and Jenny went to get ready to leave the house to go to the shop.

The children's chatter at breakfast-time had distracted her from the problem about Mr Briggs, or Joshua. How could she tell him without hurting him, or spoiling their close working relationship? She would have to mull this over during the next day or two. She did not want to leave it too long, especially as she was going to reject his offer.

Once arriving at the shop, all thoughts of the children and Joshua were put away as she concentrated on her business. She had a business meeting with Sarah this morning. Jenny had inherited Sarah with the shop. She had been a slight young girl then, who had been underfed and mistreated by Bruce. It had been a privilege to watch her grow to womanhood. Sarah's first area of responsibility had been to look after young George, Marian's baby, whilst Marian worked in the shop.

Later, Sarah had developed the shoe department, as this had been a favourite area in the shop for her. Gradually, she had taken over responsibility for larger areas of the shop and now was Jenny's second in command in the shop.

After the main business of the day was done, Jenny made Sarah laugh about the hopes and desires of her children.

'You will have to look out for your job, Sarah. Rachel thinks that she is almost ready for it!' said Jenny.

'Oh well, at least I know I have got competition,' Sarah joked back. 'Seriously though Jenny, will you let her come into the shop?'

'I don't know. I haven't thought it through yet. I suppose if she wants to, she can, but as she is only eight, I'll leave it to worry about for another day. I think your job is safe for a little while yet.'

'Are you here all day today, Jenny?'

'No, I intend to leave shortly after lunch. I have told the children we will do something together. They see little enough of me at times. Will you lock up for me, Sarah?'

'Yes, of course. I will see you on Monday, then. Enjoy your time with the children.'

'I will, thanks.' Sarah closed the door quietly behind her. Jenny gave a grateful sigh of relief that she had such a competent person whom she could leave in charge. She got out the balance figures for the last month. As ever, they were very healthy, despite all the staff that she employed, and despite giving them all percentage bonuses in their wages. There was a very small turnover in staff, as the wages and conditions, which she gave, were more generous than any other similar establishment. Her staff were loyal to her, especially as many of them were from the workhouse and would not have had such a good post or standard of living without Jenny.

Jenny would never be tired of the shop, it had given her the chance to live a decent life, but she could never be complacent. She must always strive to keep abreast of the changes in fashion, and changes also, in other shops.

There was no room for expansion on either side of her shop. Mr Nettleton was on one side and an alleyway on the other. If she needed to expand, then it would mean moving to another shop. Did she want to expand? Perhaps she would need to as her shop developed more departments. Perhaps she should start looking round for bigger premises. Or even expand by starting another shop.

Perhaps even in another town. Blackburn, or Burnley would be ideal. They would both benefit from having another large select gown shop. Yes, she must think about this soon. Perhaps put some discreet feelers out amongst her trade connections. Perhaps Joshua might know of somewhere. Thinking of Joshua reminded her of the unpleasant duty which she had to perform. The sooner, the better. She stood up from her desk, reached for her winter coat and bonnet and set off for home. The sooner she got home to her children, the better that would be, too.

As she opened the door, Ellen rushed towards her, nearly knocking her off her feet.

'Mummy, mummy, Aunty Marian has asked us all to tea. Oh, do say that we can go, please do.'

'Yes, all right. Is that what you all want to do?'

'Yes, and we were good for Mr Marsden, too. He said to tell you that we were all improving.'

'Really? That is a surprise,' said Jenny dryly. 'Have you told Cook that we have been invited out for tea?'

'Yes and she said that was fine.'

'Well, you seem to have got it all organised Ellen. What time do we have to be there?'

'Three of the clock.'

'I had better get changed out of my work clothes then. It is almost two of the clock now. Where are the others?'

Ellen looked sheepish. 'They have already gone to Aunty Marian's. Roger was going to get the horse some new shoes and they got a lift.'

'I see. Well, we had better hurry up then, hadn't we? Is Roger back with the horse yet?'

'No, but we can walk can't we?'

'Yes, it is a nice crisp afternoon. It will do us good to walk.' Jenny went upstairs to change her clothes and then she and Ellen set out to walk up Waddington Road and on to Pimlico Road where Marian and Will had just moved to a new, larger house.

Will had taken all the children for a walk, so whilst Ellen played upstairs in the playroom, Jenny and Marian settled down for a good talk, as they got little enough time to talk nowadays.

'How is young Master Jonny?' asked Marian.

'Oh he is well. He is so beautiful,' enthused Jenny.

'There speaks the devoted godmother,' teased Marian. 'And speaking of godmothers, I may be needing one myself soon.'

'You? Why, Marian, are you expecting again?'

'Yes,' replied Marian. 'I hope that I carry this one safely this time.' Marian had lost her last baby at seven months. It had been a little girl and Marian was very sad as she had wanted a girl to complement her two boys.

'When is the baby due?'

'Around Easter time. I didn't tell anyone for a while, just in case. I haven't told the boys of course. Time enough to tell them if they notice anything different about my shape,' laughed Marian ruefully. 'I wanted to tell you before I told Sarah, as it will soon become obvious when I no longer want to come to the shop.'

'I am so pleased for you.

'Thank you. I'm pleased too. I would like four children ideally. But you get what you are given don't you?'

'That is true. At the rate Jonny and I were going, I think we would have had about six by now, even more if we had had any more twins! I was beginning to wonder about how to stop babies coming.'

'Oh Jenny, you can't. Well, not unless, you, er, you know, abstain.'

'Oh yes you can. There are ways and means, but nobody tells you about them. I am sure that there are people who would help other women. Some women are just worn out by childbearing, year after year. And then the children often don't survive. Surely it is far better to have fewer children who are healthy, and you can afford to feed and clothe them properly.'

'My goodness, Jenny. Don't you know that you can be prosecuted for stopping babies coming? You sound very radical. You will be joining those Suffragist women next.'

'I wouldn't mind. I think it is about time that women got the vote. I pay tax, own three businesses and a house, but I am not allowed to vote. It is not that long since women gained the right to own property in their own right, too, without it becoming the property of the husbands on marriage. It is not fair.'

'That is true, but would women want to vote? I certainly wouldn't. I would prefer to leave it all to Will. He can vote for me. I make my feelings known to him.'

'But what if you disagreed? What if he voted for something that you really were violently opposed to?'

'I am sure he wouldn't do.' said Marian sullenly.

'But wouldn't it be better if you could vote yourself?'

'I am not interested really. I think all that sort of thing is for men. A woman's work is her children and looking after her husband and the home, not fretting about governments.'

'Oh Marian, you are so old-fashioned. It is nearly the twentieth century. It is time women's voices were heard.'

'Well, I am still not sure. I don't know any women who want to vote.'

'Yes, you do.'

'Who?'

'Me!'

'Oh you, I mean besides you.'

'I think many of our workforce would be interested. Look at the way the mill girls of Lancashire are rising up to join the Suffragists. I am sure there is much interest in Clitheroe, especially in the mills.'

'You wouldn't, Jenny?'

'Wouldn't what?'

'You know what I mean, join the Suffragists.'

'I might. But I probably won't, but I am very sympathetic to their cause. I would help any of my staff if they wanted to campaign. I would give money too. In fact, I already have.'

'No,' said Marian disbelievingly, 'when?'

'Today, after Captain Parker said that I probably wouldn't get on the Board of Governors at the workhouse because I am a woman!'

'Be careful Jenny. It might not be wise. It could harm your business.'

'It will take more than an interest in the Suffragists to ruin my business, Marian, so don't you worry. Yours and Will's jobs are safe with me. I wouldn't go as far as to compromise the business. It means everything to me. Besides, I need to leave it in good order ready for Rachel.'

'For Rachel? What about the others?'

'Oh, Rachel has all the future planned. She wants to leave school now, as she knows enough to be able to run a shop and take over fairly soon. She reminded me that I wouldn't always be around. It was quite a shock to hear her say it, I can tell you.'

'I wouldn't have thought that Rachel would be interested in the shop,' replied Marian.

'No, neither did I. It was a surprise.'

'And what about the others?'

'Ben wants to be an engineer and Ellen wants to stay at home with me and have a pony.'

'Is Ellen asking about having a pony again?'

'Sadly, yes. But I am not giving in. She is far too young yet.'

'Well at least my children aren't giving me problems. George wants to be an engine driver on the railway.'

Jenny laughed. 'That must be all the journeys you used to take him on when he was tiny. What about Luke?'

'Now that is a surprise. He wants to be a teacher.'

'At least he will always have employment, especially now that children are forced to go to school. What has made him interested in becoming a teacher?'

'He just loves school. He would go there at weekends if he got the chance. He always has his nose in a book.'

'I knew he was good at school: my children tell me that about him. But a teacher! And yet, why not? I hope that he will achieve it, and if there is anything I can do to help, just let me know.'

'I am sure we can manage ourselves, Jenny. We owe you enough already. But thank you for the offer anyway.'

A noise at the door interrupted the talk. The children clattered into the room, followed by Will.

'Mum, mum, we have seen a horseless carriage. Doctor Dunlop was driving it. It looked very smart. Can we have one?'

'No Ben, we can't. Was it not noisy and frightening?'

'Not at all, it looked fun.'

'It was very noisy and looked very frightening, Jenny. It seemed to be going very fast,' said Will. 'Do not take any notice of Ben. He would have run after Doctor Dunlop and begged a ride if I hadn't restrained him.'

'You mustn't do that, Ben. It would be rude to ask. I would be frightened to go in one anyway,' said Jenny.

'Your mummy was frightened to go on a railway when she was younger, so don't ask her about a horseless carriage. It will take her years to get in one,' teased Marian.

The maid arrived at that point to say that tea was ready. They all went into the next-door room to eat their tea. After tea, the children went upstairs to play and Will went into the backyard to smoke his pipe. The friends were alone again and able to continue talking.

'Well Marian, where did you get that maid from? You kept that quiet. Fancy you having a maid,' said Jenny.

Marian blushed, and then rallied. 'Katy, you mean? I got the idea from a friend of mine who has several servants,' Marian replied in a false mincing voice. 'And like my friend, I got my maid from the workhouse. What is good enough for my friend, is good enough for me.'

'Really?' said Jenny, ignoring the sarcasm, 'that is good. How long have you had her?'

'Two days! But Katy is so grateful for getting a job out of the workhouse. We know how she feels, don't we?'

'We certainly do. Does she know that you and I were in the workhouse as well?'

'Yes, she couldn't believe it. She thinks that Will and I are quite well-to-do. I said to wait until she met my friend, meaning you.'

Jenny giggled. 'We were so lucky to escape. I am glad you are able to help people escape, too.'

'When you gave Will his last pay rise, we decided that we would look around for a suitable person, especially as I am going to need some help soon,' she said patting her tummy. 'It was Will's idea to go to the workhouse actually.'

'Who would have thought that we would be sat around discussing the servants, like they used to do at Ormerod Hall?'

'At least we treat them better than they did at Ormerod Hall, although we didn't feel badly done to after having lived in the workhouse. It was just bliss to get well fed instead of the terrible food they gave us at the workhouse.'

Will returned to the living room and asked if the children could stay overnight.

'Oh no, it is not fair on Marian. They will be too much trouble.'

'They will be no trouble,' said Will. 'And besides, we have a maid now. She will help Marian. She is not much older than the children. She will probably like playing with them, never mind looking after them!'

The children entered the room at that point and begged to be allowed to stay, so Jenny relented. She bade farewell to them all and decided to walk back home herself.

As she got to the junction of Pimlico Road and Waddington Road, she decided on impulse to go back to the shop. She could ring Maggie from the shop and warn her that the children weren't coming home tonight. In fact she could tell Maggie to let Megan have a night off. Megan could then go home to her mother's house for the rest of the weekend. Jenny turned towards the town centre and quickened her pace as she neared the shop.

Chapter 10

Sarah was just locking up as Jenny arrived at the shop. Sarah jumped. 'Oh Jenny, I didn't expect to see you here tonight. Is anything the matter?'

'No, I am suddenly childless,' she laughed. 'We have been to Marian's for tea and the children asked to stay for the night. So I thought that I would come back here and do some thinking. But don't let me keep you. You are already late going home as it is.'

'Oh, there was a problem with the final balances of the day. It took a while to sort out. But it is correct now. What sort of planning are you doing?'

'I just wanted to take a look at the shop and think how I could improve it.'

'Do you want some help? Or do you think better on your own?'

'Why? Do you have some ideas?'

'I think that the shop grew in a sort of haphazard way. We thought of a new department, so we started one. There isn't much continuity to the shop.'

'Sarah, that is exactly what I had been thinking, but life is so busy that I couldn't put my finger on what was wrong. Are you going anywhere tonight?'

'No, as you know, my fiancé is in the army and he does not come home for three months. I have nothing better to do this evening.'

'Help me then Sarah, if you like.'

'Yes, I would like that Jenny. Thanks. Where shall we start?'

'I thought that I would get the measurements out first and write down all the departments and then see if I could make some sense out of them. If you write all the departments down now, I will go and get the plans that we had drawn up for the deeds of the shop.'

Jenny returned with the plans and spread them out on her office desk. Sarah had the list of departments ready. Slowly they worked through the shop, trying to make more sense of where everything could go. Jenny sighed.

'Really, we need more room, but there are no more neighbouring shops to buy up.'

'Yes, space is a problem. Do you still use the upstairs rooms?' asked Sarah innocently. Jenny froze. Her rooms upstairs. She didn't use them anymore and hadn't done since she and Jonny had bought the house on Waddington Road. But she had never thought of using them, they held too many memories of the time she had spent with Jonny before the children had come.

'Jenny? Are you all right?' asked Sarah, worried by the look on Jenny's face.

'Yes, yes, I am all right Sarah. I was just remembering. No, I suppose I don't use the rooms anymore. I could open them up to make more room for the shop.'

'Shall we go up and look at them now, so that we can add them to our plans?'

'No,' said Jenny sharply. 'No, we can't go and look at them.'

'I am sorry, did I say something wrong.'

'No, nothing wrong. It's just that those rooms bring back many memories to me. Suffice it to say that there is as much space on the top floor as there is on the other floors. We would have to change all the rooms around anyway, so we could make a large sales area at the top.'

'What about putting all the staff areas and the kitchen and tearoom on the top floor?'

'But how would all our elderly customers get up there? They have enough trouble getting to the ladies department on the second floor sometimes,' said Jenny. They sat in silence for a while. Then Jenny remembered a conversation that she had held with her son Ben.

'Sarah, my son was telling me that some shops are installing special platforms into shops, which can take passengers up to the next floor. That might be the answer. It might even increase our trade if customers know that they can easily get from one floor to another.'

'We always offer to bring the goods down to the sitting room on the ground floor if they struggle with the stairs,' said Sarah haughtily.

'I know you do, Sarah, and I am not criticising that, but the ladies would far rather go upstairs themselves. This could be a major feature in the refurbished shop.'

'Wouldn't the building of this moving platform cause a lot of extra work?'

'Yes, it would I suppose. We would have to close the shop for a week or two, I think. I don't know. I would have to find out some details. But we could have the moving platform done first before we did the other alterations.'

'It all seems a lot of work and trouble.'

'Yes, but it will be worth it in the long run. Much of the shop needs repainting anyway, so it would be a good opportunity to give everything a new look. We could even change the colour scheme. Are you not fed up with brown and cream?'

'No, I quite like it. I think it gives the shop a distinctive look. People recognise the shop by the colours.'

'I won't change the colours then,' said Jenny laughing. 'I might even make you a wedding gown in brown and cream if you like the colours so much,' she teased.

'I don't like them enough to be married in them, but I think it makes us look very smart, but not too severe, which black and white might do.'

'That is true. I will probably leave the colour scheme as it is, then. Now I think we have done enough tonight. Perhaps we can have another meeting when I have had the engineers in to give an estimate to see if they can build a moving platform. And I will want Mr Aggett in to give an estimate for the repainting. Leave it with me for now, but if you have any more good ideas, let me know. You have really helped me to clarify what I want to do tonight.'

'Shall we walk home together, Jenny?'

'No Sarah. I think I will stay a little longer and then telephone for Roger to come and pick me up. Will you be all right on your own?'

'Yes, I haven't far to go, have I,' laughed Sarah. Sarah lived in a small terraced house at the back of the shop, down on Lowergate.

'No, you haven't. Well, go carefully and thank you again for tonight.'

'Anytime, Jenny. Good night.'

Jenny locked the main door after Sarah had gone and then slowly turned towards the fourth floor of the shop. She would have a fresh look around this top floor and try and plan what it would look like with a different layout from what it now had.

As she walked around the area, Jenny remembered the first time that she had seen this suite of rooms, which had belonged to her mother. It was the first time that she had realised whose daughter she was, and the information had not pleased her at the time. She looked again at the picture of her mother and the old Lord Ormerod, her father.

The lounge was decorated in a sumptuous fashion: perhaps something of this room could be kept and used as a sitting room on the top floor when she reorganised her shop. Perhaps it could even become the tearoom?

Yes, this had distinct possibilities, thought Jenny to herself. She moved into the bedroom and looked again at the wall of mirrors along one side of the room. She remembered how shocked she had been when she first saw them, saying that the mirrors made it look like a boudoir but Jonny had made her realise that it was a precious tribute to her parent's love.

Well, they can't stay as they are, thought Jenny. It would be too embarrassing to have them on show. But how would she get them removed to another room? It would be difficult. It would have to be someone that she trusted. Mr Aggett would be best. She would call him in and show him the whole suite and ask his advice on how to use the rooms to best advantage.

The bathroom could stay, as this would make an extra bathroom for the staff or customers to use. As could the kitchen, or should the kitchen be made much larger by using the lounge? And what about her old bedroom from when she was a baby? Jenny wandered into the bedroom and the painting over the fireplace caught her gaze. It was of herself as a toddler, beautifully dressed, running towards someone with glee. She sighed.

Jenny had no memory of this time in her life, nor indeed of her mother. She would take this picture to her house before she changed the use of the rooms and put it in her bedroom. What she would do with the picture of her mother and father, she did not know. It would obviously have to come out of the suite, but she could not have the painting hung at home without causing some questions to be asked.

The other room was a workroom, which her mother had used in the evenings. This was only a small room, so perhaps the whole floor could be re-arranged. But first she would contact Mr Aggett for his advice and swear him to secrecy about the contents of the suite. She would contact him on Monday, although it was a little near Christmas now.

Also on Monday, she must contact Joshua. In all the excitement of the weekend, she had forgotten that she had to give him an answer to the marriage proposal, which he had made.

Jenny rang Roger and asked him to come and collect her from the shop. When he arrived, he told Jenny that Mr Marsden had called with a letter.

'What is it about?' asked Jenny.

'I don't know. He just left it for you.'

'I hope the children haven't been misbehaving.'

'I don't think so. It seemed urgent, or else why would he bring it tonight instead of next Saturday?'

'Hmm. True. Well, I will see what it is when I get home.'

They drove the short distance to Waddington Road and Maggie brought in a tray of tea, with the aforesaid letter perched on the tray.

Jenny opened the letter. Mr Marsden was asking if the children could go with him to Mearly Hall, to the home of Lord Thievely on New Years Eve to perform a short concert for his guests. Jenny would also be welcome to attend with them. Some of his other pupils would also be performing.

Well, this was quite unexpected. Her children performing in a concert! She hoped that they would behave. Perhaps they would practice a little more often if they were making an appearance for someone else, she thought. There was no reason why they could not go, and so she wrote a reply to Mr Marsden and asked Roger to deliver the letter after church tomorrow morning.

Next day, after the children returned from Marian's, they all groaned when Jenny told them what she had done. But being fairly obedient children, they all promised to practice a little extra every day until the concert.

On the Monday, Jenny asked Joshua to call on her that evening. She gently told him that she could not marry him, and he took it quietly.

'I didn't expect you to say yes, but I had to ask. I hope you are not offended?'

'Certainly not. I am most honoured that you asked me. But I hope that we may remain friends?'

'Of course. We have known each other too long to let this spoil our friendship.'

'Thank you. I was worried that you would be offended and would not let us keep the same relationship, which we have always enjoyed. I do rely on you so much.'

'And I will continue to serve you in whatever capacity that you need me to. Friends?' he said, offering her his hand.

She took his hand. 'Yes, friends. Very good friends.'

Suddenly Joshua jumped up and said that he must be going as he had another errand. They parted amicably, but as he left, Jenny felt miserable because she had upset him and could not acquiesce to his proposal.

It was soon Christmas Day and Jenny invited Marian, Will and the children, and also Mr and Mrs Marshall, her parents-in-law, and Susy and Arthur and baby Jonny.

The table groaned under the excess of food. An extra wing had had to be laid in the table to accommodate everyone. As soon as the food was cooked, Jenny told all the servants to come and join them for the meal, sitting down at the same table with the family. As soon as they had eaten, Jenny sent all of her staff home, or to their quarters. The rest of the day was for them to enjoy alone. Within half an hour, all the servants were gone and Jenny detailed all the children to start clearing the table. Amidst groans, the children carried the dishes out into the kitchen.

'All ready?' asked Jenny.

'Ready for what, mummy?' asked Rachel.

'Ready for washing up.'

'But we don't know how to do it,' replied Ben and Luke.

'Then it is high time that you learnt. Now all of you help each other out, whilst we adults have a chat and enjoy a cup of tea. Afterwards we will play some games, but not until the washing up is done.'

'Can't we leave it for the servants until tomorrow?' asked Rachel.

'No we can't, Rachel. Would you like to have to wash up all this lot tomorrow?' Rachel shook her head vigorously. 'And neither would they. So get on with it.' The children went reluctantly to the kitchen and started the allotted task. The whole job was done very quickly and Jenny thought that she would have to go into the kitchen tonight and check what sort of mess they had made, but for now, she just thanked the children.

They played riotous games for the rest of the evening. Little Jonny watched the older children, sat upon his mother's knee, looking like he would like to join in all the festivities. Next year, he would be with the other children, tottering around and trying to keep up with them. And perhaps Marian would have her little girl. As the children drifted to bed, and the others left, Jenny reflected on what a happy Christmas time it had been. Another happy memory that no one could take away from her.

Chapter 11

By five of the clock on New Years Eve, the children were getting excited. They had never performed in public before. Also, they felt very important to be getting to stay up until midnight on New Year's Eve. Mr Marsden arrived and they set off in the carriage. Jenny talked to him about where they were going.

'Whose house are we going to? Where do they live?' she asked.

'It is the house of Lord Thievely. He has only been the Lord for one year since the death of his uncle, who died childless. There was not a lot of money left with the estate and also heavy death duties. It is said that the uncle was quite profligate. The Lord was not brought up in the house, but only moved here on his inheritance.'

'You seem to know quite a lot about him,' said Jenny. He laughed before replying.

'I teach his little sister Jemima and she is quite a chatterbox. I am sure that the family don't realise how much she talks about them whilst I am trying to instil the rudiments of music into her.'

The rest of the journey passed companionably and they soon arrived at Mearley Hall.

The lights were shining brightly from all the windows, giving a welcoming air to the house. A butler was waiting at the top of the stairs and invited them into the house. He led them into a small drawing room. Jenny noticed that the room looked shabby. The curtains looked old and faded and the furniture was marked and the cushions threadbare. Suddenly, a cultured, charming voice broke into her survey of the room.

'Good evening Mr Marsden. How kind of you to come and to bring your pupils. And who is this charming lady?'

'Ah, Lord Thievely, thank you for inviting us. This is Mrs Marshall, the mother of three of the children who will be performing for you.' Lord Thievely took hold of her hand and kissed it in the French fashion, making Jenny blush.

'And is Mr Marshall with you tonight?' Jenny instantly withdrew her hand from his.

'No, I am a widow,' replied Jenny with haughty pride.

'I am sorry, I didn't know. I didn't mean to offend you,' he said with solicitude.

'That is all right. You weren't to know.'

'He must have died young.'

'Yes. He was killed in an accident.'

'It must be hard caring for small children on your own.'

'I have good staff and friends to help me. But yes, it is hard. Especially with having businesses to run, but it keeps me busy. '

'Business? You have a business?' he said with amazement.

'I own a gown shop in Clitheroe, amongst other things.'

At that point a lady entering the room interrupted them.

'Theobald, there you are. We are waiting to start supper.'

'Ah Mildred. Come and meet our entertainers for the evening. Mr Marsden you will already know. This is Mrs Marshall who owns a gown shop in Clitheroe. This is my sister, Lady Pennington,' he said turning to Jenny.

'Pleased to meet you,' said Jenny.

'Where exactly is your gown shop?'

'On Castle Street, one of the main shopping streets in Clitheroe.'

'Then I will have to come and visit you. One can never have enough gowns. Is it just gowns that you sell?'

'Not any more. We have expanded and sell all kinds of accessories. Do come and see the shop and I will be pleased to show you around. You could take tea with me as well.'

'Thank you. I will look forward to that. Now come along Theobald. Our guests are waiting.'

'Yes, I am sorry Mildred. Until later then,' he said looking straight at Jenny.

Jenny hurriedly took to checking her children when the brother and sister had left the room. She straightened their hair and tweaked their clothing until they were to her satisfaction, but it was more to distract everyone from the attention that Lord Thievely had given her so pointedly.

A maid then entered the room bringing light refreshments for them all. When they had partaken of them, the butler returned to take them into the long gallery where the children were to perform. There were six children in all. The others were all older than her children.

The children were taken to the front of the room where a small bench was situated behind the piano. The oldest child sat at the piano, ready to begin her recital. Jenny and Mr Marsden took their seats at the side of the piano near the children.

Slowly the room filled up as the guests drifted in from the dining room. Lord Theobald called for Jenny to go and sit over by him and

Lady Pennington. At first she declined but Lady Pennington came over and drew Jenny over to the front row of the audience.

Once they were settled, the children began their recital. The oldest child gave a competent rendering of a Chopin nocturne. Jenny's heart gave a lurch. Her children were nowhere near that standard. But later, when her children performed, she was pleasantly surprised. The children were more capable than she had perceived. They had obviously worked harder with Mr Marsden present, than when she oversaw their practice sessions.

The final player was the youngest sister of Lord Theobald and Lady Pennington, called Jemima. She was only nine years old, but already was a competent player.

The guests gave polite applause at the end of the recital and the children looked suitably pleased. It was then approaching midnight so the revelries concentrated on welcoming the New Year of 1896 in. Everyone was wished a Happy New Year and gave each other good wishes for the coming year. Some of the adults even gave the children small coins as a thank you for their efforts during the recital. Jenny and the children made their way home soon afterwards.

Ben especially grinned at the amount of coins that he had received and the children were busy planning what they would spend their money on, whilst the carriage was driving home.

Jenny sat quietly during the journey, thinking about the brother and sister that she had met tonight. Lord Theobald and his house appeared shabby and yet Lady Pennington was the epitome of elegance, wearing the height of fashion. Obviously she had a rich husband who could keep her in such costly apparel and yet there was no sign of him tonight.

The brother and sister didn't even have the same colouring, Jenny reflected. Lord Theobald was tall, slim, with jet-black hair, and an aristocratic bearing in his manner. Lady Pennington was tall and slim, with an abundance of long blond hair. But they were both charming. That was one thing that they had in common.

The children had all fallen asleep during the journey home, not being used to be being awake at that time of the night. At least they had no school in the morning and Jenny had decided not to open the shop on New Years Day but to give everyone a holiday. To be honest, it was more for her own benefit than from any philanthropic reason. She got little enough time with her children as it was.

The next day was spent leisurely around the house: the children finding lots of activities to do together in their bedrooms. A special meal rounded off this day of rest and then the children went to bed early after their late night, or rather early morning, the previous day.

A few days later, whilst Jenny was busy working in her office, she got a message that a lady wished to see her, and was waiting in the front entrance of the shop, on the ground floor. Jenny asked who it was, but the messenger did not know. Unusually irritated, Jenny was sharp with the young shop assistant, telling her to find out next time who it was. The young girl looked quite shocked to be told off by Jenny, but nodded her agreement and left the room quickly.

Jenny hurried down the stairs to the ground floor, still feeling slightly aggrieved that she had been disturbed in her wedding planning session. She was surprised therefore, to see Lady Mildred Pennington.

'Good morning Lady Pennington. How kind of you to call. Would you like to come to my office for a cup of tea?'

'Good morning, Mrs Marshall. No, I would like to see round your shop first, if I may. Later I would like a cup of tea, when my brother joins me. He has just gone to Cosgrove's menswear shop and will be joining me shortly.'

'That will be fine. Shall we start looking around then? Is there anything specific which you want to look at?'

'Oh no, I want to look at it all. I buy most of my clothes in London, but I must admit, whilst I have been staying at my brothers, I have talked to several women and asked about local shops and they have all mentioned you. I have become quite intrigued by you. I was so glad that Mr Marsden brought you to my brother's house. It gave me an excuse to come to your shop, Mrs Marshall.'

'Thank you. That is most kind of you. You are welcome in my shop at any time. You don't have to wait for an invitation and please call me Jenny. Everyone else does. We don't stand on ceremony here. All the staff call me Jenny.'

'Jenny, then, and thank you. Now before my brother comes, there is one area that I would like to see first. I believe that you specialise in gowns for when a lady is in an interesting condition, if you understand what I mean.'

'I most certainly do and may I offer you my congratulations. Is it your first baby?'

'Yes, I have only just had it confirmed by the doctor.'

'I am sure that your husband is delighted.'

'He doesn't even know yet,' Lady Pennington laughed. 'He has gone on an expedition to darkest Africa. He went last November and won't be back until April, by which time I shall be huge.'

'I will take you to our mother-to-be department first then. What did you have in mind?'

'Oh, lots of things, for different stages. It is most difficult in London to get anything special for times like these. It seems that in London one isn't supposed to be seen at all whilst one is expecting, but vegetate at home or in the country seat.'

'Here we are then. I will get my second in command, Sarah, to attend you. Please sit down on this couch and she will bring some things to show you.'

Lady Mildred sat down on the brown and cream couch, looking around her with interest. Sarah came along presently with a selection of clothes, which had expanding waistlines for later in the pregnancy. Also there were gowns that could be let out. Other gowns were presented which had a flattering high-busted style, but loose under the bust, which hid the enlarging tummy.

Lady Mildred looked at each one in turn, showing surprise but pleasure at the ingenuity of the gowns and the high standard of workmanship.

'Is there anything here which you would like to try on, Lady Mildred? Or if there is nothing to your taste my girls can make some garments up to your own specification,' Jenny offered nervously.

'I like everything that I have seen. Even ball gowns! I never thought that I would be able to go to a ball until after the baby was born, but in your gowns I will be able to continue being seen in public much later. This is marvellous. You should open a shop in London. You would make a fortune.'

'Why thank you. I will think about that. But Clitheroe is enough for me at this time.'

'I will just have to send all my friends to you then, when they need you. How would that be?'

'I would be most grateful for their custom and thank you again.'

'Now, can I have all that you have shown me, please?'

'All?' said Jenny aghast.

'Oh yes, I will need all of these garments during my time in Lancashire and when I go back to Tamworth in April.'

'Are you staying here until your husband returns?'

'Yes. It is rather lonely on the estate in Tamworth, and now that I am having a baby, I could not be seen in the salons of London after the next few weeks.'

'Would you like to try any of these on so that we can alter them for you?'

'Yes, that would be a good idea, although some of them I want for much later and they will be far too big at the present moment. But I will try them all on now. Thank you. Where is your fitting room?'

'Over here, at the back of the shop. Will you come this way, please?' They walked across the shop and Sarah carried the garments into the fitting room and helped Lady Mildred on with them.

'They are all satisfactory. Could you deliver them for me?' said Lady Mildred at the end of the fitting session.

'Certainly. We will send them out to you tomorrow. Will that be early enough?'

Yes, tomorrow will be satisfactory. Perhaps you could come with the delivery and take tea with me, Jenny? I have so few friends here in this area. I really miss my husband and our social set.'

'Of course, that would be lovely. I don't often get out of the shop, so a trip out on business would be doubly beneficial. Would eleven of the clock suit you, or is that too early?'

'No, that is a good time, I can face the world without being sick by that time,' she laughed.

'I remember that so well,' replied Jenny with feeling.

'And what are you two laughing at?' asked a male voice. It was Lord Thievely.

'Oh hello Theobald. It was women's talk, so no concern of yours. Have you done your shopping?'

'Yes, I just wanted a new waistcoat for a ball that I have been invited to. Did you get a ball gown?'

'I got more than a ball gown. I actually got enough clothes for the next few months. I am very pleased with Jenny's shop. It is quite the latest fashion and yet it is in the dullest backwater imaginable. It has been a lovely surprise. Now I suggest that you go and find a reading room, as I have only looked around one department and am not ready for your company yet. Come back in half and hour and then we can have tea together in Jenny's tearooms.'

Begrudgingly, he agreed to the suggestion, but as he was leaving he said, 'Half an hour, think on. I am ready for a cup of tea.' Jenny and

Lady Mildred laughed as they watched him leave the shop, then got back to the more important business of shopping and selling: shopper and salesperson.

By the end of the visit, Lady Mildred had amassed a great amount of shopping, from virtually every department in the shop. She had not bought any baby garments as she felt that it was too soon, but promised to come back and order a baby layette from Jenny, before she left for the country when her husband came back.

Jenny took Lady Mildred to the tearoom and Lord Thievely later joined them.

'What did you buy? Just a waistcoat?'

'Yes, I haven't a rich spouse like you. You have probably spent more today than I spend all year on my servants wages.'

Jenny mentally calculated that he had probably underestimated, and that she had spent far more than that, but said nothing.

'Well I will need a lot of new garments for the coming months, won't I? I don't intend hiding away for the next few months. It is so silly to pretend that it is not happening, when everyone knows that it is.'

'You are such a modern miss, Mildred. I suppose you will be agitating for the vote next,' laughed her brother.

'Oh yes, that is true. Very important, don't you think, Jenny?'

'I certainly do. There is a very strong movement in Lancashire amongst the mill girls. I fully support them.'

'Poppycock,' said Lord Thievely. 'Utter poppycock. Women are for breeding and homemaking. Their men can vote for them.'

'But I haven't got a man to vote for me. I pay rates, taxes and employ many people in the town, so why shouldn't I get a vote?' said Jenny forcefully.

'I'm sorry Mrs Marshall. I always seem to remind you that you are a widow. It wasn't my intention to hurt you again. Come Mildred. We have outstayed our welcome by my clumsy opinions. Goodbye Mrs Marshall.' He stood up and made to leave.

Jenny stood up too, and remonstrated with him to stay, but to no avail. He went out of the shop, obviously expecting Lady Mildred to follow.

'I do apologise for my brother. He is always embarrassed if he makes a faux pas. I will see you tomorrow?'

'Yes, at eleven of the clock. Shall I bring your brother's purchase from Cosgroves, to save them making a single delivery?'

'That is most thoughtful of you, Jenny. I am sure that he will appreciate that gesture and will feel that you have not taken against him for what he said.'

'Not at all. It just makes more sense to save a delivery. I will send a girl round to Cosgroves now with the suggestion.'

'Thank you. Until tomorrow, then?'

'Until tomorrow.'

Lady Mildred left the shop and Jenny went to find Sarah to tell her what the arrangements were and to send someone to Cosgroves.

'She has spent over one hundred pounds, just in one shopping spree,' said Sarah with utter amazement.

'I know, and she has ordered a layette for later.'

'Who was the man with her? The one that looks as if he would like to eat you?'

'Sarah! What a thing to say. What do you mean?'

'You know very well what I mean Jenny. Stop being coy. Who was he?'

'Her brother, Lord Thievely. He inherited the house and title at Mearly Hall. She is staying with him whilst her husband is away on an expedition to Africa.'

'You seem to know a lot about them, Jenny.'

'I think that she is quite lonely. She is staying with her brother whilst she is waiting for the baby and is missing her friends. By the way, she suggests that I open a shop for mothers-to-be in London. What do you think about that?'

'In London? That would be marvellous. Are you going to?'

'Certainly not,' laughed Jenny. 'I have enough to do here, but it has certainly made me think again about expanding to another shop in Burnley or perhaps Blackburn. Maybe London next year, if those go well!' she pondered. 'Now, let's get this order ready. I have to take it to their house tomorrow and I have a lot of other work to do today.'

Jenny and Sarah both went back to their respective work and the day passed quickly for both of them.

Chapter 12

Robert arrived at Jenny's office at a quarter before ten of the clock next morning.

'Good morning Jenny. I believe we are going together on a single delivery this morning? I have loaded the carriage up, but there seems to be a large amount of parcels for one order. Have they made a mistake?'

'No mistake, just a very generous lady, who needs a lot of clothes, or thinks she does.'

'That is good then, less delivery time if we are only going to one house call.'

'Yes and we are delivering for Cosgroves as well. Her brother ordered one garment from Cosgroves and I offered to bring them both over to save a special delivery.'

'Only one garment compared to her many? The lady obviously doesn't get her shopping habits from her brother, then.'

'Obviously not,' replied Jenny laughing. 'Shall we set off? It is a fair way to go and I said that we would be there by eleven of the clock.'

'Right. Let us go.'

Jenny looked at the pile of brown and cream boxes and packages piled on the carriage. It contrasted sharply with the one black package from Cosgroves.

She was glad that she had chosen the brown and cream colour scheme for all her packaging and furnishings. It made the shop look cared about and co-ordinated. Even her carriage was in the same colours and the staff wore the colours for their work clothes.

Jenny thought about the new schemes for the shop, but decided finally that she would keep the present colour scheme rather than change it. Townspeople knew her by the colours now. They contrasted favourably with the Cosgrove's bag, which was plain black, but she presumed that men would not want more decorative packaging.

Robert and Jenny talked idly about the countryside whilst they travelled along the roads. Fortunately for the time of year, the roads were clear and not too muddy or full of holes. Neither had it snowed recently so they made a good journey to Mearly Hall.

On arrival, Jenny deliberated whether to go to the front door or the back door, but before they had decided, Lord Thievely came dashing in on his all-black steed.

'Greetings, Mrs Marshall. I trust that you had a good journey? Do come and park your carriage in the stable with my horse. It is round the back of the house. My groom will look after the horse and show your man where to get a drink from Cook. Allow me to take the parcels in,' he said reaching over to the back of the carriage.

'Begging your pardon, my Lord,' said Robert, 'I think that there may be too many packages for you. I will get the groom to bring them all in with me, if it is all the same with you. These are all for your house,' continued Robert as he waved his hand over the carriage full of packages.

Lord Thievely paled. 'Yes, I see what you mean. Did my sister buy up your entire stock, Mrs Marshall? It certainly looks like it.'

'Not quite, but she did buy quite a lot. Now where would you like Robert to put the packages?'

'Oh, in the hallway to the kitchen and then the maids can take them up to my sister's room. Will you walk this way, Mrs Marshall? I will order some refreshments. Ah Agnes,' he said to the maid who had answered his summons, 'tell Lady Pennington that our visitor is here and then bring us all some refreshments. Now do sit here Mrs Marshall,' leading Jenny to a long settee near the large fireplace. The fire was roaring in the grate and Jenny was glad of the warmth after the cold journey in the draughty carriage.

Soon afterwards, Lady Pennington arrived and also made a fuss of Jenny as if she was an old friend and one of her own set rather than a tradesperson. Jenny felt rather gratified to be so treated. She liked this lady and enjoyed her company. She quite liked the brother as well, even though he was rather overbearing at times. But then, so were many of the gentry, as she knew full well. But they were both very charming and pleasant company to be in.

'I have been to see all my packages,' said Lady Pennington. 'It looks exciting, just like Christmas Day. Did I really buy so many garments? And then I saw Theobald's little package. It looked quite pathetic next to mine. Is that all you bought?'

'Yes, I don't have a dress allowance like you. New clothes come well down on my priority list of spending.'

'It is a nice waistcoat though. I approve of it. It will look splendid with your evening dinner suit. When is the ball?' replied his sister.

'In three weeks, at the end of January. I am quite looking forward to it. There is little enough in the way of balls in the winter in this area, or I don't get asked to them. I don't know which it is. What about you, Mrs Marshall? Do you go to many balls?'

Jenny laughed. 'I most certainly do not. I have lived here for over seven years and this Christmas was the first time that I managed to go to the Clitheroe Ball.'

'Why ever not?' he asked. 'Did you not get asked?'

'Oh yes, but it was always difficult. Either it was because I was having one of the children or being in mourning. I just didn't seem to make it.'

'What about coming to the ball with us, then?' he asked Jenny. 'We can take another guest as the invitation said *and friend* for Mildred, because of her husband being away.'

'Yes, do come, Jenny. It will be so nice to have a companion to talk to. Much as I love my little sister, she is too young for sensible female conversation.'

'Well, I, er, I don't think I . .'

'Oh say yes, please,' interrupted Lady Pennington. 'I really would like you to come with me.'

Jenny wavered. She had so enjoyed the ball at Christmas. She too, sometimes missed adult conversation.

'Please come Mrs Marshall,' said Lord Thievely quietly. It was so unlike his usual manner that Jenny was surprised.

'Yes, thank you, I will come then,' she replied before she realised what she had said.

'And now it is time for tea,' said Lady Mildred. She got up to ring the bell for the servants and they chatted about the weather until the maid brought the tray of tea in and placed it on to the small side table.

Lord Thieveley brought Jenny a cup of tea and appeared to hold her hand steady whilst he made sure that she had hold of the cup. Just a shade too long for comfort, thought Jenny. She smiled briefly at him and withdrew her hand. She was beginning to wonder if agreeing to go to the ball had been a good idea.

'Where did you say the ball was being held at?' said Jenny, trying to remain calm.

'I don't think that I did.' replied Lord Thievely. 'It is at Langho. At the Carroll's place.'

'Oh,' said Jenny, quite surprised.

'Why,' said Lady Mildred, 'do you know them? You looked quite surprised then.'

'Only through the shop. When old Lord Carroll died I made all the mourning clothes for the family. I think that they will remember me.' Oh dear, she thought to herself. That could be embarrassing if they see me as a tradesperson.

'Excellent,' said Lord Thievely. 'They will fully approve of our taking you.' Jenny was not so sure, but weakly smiled her acquiescence.

'I will probably need to come to your shop again Jenny, before the ball,' said Lady Mildred. 'I have no accessories with me for going to balls. I thought that I would be hidden away up here, like I was in London, but with it being so early, and due to your flattering ball gowns, I will get away with attending. Now let me see, I will need slippers and shawls and handbags. I will call again next week. What will you be wearing, Jenny?'

'I will probably wear the ball gown which I wore at Christmas. I don't have a need for many ball gowns.'

'What colour is it?'

'Lilac.'

'Of course, you are still in mourning,' said Lord Thievely.

'Well not really, nearly three years have passed now, but I didn't want to shock everyone by going out to a ball for the first time in a bright shade.'

'Well I shall wear the pale blue one, so we will look quite the modern matrons together in pale colours. We will leave the bright colours to the other younger girls,' said Lady Mildred.

'Most of the young girls still wear white in this area for balls. We are quite old-fashioned really,' replied Jenny.

'You seem to have a very up-to-date gown shop, even though you say that it is in a backwater. I was very favourably impressed, wasn't I Theo?' said Lady Mildred.

'You certainly looked happy when you returned after spending the equivalent of a years servant salary in one shopping expedition,' replied Lord Thievely in a droll manner. 'May I get you another cup of tea, Mrs Marshall?'

'Oh, do call me Jenny. I have told your sister as well. I am rarely called by my full name, even in the shop.'

'Why thank you. Jenny it is,' said Lord Thievely, 'and you must call me Theo. I prefer it to Theobold.'

'Theo it is then, but no thank you, in answer to your question. I must get back to the shop. Thank you for your hospitality.'

'No, it is we that must thank you. For coming all this way with the packages.' Lord Thievely rang the bell as he spoke. A maid came scurrying into the room and curtsied.

'You rang, Sir?'

'Mrs Marshall is going, Matty. Please bring her outer clothes.'

'Yessir, straight away, Sir,' replied the maid, who scurried out again, soon returning with Jenny's clothes. Robert also came into the room behind her.

'Robert, I trust that you have been looked after well?' asked Lord Thievely.

'Very well, My Lord. Thank you,' Robert replied, giving a slight bow.

'I hope that you will come again, Jenny. I do miss female company. Theo is no use at all when it comes to conversation,' said Lady Mildred whilst Jenny was putting her coat on.

'I will try, but I have very little time to spare, what with the businesses and the children. It is easier if you come to me at the shop, or come to my house.'

'Thank you, I will. I had hoped that Theo would have made quite a few acquaintances when I got here, but he hasn't. He only knows Robert Carroll from Eton. He hasn't met anyone here at all.'

'I have been too busy sorting the estate out and trying to salvage what is left after death duties. Anyway, you say that it's more interesting here than being incarcerated in your country estate on your own.'

·'Theo, I am not complaining. Just stating facts. We are keeping Jenny from her work. Goodbye for now and thank you once again.'

Jenny and Robert took their leave and travelled back to the shop. On the way, Robert regaled Jenny with tales that he had heard whilst waiting in the servants' quarters about how financially embarrassed Lord Thievely was, and how rich his sister's husband was in contrast.

Jenny made no comment but thought that as Lord Thievely had inherited all the estate, he couldn't be too hard up. He should sell up and buy a smaller house, she mused, but as he had inherited the title, the house could be entailed as well, so she supposed he couldn't do that.

Eventually they arrived back at Clitheroe and Robert returned to the delivery office, whilst Jenny went back to her desk and her backlog of work.

Chapter 13

Later in the day Marian came into Jenny's office. She told her about the ball at the Carroll's place. Marian had attended the Carroll's with Jenny when the bereavement had taken place some years ago, when Jenny had only just inherited the shop.

'So you will be in need of a new ball gown, then. I will make you one. When is the ball?' asked Marian.

'No, I will wear my lilac one from Christmas. After all, it has only been worn once, and I don't have much occasion to wear ball gowns.' Marian was horrified.

'You can't be seen in the same ball gown as last time! What will everyone think? You are Miss Mitchell of Mitchell Modes. You have standards to set.'

Jenny laughed. 'I seem to remember you saying something like that when we got married. I thought I was having a plain grey suit and you produced a lovely wedding dress on the very morning.' Jenny and Marian had had a double wedding and Marian had secretly made wedding gowns for both of them, instead of the practical suits that they had planned.

'And I will make you a secret ball gown for this ball if you say you are going to wear the same gown again. Now when is the ball?'

The end of January,' said Jenny meekly. She knew when she was beaten with Marian. 'But not pale blue. That is what Lady Mildred is wearing.'

'Leave the colour to me. I will think of something. And now I must go. I have a ball gown to design and it is for a very special customer.' Marian laughed as she walked away, leaving Jenny shaking her head.

Having missed her lunch, Jenny rang through to the kitchen to ask if she could have a sandwich. This was brought up promptly, so Jenny carried on working; checking sales figures whilst munching her sandwich.

She was having her second cup of tea when a knock came at the door.

'Come in,' she called, and in came Emily, fiancée of Robert.

'Ah Emily, thanks for coming. Now just sit down and I'll find the plans that I have made for you. Would you like a cup of tea?'

'Only if it is no trouble, Mrs Marshall,' said Emily nervously.

'Now Emily, I thought we agreed that it was Jenny?' she chided gently.

'I feel awkward speaking your first name when you are Robert's boss.'

'We don't worry about things like that here. We all use first names. I don't think I know some of the staff's surnames anyway,' she laughed. 'Now where did I put those plans? Just help yourself to a cup of tea whilst I search for them.'

'If it is not convenient I can call another day, Jenny,' said Emily.

'Certainly not. I have them here somewhere. And anyway, you don't have much time off so you can't waste a journey. Oh here they are. Now what did I tell you last time?'

'Just that you would make both me and the bridesmaids blue dresses. You told me the style for the bridesmaids dresses, but someone came in before you told me about mine.'

'Yes, I remember. A bereavement call. Well, have a look at this sketch and see what you think. The dress would have a definite waistline to emphasise your small waist. The whole of the front and back would be pin-tucked, from neck to waist. This would give the dress an air of being fancy but not too ornate that you couldn't wear it for church every Sunday. Is that satisfactory so far?'

'Oh yes, it looks lovely. Far too fancy for the likes of me.'

'Nonsense. It will look lovely and yet be practical. Now, about the skirt. Because of the fussy bodice, the skirt will be completely plain and fairly straight, not a bustle in sight. The top of the sleeves will be pin-tucked to match the bodice, and then will be tight fitting down to the cuffs, which will be trimmed with delicate ribbon. The same ribbon will be used as a waistband. Oh, and the neck will be round and also have a ribbon trim as well. There what do you think?'

'Oh Jenny, it is beautiful. I will feel like a princess and yet you are right, I will be able to wear it again afterwards for special occasions. Thank you so much.' At that Emily burst into tears.

'What is the matter, Emily? What is wrong? Do you not like the dress?'

'I am just so happy to be having such a beautiful dress. I just wish my family were here to see it.'

'I know just how you feel, Emily. I had no family at my wedding either, but I did have my three good friends.'

'From the workhouse?'

'Yes, two of them were, Robert may have told you about Marian and Susy who first helped me in the shop. They were my friends from the workhouse but the other one, Martha, was from the house I worked in at Burnley. She could have come to work for me here, but her family are all in Burnley and she didn't want to move over here.'

'I can't blame her. If I had family, I wouldn't move away, whatever the offer.'

'Now is there anything else, Emily?'

'Will I be wearing a veil? Only it might look daft with a blue dress, begging your pardon, Jenny.' Jenny laughed.

'You are right Emily. No, I think a nice blue bonnet to match the dress would look much better, don't you?'

'Yes, it would. And I could wear that for church afterwards as well,' laughed Emily back.

'Now you are getting into the spirit of things, Emily. I will also make you a dark blue long coat to go with the dress for the wintertime. Obviously you won't need it for the wedding, with it being in August.'

'No, that is too much. You are doing enough already,' protested Emily.

'Nevertheless, I will see that there is a coat to go with your outfit. The long coats are becoming more fashionable than cloaks now that bustles are disappearing. Now anything else?'

'Well, er, .. er..'

'What is it?' interjected Jenny.

'Robert mentioned that I may be able to have a job here,' gasped Emily all in one breath.

'That is right. Yes, I forgot for the moment. I am glad you mentioned it. Now where would you like to work?'

'Anywhere, Jenny. Truly, anywhere.'

'We have shop work or kitchen work or working in the offices, working out the accounts and keeping up to date with ordering.'

Emily pulled a face at the last suggestion.

'I can't do sums Jenny. They just don't seem to make sense to me. All those figures dancing around the page.'

Jenny laughed. 'No, it is not my strong point either. I would much rather plan a wedding or suggest an outfit any day. The book keeping is quite tiresome, but now that I have a lot of staff, there is always someone to do it for me.'

'Shop or kitchen work is fine. I know I can do kitchen work, but I haven't worked in a shop before.'

'Would you like to?'

'Oh yes. I would love to work with ladies clothes. I loved helping out in the laundry and pressing and goffering the fine linens. Sometimes, I got to help dress the young mistresses if they were going out. I liked that as well.'

'Can you sew?'

'Yes, the mistress insisted that I was taught.'

'Good. I will have a word with Sarah, my deputy, and see where she thinks you would fit in. Leave it with me, Emily.'

'Thank you Jenny. I can't tell you how happy I am. Really, really happy. And to marry Robert as well. I feel like I will burst sometimes. I am so happy.'

Jenny looked at the radiant smile of this young girl and envied her. She too had been as happy as this when she was marrying Jonny. Thinking of him brought a little pang to her heart, but she brushed the thoughts away. She had had her time, now it was Emily's and Robert's time.

Swallowing quickly to control her tears, Jenny told Emily to go downstairs to get measured by Marian's team of seamstresses and ask them to refer to Jenny for the sketches to make up the dress.

Emily thanked Jenny again and left the office, almost skipping. Watching the little skip made Jenny smile. She was able to put her own troubles behind her, and pulling her pile of letters forwards, immersed herself in her work.

Chapter 14

A week later, Jenny had a visit from Joshua. He said that he had some news for her. As they waited for a cup of tea, he told Jenny that she had been unsuccessful in gaining a place on the Board of Governors at the workhouse.

'I am not surprised. I suppose it was Captain Parker who spoke against me?' She was surprised when Joshua laughed.

'Not at all. He was very much in your favour. I don't know what you said to him at the ball, but he had certainly thought about it and was recommending you for a place on the Board.'

'That is amazing,' replied Jenny. 'Who would have thought it? I was sure that he had taken against me for being so outspoken.'

'Obviously not. I think that he will support you in the future as well, if you should apply again.'

'Oh, I will be applying again, make no mistake about that. As soon as there is a vacancy.'

'I will support you as well, Jenny. You do deserve to be on that Board. I too, have thought about what you said.'

They drank their tea and chatted about the various townspeople that they knew in common. Jenny was pleased that their old relationship had returned and there was no hint of bitterness on Joshua's side since her refusal of his marriage proposal.

After he had left, Jenny's thoughts returned to the subject of the workhouse. Ever since Jenny had been to the Bradford workhouse and found her father-in-law, she had been perturbed by the story Bruce had told her about her own daughter. Jenny knew what it felt like to be abandoned to fate in a place with people that didn't care for you.

More and more, she thought about the girl and wondered what had become of her. She decided that her curiosity was too great. Besides, if she was still in the workhouse, perhaps Jenny could offer her a job in her shop and make her life happier. Although Bruce had treated Jenny badly, she had also treated her own daughter worse and nobody deserved that. Jenny resolved to take a trip to Blackburn workhouse at the first available opportunity.

The following week Jenny took a train from Clitheroe station to Blackburn. Upon her arrival there, she asked a porter where the workhouse was. On being told that it was up a very steep hill on the outskirts of town, Jenny asked him to engage her a carriage, which he willingly did.

The journey from the station to the workhouse on the Haslingden Road was not a long distance, but the hill was so steep that it took the horses quite a while to pull the carriage up the steep incline. Jenny paid the man and stood looking down at the whole of Blackburn town stretched out before her. The wind was blowing a gale and Jenny did not stay looking for long. She walked towards the door and rang the bell.

After a short while, the door was opened and a maid curtsied at Jenny and asked her business.

'I would like to see the matron, if I may.'

'Certainly Madam,' replied the nervous maid, curtsying again. 'What name shall I say?'

'Mrs Marshall of Clitheroe.'

'Is she expecting you?'

'No. I am calling whilst I am visiting Blackburn,' replied Jenny. No need to tell them that this is an impulse visit, she thought to herself. She followed the maid into a sitting room and waited for a few minutes.

The door opened and a large slovenly woman came into the room.

'Mrs Marshall?' said the woman suspiciously.

'Yes, thank you for seeing me without an appointment,' said Jenny at her charming best. 'I was on business in Blackburn and came to make an inquiry.'

'How can I help you?'

'How long have you worked here, matron?' Matron bristled.

'A long time. Why? Is there a complaint?'

'Oh no, I am trying to trace someone who lived here.'

'What name and when did they live here?'

'Bruce. It was a mother and daughter and the daughter was left here in the late seventies or early eighties.'

'Yes I remember them. The daughter was told that her mother was coming back, but she never did. But then she wouldn't would she? Not if she had left and got herself a new life.'

'Is Miss Bruce still here, then?'

'No, she left here three years ago. Gone to Preston workhouse. And good riddance to her. Always causing trouble.' The venom in the tone with which the woman spoke about Bruce's daughter shocked Jenny. Mind you, if Miss Bruce had been anything like her mother, perhaps Jenny could understand. Suddenly, she didn't want to be with this matron any longer. She thanked her quickly and left by the front door. It was only then that she realised that she had no return carriage waiting.

Determined that she wasn't going back to the woman to request a carriage, Jenny set off walking back to the station. It didn't take her very long – it was all downhill! But as she arrived at the Boulevard, where the train station was, the Clitheroe train had just gone and there wasn't another one for nearly an hour. By this time, Jenny was ready for a drink of tea and preferably something to eat.

Setting off towards the shops, Jenny found a nice little tearoom on Penny Street. After a reviving cup of tea and a bun, Jenny sauntered back to the Boulevard, but noticed that a shop was for sale on King Street. Looking at the window, Jenny thought how good that shop would be for a ladies gown shop like hers. She had often toyed with the idea of opening another shop. This would be an ideal site. Right in the centre of town with all the local shops around it. She looked up at the name of the vendor and asked a passing lady where the address of the vendor was. It was just around the corner on Darwen Street.

Going around the corner, Jenny went into the office and asked about the property. She could tell that the man was not too happy to deal with a woman, but after she told him that she was the successful owner of a larger shop in Clitheroe, he treated her somewhat differently. He took her across to King Street and showed her the shop. Jenny was thrilled. Although the premises seemed to have been empty for some time, she already had plans for the new shop forming in her mind.

After he had shown her around, he asked if she would be bringing her husband to look at the property.

'Certainly not. I am a widow,' she replied haughtily. 'I will buy this shop, but as it has been empty for some time, I will offer you less than is being asked for. It will be a cash transaction, of course.'

The vendor started to huff and puff, so Jenny gracefully stood up, drew her gloves on, and said good day. The man changed his tune immediately, and offered the property at the price that she had suggested. Jenny sat down again and smiled at the man. Agreements were made and Jenny agreed to use his own solicitor to speed up the transaction. A short time later, Jenny walked out of the office, the owner of another shop. She chuckled to herself on the train returning to Clitheroe at how she had made the man change his tune.

On the way home, Jenny started thinking about the reason that had taken her to Blackburn. Perhaps she would go to Preston to try and find out why Miss Bruce had been sent to another workhouse and if she could still help her. Why, Jenny thought to herself, she could even put Miss Bruce in charge of the Blackburn shop. Or should she? Perhaps Miss Bruce would turn out to be like her mother, in which case she would not leave her in charge of anything. But for some reason, Jenny had a curious interest in this young woman who had been abandoned by the same woman as herself.

It was another week before Jenny could go to Preston. Robert was going to collect a delivery of some new hats from a warehouse in Preston, so Jenny rode with him. Besides, it would make good business sense for her to meet the proprietors of the Preston warehouse. It was always a good business move to speak to people rather than deal on paper.

Robert took her to the Fulwood area of Preston where the workhouse was situated. He waited outside rather than have Jenny waiting for him whilst he did his errands. Jenny was happy about this arrangement after being left stranded at the workhouse in Blackburn.

Jenny knocked on the door and waited until it was opened. She was led into a beautiful large hallway, with sweeping stairs going up several flights. It was a much larger workhouse than Clitheroe, and even than Blackburn. 'I bet the rest of the workhouse isn't as glamorous as this,' thought Jenny cynically.

'How may I help you?' asked the man who opened the door.

'I am looking for a Miss Bruce who came here from Blackburn workhouse. Do you have someone by that name?'

'Yes, I will just get her. If you will sit down here, madam,' he said, indicating a comfortable chair.

After a short time, an elegant, tall lady came down the stairs, of a similar age to Jenny.   This must be the matron, thought Jenny to herself and stood up to greet her.

'You were asking for a Miss Bruce?' the lady said.

'Yes, do you know of her?'

'I am Miss Bruce. Who are you and why do you wish to see me?' Jenny stared in amazement. She was expecting a poor downtrodden woman, who was ill thought of at her last place of work. Perhaps sullen or ignorant. But instead, here was a polished, well-spoken matron.

'My name is Jenny Marshall,' Jenny stuttered. 'You don't know me, but I knew your mother.'

'My mother? You knew my mother? Then I question your choice of friends,' replied the lady in a cutting manner.

'I am afraid that she was no friend of mine, but she became involved in my life.'

'Well, that is more than she did in my life, then,' the matron replied sharply. 'All my childhood I waited for her to come back for me, but she never did. I don't even know where she is, or whether she is dead or alive.'

Jenny gulped. 'I am afraid I know the answer to that. Your mother is no longer with us.'

'Dead? Is she dead?'

'Yes.'

'How do you know?'

'I was there when she passed away.'

'I thought that you weren't her friend? You must have been if you were there when she died.'

'No. She sent for me to apologise for what she did to me.'

'What do you mean? What did she do to you? She never apologised to me.'

Jenny sighed. 'It is a long story. May I sit down?'

'Mrs Marshall, I am so sorry. You have given me such a shock that I have forgotten my manners. Come to my office and I will make us some tea.' Jenny followed Miss Bruce into her office and sat down gratefully. Miss Bruce put the kettle on the fire and set the cups out ready.

'Now do tell me why you are here. I am intrigued, Mrs Marshall.'

'I lived in a shop with my mother. She owned the shop and was going to be confined again. Her protector,' here Jenny looked down away from Miss Bruce's direct gaze, 'hired your mother to help run the shop. My mother died in childbirth and your mother put me in the workhouse saying that I had no relatives.'

There was a protracted silence.

'What about your mother's protector?' Miss Bruce eventually asked.

'He lived some miles away and by the time he heard about my mother, I was in the workhouse. He was not in a position to look after me, so he left me in the workhouse.'

'Too frightened of his wife, I suppose?'

'Yes.'

'But what happened then. You are obviously a woman of means.'

'When I was about twelve years old, I was taken to work in a large house in Burnley as a scullery maid. When I was eighteen years of age I inherited the shop, where your mother was the manageress.'

'And what was my mother's reaction to you when you came to claim your inheritance?'

'Surprised, I would say. She ran off that night, along with most of my stock and a lot of money that should have been in my pocket.'

'That does not surprise me. But how did you come to be there when she died?'

'Many years passed and I must say that they were very successful years for me in the shop. I married and had children, but then my husband was killed . .'

'Oh, I am so sorry,' interrupted Miss Bruce. 'Please do not continue this story if it is too painful.'

'No, it is an important part of the story. Many years later, I received a letter from Bradford workhouse asking if I would attend your mother who urgently wanted to see me before she died.'

'How did you feel about that?'

'At first, I must be honest, I didn't want to go. I was so angry. But then I realised that your mother was the only one who could tell me more about my own mother. So I went. But I am so glad that I did, as my father-in-law was in the same workhouse as well. He had been ill and unable to make a home for his family. He was too ashamed to contact his family and tell them where he was. I was able to restore him to the family. It was very precious.'

'What did she say to you?'

'Just that she was jealous of my mother, because her protector had kept her and looked after her. Your mother had been in the same situation with you, but your father turned her out without a reference or any money and she was desperate. When she went to the job with my mother, she fully intended to send for you, but she didn't get around to it.'

'Obviously not,' said Miss Bruce. 'And you say that she died in the workhouse? How did she end up in there if she had taken a lot of your money?'

'She set up a shop and met a man, who robbed her of everything. Then she became unwell.'

'She got what she deserved then? Retribution for deserting you.'

Jenny remained silent, not sure what to say, even though that had been her own thoughts exactly.

'Thank you for telling me. But why did you come to find me? You have obviously been sent here from Blackburn.'

'I thought that you might still be in the workhouse – I know how hard it is to get out. I hated the thought that you might have an awful life and I wanted to help.'

'Why?'

'I try to get as many people out of the workhouse as I can and give them employment in my shop.'

'And is that what you are offering to me now?'

'If you should wish it.'

'I am overwhelmed by your kindness. I am not sure that I would have been as kind to you as you have been to me. Thank you.'

'You just stayed on my mind. I kept thinking about you. You had the same start as me, but I was lucky. I hated to think that you were still in the workhouse, having a hard life, when I had been so fortunate.'

'I was very unhappy at Blackburn. I got promoted to head of the hospital eventually, but I didn't see eye to eye with the matron. She is very careless and slovenly. Fortunately I was recommended by one of the governors for this post here and I really enjoy it. I have made a lot of difference to the inmates' lives here and I want to continue doing that. I really enjoy my work.'

'I am pleased about that Miss Bruce. I am sorry if I have taken up your valuable time.'

'Please, call me Mary. I have enjoyed talking to you.'

'And I am Jenny. If ever you need a new gown, you know where to come,' Jenny laughed.

'I may just do that. Although I love my job, it is quite lonely. I have a weeks holiday soon but I will probably stay here as I have no family and nowhere to go.'

'You have now. You must come to my house and have a holiday. My children will aggravate you so much that you will be glad to go home to your lonely but peaceful home,' Jenny laughed.

'Are you serious?'

'Yes. Please come. Although I am busy all day at work and then have the children chattering at teatime, I am often quite lonely in the evenings. It would be a pleasure for me too.'

Jenny watched the emotion flickering over Mary's face and was pleased when she eventually accepted the invitation. Jenny wrote her address down and told her that Robert would come to pick her up in two weeks time. The two women embraced and then Jenny went to find Robert, who by this time had gone into the workhouse and found the kitchen.

Chapter 15

The night of the ball soon came round. Jenny had alternate feelings of misgivings and excitement. She had not been out on her own without the children since the Christmas ball, although that was only six weeks ago. In fact, she rarely went out without the children anyway.

Marian had made her an unusual ball gown. It was almost a throwback to the 1820's. It was made of fine gossamer material in a delicate shade of peach, with quite a low neckline, which Jenny wasn't sure about. It was gathered under the bust in the regency style and the skirt was loose and flowing under the bust. The sleeves were short and puffy, leaving all her shoulders bare. A frill in the same material around the bottom of the skirt was the only adornment.

After Jenny complained about the neckline, Marian made her a matching shawl to cover her modesty. Jenny tried it on again at home and looked in the large bedroom mirror. Marian was right. It was beautiful and it made Jenny look beautiful. The colour of the dress, although delicate, made Jenny's cheeks glow.

On the night of the ball, Megan came in to dress her hair and carefully placed the small peach coloured rosebuds in her hair. Jenny wore white shoes and bag, as she felt that too much of the peach colour would spoil the effect. She was right. The whiteness of the accessories only enhanced the peach colour.

She came down the stairs to find all the children waiting in a row at the bottom of the stairs.

'Mummy, you look like a princess,' said Ellen in a breathy voice.

'Why thank you, Ellen. I feel like one, too.'

'When will we be able to go to balls, mummy?' asked Rachel peevishly.

'In a few more years, Rachel. You are only eight years old.'

'I am nearly nine,' reminded Rachel.

'Well, nearly nine, then. But nowhere near old enough to go to a ball. Your turn will come. We have had this conversation only a few weeks ago, if you remember.'

There was a knock at the door. Maggie went to answer it and found Lord Thievely's groom had arrived.

'Is Mrs Marshall ready?' he said quietly. Maggie nodded and called Jenny gently. The children clung to Jenny and begged her not to leave them. Jenny chided them and reminded them that she would only be away for one night and would be back to tell them all about it in the morning.

The groom led Jenny into the carriage and there she found Lady Mildred and Lord Thievely in the back. Lady Mildred instantly admired the colour of Jenny's outfit, even though she could only see the hem of her dress under her black velvet evening cloak.

Lord Thievely said nothing. He sat and stared at Jenny until she became uncomfortable, so she engaged Lady Mildred in a conversation about the children. The two of them chatted all the way to Langho; Lord Thievely remained unnaturally quiet.

On arrival, the groom helped Jenny out of the coach, and then Lord Thievely took her hand and Lady Mildred's hand and tucked them in the crook of his arms.

Whilst waiting to be announced, Lord Thievely began to talk again, once more becoming the charming man that Jenny had become used to. The Master of the Ceremony announced their arrival and they all went into the large ballroom.

The room was full of people that Jenny didn't know, although she was pleased to see that she recognised some of the gowns that were there, as being from Mitchell Modes. She had a small smile to herself.

'What amuses you, Jenny?' asked Lord Thievely quietly.

'Oh, business as usual, Theo. I am noting that several of the gowns are from my shop. It is quite gratifying.'

'Well I think that we are by far two of the smartest matrons in the room,' said Lady Mildred. 'We both look so elegant in our gowns. What do you think, Theo?'

'I agree wholeheartedly. There are not any more beautiful gowns or people than you two in this room. You are both quite my favourite people,' replied Theo, but looking only at Jenny.

Jenny blushed. She was not used to such fulsome praise, except from her children.

'Why, you are blushing, Jenny,' he teased. 'Are you not used to being told that you are beautiful?'

'Only by my children,' said Jenny, blushing even further. 'And I suppose they don't count in the scheme of things. There is usually an ulterior motive.'

'Surely not?' asked Lady Mildred, 'your children looked like young angels on the night before the New Year.'

'Well they are not angels all of the time, I can assure you. Why, for my birthday last year they bought me a puppy. Now did I want a puppy? No, I did not. It was them that wanted a puppy, but they bought it for my birthday, so what could I say? Angels indeed!'

'When is your birthday, Jenny' asked Lady Mildred.

'In March. When is yours?'

'So is mine!' Lady Mildred exclaimed. 'What date?'

'The twenty-seventh.'

'Oh mine is the fourth. We could have a joint birthday party. Wouldn't that be fun, Jenny?'

'I will probably spend my birthday with my children,' replied Jenny.

'Yes, but we can have an adult party on another day, somewhere between the two dates. Oh please say you will. I will be enormous by then and won't be able to go out in public, so I will need some amusement to keep me alive.'

'I suppose so, but it can't be on my birthday itself. I must spend that with my children.'

'Don't you have maids to do that sort of thing?' asked Lord Thievely.

'What sort of thing?' countered Jenny.

'Well, the children thing. Aren't they looked after by the maids? Isn't that what you pay them for?'

'Certainly not,' retorted Jenny sharply. 'I love spending time with my children, but I have businesses to run. I need help.'

'I am sorry Jenny. I did not mean to upset you. Come, the dancing is starting. Come and dance with me.'

Jenny was led on to the dance floor by Lord Thievely, but she held herself rigidly away from him at the beginning of the dance. However, as the music played, she found herself relaxing and held herself less rigidly and started enjoying the dance. All too soon it was ended. Theo thanked her and led her back to Mildred, and bowed low over her hand.

'I must go and dance with some others now, but I will come back later. Then I will dance with you as well Mildred.'

'I may be too busy and fully engaged by then,' said Mildred haughtily. Theo smiled and left them. Theo was wearing an old suit that looked as if it had seen better days. Only his new waistcoat looked splendid and lifted the rest of the outfit.

Jenny picked up her fan and fanned herself. It had been quite a vigorous dance. She watched Theo as he danced with several other ladies. He was a good dancer and seemed to have all the ladies laughing and flirting outrageously with him, especially the married ones. Jenny was mildly shocked. She had never seen such public flirting before and was a little embarrassed. Perhaps this was what went on in so-called good society, thought Jenny uncomfortably to herself.

At that point, a voice asked her for a dance. Mildred had just been taken on to the floor, so Jenny agreed. It was Lord Robert Carroll, her host.

'I am sorry my dear, I do not know your name. Have you come with the Thievely party?'

'Yes, Lord Carroll, I have come with them. My name is Jenny Marshall.'

'Marshall, Marshall? Can't say I know the name,' he said rather pompously. 'Oh yes, there are some Marshalls in Cheshire. Are you one of the Cheshire Marshalls?'

'Er, no, I don't think so. My husband came from Clitheroe.'

'Never heard of any Clitheroe Marshalls. Would I know your husband? Is he not here?'

'I am a widow,' said Jenny quietly.

'I am sorry, please forgive me. How do you know the Thievelys then? I was at Eton with Theo. Best years of our lives, what ho? But we didn't think so then. No, we hated it most of the time. But I have got my boys names down. One has to send them away, hasn't one? Have you got children?'

'Yes, two girls and a boy.'

'Is your boy going to Eton?'

'No, he will be going to Clitheroe Grammar School.'

'Oh, I say, whatever for? Keeping him around your skirts won't give him any stand in life. They need that discipline in life.'

'I prefer to keep my children at home. They will not be going away to school. I am perfectly satisfied with how they are being educated in Clitheroe.'

Lord Carroll remained silent after this conversation and gave the appearance of boredom, but of course, was too polite to say so. He probably thinks I am an imbecile, thought Jenny sadly, but I don't care. Those children are my life.

Fortunately, the dance soon ended and Jenny was glad to get away from Lord Carroll. She hurried back to Mildred and Theo, who had both relinquished their partners. It was soon time for supper and Theo asked Jenny if he could have the next dance. She acquiesced and felt quite pleased that he had asked her. She was looking forward to being in his arms again.

During the evening, Jenny and Mildred danced with several partners, but none as easy to dance with as Theo. They seemed to mould into one another when they were dancing. Jenny hadn't felt like that for some time, if ever. Even Mildred commented on how good Theo was at dancing and Jenny could only agree.

'Mind you,' laughed Mildred, 'he didn't think so when I kept trying to get him to practice with me, up on the nursery floor. Especially with Nanny clapping the rhythms.'

'I can just imagine you both. I bet you teased him mercilessly,' replied Jenny.

'For a long time, he used to accidentally stand on my feet, or twist my arm, but when he went to his first ball and was an accomplished dancer in comparison with his friends, he was delighted. Not that he ever thanked me, but then that is the way of brothers. Although he was very pleased when I started bringing my friends home from finishing school.'

'And yet he has never married?'

'No, he came close once. He fell in love with a young girl, but her family would have none of it. He was far too lowly as a suitor and with no expectations of any inheritance at that time; he wasn't deemed suitable for their daughter. Since then there has been no one that he has seemed interested in, until now of course.'

Jenny looked around the ballroom; trying to decide which of the young ladies may have caught his eye.

'Is there someone in whom he is interested now?' asked Jenny. Lady Mildred laughed out loud.

'Oh Jenny, you are so funny. That is what I like about you.' Bewildered, Jenny asked what she meant.

'Why, you don't need me to tell you who Theo is interested in, do you?' Mildred asked. Jenny nodded.

'Why, you goose, it is you. Why do you think that he invited you to the ball? Just to keep me company?'

'Well yes,' replied Jenny.

'It is because he is enamoured of you. I am quite delighted. It is the first time that he has shown interest for some time. You really have made an impression on him.'

'Surely not. Me, a widow? What would Theo be interested in me for?'

'Don't be so coy. Have you not looked in the mirror recently? You are a fine looking woman and have made such a success in life, despite your humble beginnings.'

Jenny remained silent, lost in thought about what Mildred had said. Surely he could not really be interested in her? And yet Mildred insisted that he was. Jenny felt a warm glow in her heart, which appeared to be running a little faster than usual for some reason.

Looking up at Theo who was dancing with a young woman, Jenny watched him for a while, but withdrew her eyes when he looked across at her and caught her looking at him. He merely inclined his head gently, without seeming to distance himself from his partner, but this simple action set Jenny's heart racing. She chided herself for being silly. You are behaving like a young schoolgirl, she said to herself and was grateful when a gentleman asked her for a dance.

The end of the ball came all too soon for Jenny, even though it lasted until two of the clock, next morning. Then they were being escorted home in the carriage, dropping Jenny off first at Clitheroe. As they arrived at her house, Theo jumped down and said that he was going to walk Jenny to her front door.

'What, all twenty yards?' hooted Mildred, but all she received was a black look from Theo for her trouble. 'Goodbye Jenny. Thank you for keeping me company tonight,' Mildred shouted mischievously.

Jenny said goodbye and walked up to the front door with Theo, her arm tucked under his elbow as if she was a fragile china doll. At the front door, Theo turned her round to face him, still keeping hold of her hands, and then leaning very near to her face, whispered 'Until next time, Jenny my precious one,' whilst squeezing her hands.

Jenny backed away. She couldn't believe it. He was about to kiss her, she was sure, but then something made him draw back, and he walked briskly back to the carriage and Mildred. Without waving, Jenny hurried inside; stunned at the way the evening had ended.

After checking up on the children and saying goodnight to Maggie who had waited up for her, Jenny went to bed to savour all that Theo had said by word, look or deed this evening. It was totally unexpected, but nevertheless rather pleasant to be the object of someone's regard. She could quite get used to the fuss that had been made.

As she took her ball gown off, Jenny looked at herself critically in her mirror. She was in her thirties, had given birth to four children, and was not just a young girl at her first ball. So why was she feeling like this, she asked herself? Because I am being silly, she replied to herself. It has just been the effects of the punch and the hot atmosphere. I have probably imagined it all.

Going for a brisk wash in her bathroom, Jenny got into bed and decided that tonight was a little like a pleasant dream. Lovely to have, but real life would be back in the morning on waking. Besides, she said again to herself, I am not looking to have a suitor. Nobody could replace Jonny.

Turning herself over in the bed, Jenny decided that she would wait and see. She was sure that most of what had happened was the fertile imagination going on in Mildred's head. Pulling the covers over her head, she tried to get to sleep, knowing that the children would be in her bedroom early in the morning, wanting to know what happened at the ball. But sleep was a long time coming.

Chapter 16

The children were indeed, in her bedroom very early. Jenny felt as if she had only just gone to sleep. Fortunately, it was Sunday so there was no school or work for the children and her.

Throughout breakfast the children asked Jenny questions and Jenny had to describe the ball many times. First, the girls wanted to know who was there, then what the dresses were like and how many dances Jenny had had, and who with. Ben was not interested in all this, but he wanted to know if there were any horseless carriages at the ball and was disappointed that there were none.

After church, the questions continued and Jenny was weary of the whole affair by the time that the children went to bed. She was glad that they hadn't gone to Susy and Arthur's for tea today, or else she would have had to go through the whole story with Susy as well. They were away at Arthur's family for a short holiday. She would be glad to go to work for a bit of peace tomorrow, she thought ruefully.

Part of her reluctance to talk about the ball was the mixture of emotions that she was feeling about Theo. Mentally pulling herself together, she decided that she would take a day at a time and see if anything should develop. She would certainly not contact him. A brisk walk to work tomorrow would get rid of any silly notions, she decided.

The first appointment in Jenny's diary next day was Mr Aggett. She welcomed him into her office and ordered a cup of tea for him.

'Thank you for coming to see me, Mr Aggett. I do have quite a few plans and I need your advice and help.'

'It will be a pleasure to work with you again Mrs Marshall. Is the work at your house?'

'No, here at the shop. I want to make some major changes to the shop. And then I will need you to decorate afterwards. But first I want to know if I can have your absolute word that nothing of what I tell you will go further than this room.'

'But of course,' answered Mr Aggett a little mystified.

'It is a long story,' warned Jenny. She commenced to tell him of her history, her parentage, although she didn't give their names away and how she came to inherit the shop. She also told him about not being allowed to go up to the fourth floor of the shop for three years. He was obviously shocked, but said nothing. She then told him of her plans to make a moving platform through every floor of the shop.

'They will have to do the moving platform the first week, and then you will have to decorate the shop in the second week.'

'How will I manage that with the shop being open? Am I to work at nights again?'

'No, I am going to close the shop whilst I make all these alterations.'

'That will make my job much easier.'

'Now I will take you upstairs and show you the rooms. You are the first person ever to see these rooms apart from my husband.' Mr Aggett nodded and followed her towards the fourth floor stairway.

Jenny took the large key out of her pocket and opened the door. Mr Aggett followed Jenny up the stairs and waited whilst she turned the gas mantle on. Jenny lit a taper from the mantle and lit all the lights on the corridor.

She then took Mr Aggett into the kitchen and explained how she was going to convert this entire floor into rooms for food. The tearoom would be up here, as well as the staff canteen. Mr Aggett nodded his understanding. Next they went into the lounge and Jenny was glad that she had remembered to remove the painting over the mantelpiece. It would never do for Mr Aggett to recognise who her father was.

'I think that this could stay as a lounge. It would be quite elegant for my customers to come up here and rest, whilst they are having a cup of tea, don't you think?'

'Yes, it would be a shame to spoil this room. Are they all as elegant as this?'

Jenny nodded. 'On the whole,' she said cautiously. She then led Mr Aggett into the next room, her mother's bedroom. She took a deep breath before she opened the door and said hurriedly, 'I think that there is a need to change this room more than the others.' She walked quickly into the room, so that Mr Aggett could not see her blushes. There was a stunned silence for quite some time. Eventually, Jenny turned to look at Mr Aggett. He was endeavouring to keep the shocked look off his face, whilst staring at the long wall of mirrors facing the bed.

'Yes, a very unusual room,' he said politely.

'I want all these mirrors tearing out, of course. Can you do this discreetly for me?'

'Yes, but are you throwing them away?'

'I certainly am. What else could I do with them? It is too embarrassing by far.'

'From what you have told me of the plans, they would make a special feature in the bridal room, so that brides-to-be could see the full effect of their wedding finery.'

Jenny was silent for a moment.

'Yes,' she said thoughtfully, 'you could be right. What a good idea. In that way they would never have to leave the shop with the risk that perhaps they might be seen in the street. Could you do that? Could you fit them into the bridal room?'

'I could, and perhaps I could fit them before the men come in to fit the moving platform? That way everyone will think they have been part of the refurbishment.'

'Yes, that would be good, as you could then remove the mirrors before your workmen see them. You will move them on your own, Mr Aggett? Please give me your word on that?'

'Of course. I will bring them downstairs ready for refitting during the weekend before the engineers come in to erect the moving platform.'

'Splendid. Now let me show you the rest of the rooms.' Jenny showed Mr Aggett the bathing room, the child's bedroom and the small workroom that had been her mother's. He made little comment whilst they were viewing these rooms, but made notes as to how Jenny wanted this floor to look. When they had completed looking at all the rooms, Mr Aggett turned to Jenny.

'Have you got a date in mind for all this work?'

'Yes, I thought of the first two weeks of July. I will shut the shop and give everyone two weeks holiday, and announce that I will be refitting the shop during this time. No staff will be allowed in during the two weeks, until all the work is completed. Would that be satisfactory?'

'That would be satisfactory, most satisfactory. I will look forward to working again with you, Mrs Marshall. Would you like me to make an estimate of the costs for you?'

'If you please, that would be helpful, so that I can work out the total amount that I will be spending. Thank you.'

'I will send them to you as soon as possible, Mrs Marshall. Now if I might take some measurements?'

'Of course, or better still, why don't you come back this evening at six of the clock and then you can have some privacy whilst you are doing this?'

'That would be far easier. I will return at six, then. Will you be available this evening, Mrs Marshall?'

'I can be available, I do not wish any one else to be here when you go upstairs.'

'I quite understand that. Until six, then?'

'Until six.' Jenny nodded. 'Goodbye, and thank you Mr Aggett. You have been most understanding.'

He left the shop and Jenny let out a long breath. She would be glad when the whole of the top floor was part of the shop. She had no use for it anymore.

Jenny left the shop early that afternoon so that she could return in the evening. It was a bitter cold night and Maggie fussed about Jenny going out in the dark at night.

'Haven't you been there all day without going back at night, Mrs Marshall? You will catch your death of cold.'

'No, I need to go back this evening as I need to let a tradesman in to measure the rooms upstairs.' Maggie went back to the kitchen muttering away under her breath, but Jenny didn't enlighten her any further.

After Mr Aggett had finished and gone, Jenny carefully wrapped up both the painting of herself and the painting of her parents and took them home with her. During the drive home, she asked Roger if he could hang one of the pictures on her bedroom wall.

'Not both of them, Mrs Marshall?'

'No, just the one. The other one can go in the attic for now.'

Roger made no further comment and drove home quickly.

Later in the evening Roger put the picture on Jenny's wall. Jenny had wrapped the other picture up and put it into the attic in a store cupboard, far away from prying eyes. After supper, Jenny went up to her bedroom to find Rachel sat on a stool in front of the painting of Jenny as a toddler.

'Why Rachel, what are you doing here?'

'I was looking for your lavender oil for my pillow as I have a small headache and I saw this picture. Who is it, mummy? She is beautiful.'

Jenny swallowed before answering. 'It is I, Rachel.'

'You?' said Rachel disbelievingly.

'Yes, when I was a little girl.'

'But you told me that you were brought up in the workhouse. How can this be?'

Jenny sighed. 'I wasn't always in the workhouse, Rachel. Do you remember that I told you last year that I had been taken to the workhouse by a lady when my mother died? This was a picture that my mother had painted before that.'

Rachel was quiet for a while but before she could think up any more questions, Jenny suggested that they go downstairs and have a hot drink, and then she would massage Rachel's temples to relieve the headache. The ruse worked and no more questions were asked that night.

But Jenny knew that one day the whole truth would have to come out. Rachel was very astute and had once commented that none of the children looked like Jenny. Rachel and Ben looked like the Ormerod family and Ellen looked like Jonny, but then Jenny didn't look like her parents either, but was more like her half sister, Lady Morag. It was all very strange. At least Jenny had made the right decision about the other picture of her mother and Lord Ormerod. It would cause too many questions from Rachel, not to mention the staff.

Next morning, when Jenny was busy with an accounts session with Agnes, they were disturbed by Janey.

'I know that you said that you were busy, Jenny, but I thought that you would want to be disturbed for this,' said Janey, coming into the room with a large bouquet of flowers. Jenny had the grace to blush and thanked Janey for bringing them in.

'Thank you Janey. Would you like to put them in some water for me, please?'

'Don't you want to look at the card to see who has sent them?'

'Oh very well, I will look,' said Jenny very nonchalantly, belying the rapid beating of her heart. As it was not her birthday or any other special event, she had a strong suspicion who they were from, but was embarrassed to look in front of the girls. She slowly opened the card as if it was of no import. Her gaze continued looking at the message whilst she tried to stop her heart beating too loudly. Agnes and Janey looked at her expectantly whilst she read the card.

'It is from Lady Mildred and her brother. You remember that I went to the ball with them on Saturday night?'

'Oh,' said Agnes very meaningfully, looking at Janey. 'Just from Lady Mildred and her brother. How nice.' The two of them smirked to each other.

'If you will put them in water, then please Janey?' said Jenny, her tone becoming more authoritative.

'Yes, Jenny, straight away,' Janey replied and hurried out of the room with the flowers.

'Let us carry on looking at these estimates, Agnes.' Agnes nodded and the two of them carried on working with no further mention of the flowers. However, when Jenny made her usual trip around the store, she felt that the staff were all smiling at her just a little more familiarly than other days. Or was it just in her imagination?

She was a little curt with them all for the rest of the day but it wasn't in her nature to keep it up and she soon reverted to her natural friendliness.

On arriving home with the flowers, the children were full of questions about them, commenting that no one had bought Jenny flowers before. She had hidden the card that was attached to them and kept it in her pocket away from prying eyes.

As soon as she was on her own, she read the card again. For decency's sake, the card was from both Lady Mildred and Theo, but she knew that the message was purely from Theo to her.

Beautiful flowers for a beautiful lady, as a thank you for attending the ball with us.

Jenny blushed as she read it again. She knew that she was no beauty, but right at this moment she felt beautiful. She had enjoyed the ball and especially Theo's company; she could not deny that. She had not imagined what he had said after all, and he had now made his intent clear. Jenny wasn't sure what to make of it at all, but would wait and see what happened. Neither was she sure what her feelings about Theo really were, but time would tell, she decided as she hid the card in her dressing table drawer and went back downstairs to the children.

Chapter 17

The following day, Theo and Mildred came to the shop. They pretended that Mildred wanted some more gloves, but Jenny wasn't convinced of their reason. She knew that Mildred had scores of gloves and she had bought several pairs in every colour from Jenny's shop, but no matter, she received the pair of them courteously.

Theo asked if Jenny would come to tea at Mearly Hall.

'May I bring the children?' Jenny asked.

'Of course,' replied Theo, after a moment's hesitation. It was obvious to Jenny that he had never thought of her bringing the children.

'Then we accept. When would you like us to come?'

'What about Sunday week?'

'Yes, that will be satisfactory. At what time?'

'Around four of the clock?'

'That will be a good time. Thank you.'

'Shall we send the carriage?' asked Mildred.

'No, I will come in my own transport.'

'Until Sunday, then,' replied Theo, bowing over Jenny's hand just a trifle too long for good manners. Jenny pulled her hand away, looking around the shop to see if any of her staff had noticed, but they were all busy serving customers, Jenny was relieved to see. It was only after they had left the shop that Jenny realised that they hadn't bought anything after all. So her suspicions had been right. It was just an excuse to come and invite her to tea.

Going home, she pondered what the reaction of the children would be about going to Mearly Hall. She was not pleased at their reaction.

'But we go to Aunty Marian's or Aunty Susy's for Sunday tea,' moaned Ben. 'Why do we have to go there?'

'Because we have been invited and I have accepted,' replied Jenny. 'You have been there before and will be able to renew your acquaintance with Jemima.'

'She was bossy, telling us where to sit, and she is only the same age as me,' said Rachel.

'Bossy? Just like you Rachel. You were in her house. She had every right to tell you where to sit.'

'Do they have lots of horses?' asked Ellen.

Jenny laughed. 'Yes Ellen, I think that they will have some horses, but I don't know whether there will be lots. I am sure that Jemima will take you to the stables.'

'Oh goody. I can't wait. When are we going?' Jenny smiled at Ellen, she was soon won over, but the other two didn't look convinced.

'Don't they have any boys there? Everywhere we go has girls. Can't you have some friends with boys?' said Ben petulantly.

'We will see if we can go to Aunty Marian's for tea the day before. Will that make you feel better, Ben? There are boys there.'

'Yes, it would. Do you think that Aunty Marian would let us?'

'I am sure that she would. I will telephone her when you have gone to bed.'

'Can't we telephone her now?' asked Ben.

'No, it is teatime. I will telephone later.' Ben continued to sulk so Jenny changed the subject quickly. When this didn't work, she threatened not to ring Aunty Marian if he didn't cheer up. This time it worked.

After the children were in bed, Jenny telephoned Marian. She would be delighted to have them, she said. Jenny was relieved. Really, she shouldn't have given in to their demands so quickly, but she wanted to make sure that they would go to Mearly Hall with her.

The Saturday visit to Marian's was a great success. She had made all their favourite dishes for tea and the children had a lovely time playing together. Will took them up to the Castle grounds for a walk before tea, which gave them all an enormous appetite. It gave Jenny and Marian time to catch up on their own news.

Marian only worked one day a week at the shop now, because of the children and the new baby that she was expecting, so inevitably they talked about the shop. Jenny told her of all the plans that she had for the shop and that it was going to be closed for the first two weeks of July.

'That is good,' said Marian, 'we have planned to go on a holiday those two weeks. We are going to a guest house at Blackpool. Why don't you come as well if the shop is going to be shut?'

'Oh, I can't, I need to be here for the workmen. Perhaps we can come for a day or even a weekend?'

'What are you going to do with the children while the alterations are taking place?'

'I'll just get Megan and Maggie to help with them. I won't need to be at the shop all the time. I would just get in the workmen's way,' Jenny laughed.

'What about if we take the children with us on holiday?'

'Marian, I couldn't let you. You will have a new baby by then. That will mean six children. No, it is very kind of you, but I couldn't possibly accept.'

'We will have Katy with us, so it will be easy. She can't wait. She is so excited about going on holiday to the seaside, as she has never been there before. Besides, by July, the baby will probably be sleeping through the night, so it will be getting easier.'

Jenny pondered the idea for a while. It would make sense for the children to go on holiday whilst the workmen were in, but she felt guilty about the work that Marian and Katy would have.

'Do let the children go, Jenny. It would do them good. How long is it since they had a holiday? I don't remember you going away since Jonny passed away. That is three years now. They deserve a holiday.'

'You are right, Marian. We haven't been away properly. What about if Megan came as well? I am sure that she would love a holiday as well, as she was from the workhouse like Katy. In fact, the whole family and staff could come and then they could all have a holiday. They certainly deserve it. They all work very long hours for me.'

'That is even better if Megan could come. That would really help with the children.'

'Have you booked the guest house?'

'Yes. Why?'

'I was just asking.'

'No you weren't. I can tell by the look on your face that you are planning something.'

'How well you know me! An idea has just come to me, but I would have to check it out first.'

'What idea?'

'I saw a house in Blackpool advertised in a trade journal. The owners are abroad and were offering short lets during the summer, complete with Cook and servants to look after you. There are six main bedrooms and three attic bedrooms for servants. Now, would that be enough?' said Jenny counting on her fingers.

'Enough for whom?' asked Marian bemused.

'For you and Will, George, Luke, the new baby, Rachel, Ben and Ellen. And Megan and Katy. Yes, there is enough room.'

'But what about the guest house which we have booked?'

'We could send Maggie and Roger there for two weeks and then Megan and Katy could go there for two weeks, whilst Maggie and Roger come to the house for another two weeks, with you and the children. Cook will want to go to her sisters for the fortnight. Otherwise it wouldn't be a proper holiday for the staff.'

'But Will could only have two weeks away from work. He has a very strict boss you know, Jenny,' laughed Marian.

'Will could come back to work after two weeks and then you could stay on for longer with the children.'

Marian was silent.

'Do you not like the idea, Marian? You have gone very quiet.'

'I love the idea, Jenny. I am just amazed that you could think all of that through in such a short time. But then perhaps I am not amazed. You always were able to have a long rush of thoughts like that. I don't know how you do it?'

'Then you will take my children on holiday?'

'With pleasure, but I am not sure about the full four weeks. It might be very expensive.'

'It won't cost you a penny. I am paying for everything, including the guest house.'

'No Jenny, you can't. We will pay our share,' Marian protested.

'I am paying for everything and that is final, Marian. You are taking my children on holiday and I am very grateful.'

'You could still come for a day or a weekend yourself to see the children.'

'Yes, I could. That would be excellent. Oh I am so happy. I will tell the children tonight. It will cheer them up.'

'Cheer them up? They don't look like they have a care in the world. What do they need cheering up for?'

'I was going to tell you. I, or should I say we, have been invited to Mearly Hall for tea tomorrow. They are not keen to go.'

'Mearly Hall? Lord Thievely's place?' Marian said in shocked tones.

Jenny blushed. 'Yes, he and his sister asked us for tea. You know that I went to a ball with them?'

'Of course I do. Who designed your ball gown?' laughed Marian.

'Oh yes, well they asked me for tea.'

'So you keep saying. And the children aren't keen on the idea?'

'No.'

'Why not?'

'Because it was a Sunday and they prefer to come here or go to Susy's on Sundays, they informed me.'

'Well,' said Marian expressively. 'So you bribed them to go there tomorrow by getting invited here today, is that it?'

'More or less.'

'Thank you. I know how much power I have with your children now. I am very grateful for that,' she laughed. 'And why is Lord Thievely asking you to tea, do you think?'

'I am sure that I don't know. Perhaps his sister is still lonely with being away from home.'

'Mmm,' said Marian thoughtfully, 'Or is it to do with the flowers that arrived on your desk the other day?' she asked with a twinkle.

'How do you know that?'

'Ah, that would be telling.'

'Come on Marian. How do you know? Was it Will?'

'Bless him, no. He wouldn't understand gossip if he heard it direct. It was Catherine. She came to see me with some designs. Now come on Jenny. Tell me all.'

'There is no 'all' about it. I went to the ball. I got the flowers. They have invited me to tea. That is it.'

'I will say no more for now, but I will be interested to see what develops.'

'Nothing will develop, I assure you,' Jenny said with more conviction than she actually felt.

Their tête-à-tête was interrupted by the return of Will and the children and nothing further was said. It was only as they left the house to return home that Marian leaned over to Jenny and whispered 'I will telephone you on Monday evening, if I can restrain myself until then.' With the children hovering, Jenny could only pull a face at Marian and make no comment as they left.

The Sunday visit to Mearly Hall did not start well. The children all woke up crotchety and they were late for church. Rachel developed another headache, but Jenny wasn't convinced by it and was cross with her.

The weather was bad as they were setting off and the horse was very slow, as if he too, didn't want to go. They eventually arrived at Mearly Hall a little late. Jemima was looking out of the front window, waiting for them and welcomed them into the house very politely. Jenny felt very sorry for her at that point. She must be very lonely living in this house full of adults, with no other children to play with.

'Come on upstairs all of you,' she said in greeting, and all Jenny's children trooped upstairs after her. 'We will go to the nursery,' she continued.

'Can we see your horses? Do you have a pony?' asked Ellen on the way upstairs.

'Yes, I do have a pony, but it is raining, so we can't see it at present. Besides, we are to have our tea as soon as we get to the nursery. We always have tea at four of the clock.'

'Aren't we having tea down here with Mummy?' asked Rachel.

'Of course not,' said Jemima disdainfully, 'we don't eat with the adults. We are too young.'

'We always eat with the adults,' said Rachel in an equally haughty voice. 'We are not considered too young.'

Jenny could not hear the reply from Jemima which Rachel got as they had gone round the curve in the stairs. But she was worried for the children. They were not used to being treated differently because of their ages, but Jenny knew all to well that it was how the gentry treated their offspring.

Theo and Mildred said nothing during this exchange, so Jenny took her cue from them and did not comment. They chatted aimlessly about many topics and then were served tea, just the three of them, in the small dining room.

Without the children, Jenny felt a little uncomfortable. After the meal, Theo brought out a card table, but Jenny did not know any of the games that he suggested. Instead she said that she would just watch them play and learn that way. They passed a pleasant hour playing at cards and eventually Jenny was persuaded to join in, although she was a little shocked that they were playing cards on the Sabbath.

Theo asked many questions about Jenny's life and her business. She was happy to answer them, as she was proud of the way that she had managed to make a success of her life.

Jenny, in turn, asked questions about the house and Theo's plans for it. It was obvious that he was hampered by a lack of funds and subsequently had only modest plans in mind for the immediate future. He had, inevitably, got great plans if he had more funds available, but didn't say how he was expecting to get more money.

At eight of the clock, Jenny said that she must be going home, as it was school for the children on Monday and she had to be up early for work. The coats were bought in to the parlour and the children were sent for. By the time the children had their coats on, Roger was ready at the front door with the carriage. Theo handed Jenny into the coach, making rather a fuss of tucking the blanket around her, even though it was a mild night.

'I hope that you will come again soon. We have all enjoyed having you to tea,' said Theo.

'Such a change from each other,' said Mildred.

Jenny smiled but made no commitment and thanked them for tea.

'You must come to tea at our house in return,' said Jenny vaguely.

'Thank you. When?' asked Theo.

'When what?' asked Jenny naively.

'When can we come to tea in return?'

'Oh er, well, er, what about next Sunday?'

'Yes, we are free, aren't we, Mildred?' asked Theo.

'Yes, I am sure we are. We never go out in this backwater place that you call home. Thank you Jenny. It will make a nice change to go out. As I am getting nearer my time now, it is difficult going anywhere in public.'

'Good,' said Jenny recovering quickly, 'Next Sunday it is, then. And do bring Jemima as well.'

'Jemima? Oh yes, we will bring Jemima then.' It was obvious from Theo's expression that he had not thought of bringing Jemima along. The poor child, thought Jenny again. What a miserable existence she must have.

They said goodbye and the children politely thanked Theo and Mildred for their tea.

As soon as the carriage drew away, the children turned on Jenny, demanding to know why she had invited them to tea next week.

'Because it is polite to return the favour when you have been asked out to tea. Where are your manners, children? Besides, it will be nice for Jemima to come out. I don't think that she gets much fun.'

'That is not our fault. They should take her out more,' said Rachel petulantly.

'Sadly Rachel, that is the way the upper classes treat their children sometimes. They live in the nursery and only see their parents in the evenings for an hour or two. And many children go to boarding school, especially the boys.'

'I am glad that we are not upper class then,' said Ben. 'I wouldn't like to go to boarding school. I will be quite happy going to Clitheroe Royal Grammar and coming home in the evening.'

'So am I,' echoed Rachel and Ellen together.

'But Jemima doesn't go to boarding school, she has a governess who teaches her at home,' said Rachel.

'That happens to the younger children, until they are old enough to go to boarding school. But girls are often taught at home and don't go away from home.'

The children were quiet after this, obviously reflecting on what different kinds of education there were and grateful that they were staying at home with their mother.

On arriving home, the children were hurried up to bed and nothing more was said on the matter. But Jenny pondered about Jemima for quite some time. Then she laughed to herself and decided that what Theo did with his sister's education was nothing to do with her, so why was she worrying? She had plenty of other things to worry about in life.

Chapter 18

The following morning at work, Jenny was surprised when Marian came in to see her. She didn't usually come to work on a Monday and she was hardly attending at all now, with the birth fairly imminent. Catherine, Marian's assistant, usually went to Marian's house instead.

'Marian, how nice to see you. Was it a specific visit or just a social call?'

'Just a social call. I was going into town for a few items and thought I would call in and see you, and ask you to tea next week again,' replied Marian innocently.

'Oh, of course. A social call. Nothing to do with my visit to Mearly Hall last night, then?'

'Mearly Hall? Why I had forgotten that you were going there.'

'I know you better, Marian. Well, we went, we had tea, and we came home. Is that what you want to know? Or is there anything else?'

'I was just curious, that is all.'

'Nothing much else to tell you really.'

'So you won't be going back there again, then?'

'No.'

'So no more arrangements to visit each other?'

'They are coming to tea next Sunday.

'Really? Well, that answers my other question. You won't be wanting to come to tea next Sunday as you will be too busy with the gentry for the likes of your humble friends.'

'Stop it, you goose. I will never be too busy to meet with you. In fact, you can come to tea too.'

'I can't come and meet gentry. I wouldn't feel right,' responded Marian.

'But you meet the gentry all the time at work. What is the difference in meeting them at my home?'

'I suppose I do, but it is different at home. The shop is work, this is home,' Marian replied stubbornly.

'I would like you to come though, Marian. Please. You and Will and the children.'

'But I am too near my confinement to go anywhere. I will be an embarrassment.'

'No you won't. Lady Mildred is almost as advanced as you are. You can compare notes and give her the benefit of your advice. It is her first baby.'

'Are you sure you want us, with your grand friends?'

'You are more important than any grand friends, Marian. But I would like you to come. Why don't I ask Susy and Arthur to come as well?'

'I would like that Jenny. I would feel more comfortable with Susy and family here.'

'Would you do me a favour? Would you contact Susy and invite her. It will save me time? asked Jenny.

'I'll call round to her house on my way home and let you know.' Marian was still not comfortable using the telephone that Will had just had installed for her.

'Thank you. We will have a riotous time, with all the children. It will make it easier for me, too. Until Sunday, then.'

'Until Sunday, goodbye for now,' said Marian as she left the room.

Jenny laughed to herself after Marian had gone. She could read Marian like a book. A social call indeed! Mind you, it had worked out well as she would feel much more comfortable about Theo and Mildred coming to tea if Susy, Marian and their families were present too. It would also make it easier for her own children to accept.

The week passed quickly. The children were indeed won over about the Thievely visit by the fact that all their friends were coming as well.

Cook was a little nervous about cooking for 'the Lord' as she called him, but Jenny insisted that her cooking would be as excellent as ever, and she had no need to worry. Indeed, Jenny said to her privately, she was a far better Cook than Theo's. Cook swelled with pride at this, but still retained a slight anxiety.

Sunday afternoon arrived and Jenny had deliberately asked Susy and Marian and their families to arrive before Theo and family. He was a little taken aback by the hordes of people who were already in the house and it was obvious that he had thought that there would only be their own party attending. Being of good breeding, he said nothing except a polite 'hello' to everyone in the room, introducing his sisters Mildred and Jemima.

The children all went into the other lounge and were soon playing riotous games: their shrill laughter rising and falling. Jenny was pleased that Jemima's voice was to be heard along with the other children. She was obviously having a good time, in contrast to the way her young life was restricted at Mearly Hall.

At teatime, the large dining table had been extended and the children were all seated together at the far end of the table from the adults. It was obvious that this was a novelty for Jemima, who sat watching all the adults and listening to their conversation intently during the meal.

After tea, Jenny played guessing games with the children, whilst Ben and Theo sat at one side and had a game of chess. Marian, Susy and Mildred compared notes in quiet whispers about their forthcoming confinements, as Susy had confided quietly to the other ladies that she was expecting another baby in the autumn. Will and Arthur sat in another corner discussing the world situation, especially the happenings in the Boer country, far away.

It was soon time for everyone to leave. From a lively noisy gathering, the house was soon quiet again and Jenny chivvied the children to get ready for bed. Ben commented that he had enjoyed the game of chess with Theo, and Jenny was strangely pleased that her son and this man were becoming friendlier, although she couldn't admit to herself why this pleased her.

Instead of flowers this time, Jenny received a note from Theo and Mildred, giving their thanks for her hospitality. It also contained a request for her attendance at their house in two weeks time, when a few guests would be gathering for a musical soirée. A handwritten note was added saying that it did not invite the children, as this was an evening engagement.

Jenny considered this for a while, but decided to go. She spent as much time as she could with the children and surely it was her turn to have some adult entertainment, she argued with herself. The fact that it would mean spending more time with Theo was not a consideration; she tried to tell herself forcibly.

But as she thought about him, her heart softened. It was very pleasant being treated like a lady, even though she had no intention of the friendship going any further. Or had she? How would she react if he made an advance to her? She was not sure, and blushed to herself at the thoughts which had drifted into her mind.

Putting the letter in her drawer, she took up a piece of paper and accepted the invitation, wondering already which gown she would wear for the evening. Or should she ask Catherine to make her a new gown, perhaps? After all, as Marian kept saying, she was a walking advertisement for her shop when she went out to a function.

Yes, she would have a new gown. An evening gown that would be suitable for this function and any others that Theo might invite her to. She jumped up from her chair and after asking Janey to ensure that the reply went in the post, she went and sought out Catherine's advice about a new gown. As she tripped down the stairs to Catherine's room, she felt like a young girl again, instead of a widowed mother of thirty and more years.

A few days later, Mildred called into the shop and asked to see Jenny. They went to the tearoom and ordered tea and cakes. Jenny asked Mildred how she was feeling and was assured that she had never felt in better health. She was positively blooming, thank you very much.

'I want to ask your advice about our soirée,' Mildred asked.

'I am afraid I haven't held any soirées, so I don't think that I will be of much help to you,' Jenny replied.

'Oh no, I don't mean that kind of help. As you know, Theo hasn't made many friends since he arrived here and I wondered if you could recommend anyone who might be interested. Several of his friends that he invited are unable to attend. It would be most embarrassing if no one attended, both for the soloist and the other guests.'

'I can suggest some local people to you, if you like. Who is your soloist to be?'

'It is Sally Britnell. She is most respected in these parts, so I understand.'

'Yes, indeed she is. I have heard her spoken of frequently and with high praise, although I have not heard her myself.'

'Good. It was a wise choice, then?'

'Most certainly. Now, who would be likely to accept an invitation from you? Let me see,' Jenny paused whilst thinking for a few moments. 'What about the Jolleys'? They are a good family and live in Waddington village. Then there is Captain Parker at Browsholme. He is a keen musician, I believe.'

'Jenny, could you write all these names down for me?'

'Of course, and there are the Martins at Gisburn. And the Storeys at Stonehill. Oh and what about the Duxburys? He is a mill owner down at Low Moor, but quite accepted in local society, especially since his daughter married Lord Hastings. Is that enough?'

'More than enough. Theo will be pleased. I will rush home and start writing letters today.'

'Mildred, why don't you write the letters here in my office and then you can post them. In that way, they will be delivered a day earlier and give the recipients longer to make their minds up. Also, I can help you with their correct titles and addresses.'

'If you are sure that won't be an imposition?'

'Not at all. See, sit here at this table and I will give you pen and ink.' Jenny passed the writing implements over to her and settled her down with another cup of tea.

As soon as the letters were finished, Jenny called for Janey, who took the letters straight away to the post office.

'Thank you for all your help Jenny, and please come early on the night so that we can have a chat before the other guests arrive,' said Mildred as she drew on her soft leather gloves. 'It was Theo's suggestion that you might be able to help and he was correct. You are becoming very important to our family, Jenny. I hope you know that.' With that, she swept out of the room, leaving Jenny a little embarrassed but grateful that there wasn't time to have to think up an answer to that comment.

However, it didn't stop Jenny thinking about the words that Mildred had said. Important to this family, she had said. What could she mean?

Then Jenny chided herself. I help them out when they have a problem and supply all the necessary clothes to keep Mildred happy. That is why I am important to the family. Unless she meant that . . . no. It probably wasn't a veiled hint about Theo's feelings regarding her. But yet, he had made quite a few direct comments about her looks and how he liked her.

Enough, Jenny chided herself yet again. Get on with your work and let things develop in their own time, if they are going to. But she was strangely distracted that afternoon and ended up going down to see Catherine to see how her new evening gown was progressing.

It was almost ready. It was a rich russet-coloured satin gown with black and fawn trim. It had a square neckline, with fussy lace around it, which was repeated along the hem of the fairly straight skirt. The sleeves were tight and the wrists were trimmed in the black and fawn lace, too. It was a most unusual gown and Jenny was very pleased with it. The warm tones of the russet seemed to make her face glow and she liked the effect that it had on her.

Jenny found that she was very much looking forward to the musical soirée. Only a few more days, she found herself thinking, as she tried to concentrate on her work, but it only made the days seem longer. For once, work didn't fully absorb her as it usually did.

Chapter 19

On arrival at Mearly Hall on the night of the soirée, Jenny noticed that there was quite a stir about the place, and neither Theo nor Mildred were around to receive her. She was shown into the small drawing room, which was Mildred's favourite room, but that lady was nowhere to be found. Jenny removed her evening cloak and smoothed her gown down, checking her hair in the mirror.

When the servant Matty appeared, Jenny asked where Lady Mildred was.

'There has been ever such a to-do, Mrs Marshall. Lord Pennington turned up unexpectedly, just this afternoon. It gave Lady Pennington quite a turn. She thought that he was still in darkest Africa. Quite a turn, she had.'

'And is she over the turn now?'

'Not really. They have sent for the doctor, what with her being in a delicate way, if you will pardon my forwardness, Mrs Marshall. Mind you, that gave Lord Pennington a shock, too. Apparently, he didn't know about the delicate condition, so he had quite a turn as well.'

'Are they going to continue with the soirée? Should I go home do you think?'

'Oh no, Mrs Marshall. Lady Pennington was hoping that you would come early. She wants you to be the hostess for this evening. To help her and Lord Theo out.

'Oh dear, I am not sure about this. It is not the kind of thing that I am used to doing. Surely one of the other ladies who are coming would be better suited to the task.'

'Lady Pennington said that you would say that,' grinned Matty. 'She said that I was to take you up to her room when you came.'

'Is she fit to receive visitors?'

'She was most specific that I must take you up, Mrs Marshall, even if the doctor was here.'

'Very well, then. I will go up to her room if you will take me, please.' Jenny followed Matty upstairs to Mildred's bedroom. It was a beautiful large room, which was overpoweringly hot. Another of the servants was fussing around Mildred, but Jenny's eyes were drawn to a large man sat by the bedside, tenderly stroking Mildred's forehead.

'Jenny, thank you for coming to see me. Let me present my husband, Lord Pennington, or Richard as you must call him.' At this, Lord Pennington stood up and bowed low over Jenny's hand.

'I have heard so much about you already, Mrs Marshall, I am pleased to make your acquaintance,' he said in a very rich deep low voice. He was very tall as well as large and yet had graceful movements as he moved around the bed to greet Jenny. His gaze quickly turned back to Mildred. It was obvious that he was besotted with her, and she with him.

A knock at the door stopped all further conversation. It was the doctor, who sent Jenny and Lord Pennington out of the room. Lord Pennington paced up and down the corridor like a caged tiger. Jenny tried to help him and suggested that they go downstairs but he refused to move from the door.

'I want to catch this country quack before he goes. If necessary I shall send for my man from home.'

'Actually, he is a very good doctor. He attended all my confinements. He has some very good new ideas.'

'I will make my own mind up about him,' said Lord Pennington brusquely, but turned suddenly when he heard the door opening.

'How is she?' he demanded.

'Would you like to come back into the room, Lord Pennington?' the doctor asked. They went back into the room and shut the door. Very quickly, the door opened again and the servant came out, asking Jenny if she would greet the guests for Lady Pennington. Jenny had no choice but to go downstairs and see who had arrived.

It was the soloist, with her son as her accompanist. She took them into the small breakfast room and the servant attended to their needs. They asked to be shown where they would be performing and the servant took them out into the ballroom. They had planned to use the Long Gallery upstairs, but with Lady Pennington being taken ill, they had changed the plan. Theo was still nowhere to be seen.

Eventually, Jenny asked Agnes the other servant where Theo was. The servant looked a little sheepish.

'He is in the stable, Mrs Marshall,' she replied.

'In the stable? What is he doing there? He should be here, either with his sister or awaiting his guests,' Jenny replied quite angrily.

'It's because of his mother, Mrs Marshall.'

'What is? I didn't know that he had a mother anymore.'

'No, she died in childbed. He was in the house with her alone, well, alone apart from the servants. Her husband was stuck in a snowdrift and couldn't get home and Lady Mildred and her other sisters were away with friends. She just bled to death, very quickly. But she managed to push the child out first. That was Miss Jemima.'

Jenny was stunned. 'How awful, but wasn't he grown up at the time?'

'Oh yes, but it has made him peculiar about childbirth ever since. If you went to talk to him, Mrs Marshall, I am sure that it would help him. Remind him of his duty. They are a very proud lot, the Thievelys, but they will always do their duty.'

'I see. Well, I will try, but I can't stay long if I have to greet the guests. I will go to the stable now.'

Jenny hurried along to the stable and found Theo leaning against his horse, stroking his neck.

'Theo?' she said softly. 'Are you there?'

There was no answer. She went further inside, nearer to him. 'Theo,' she said and reached out to touch his back gently. He turned around slowly and Jenny was shocked by his countenance. He looked gaunt and ill. She held his hands and tried to rub some warmth into them.

'Come back into the house, Theo. It is cold out here.' She drew him forwards out of the stable and, still holding her hands, he let himself be guided into the warmth of the kitchen.

'Get some brandy Cook, quickly now,' ordered Jenny and sat Theo down on the nearest chair.

The brandy was produced instantly and Cook poured it down Theo's throat. It had the desired effect. He gasped, took a deep breath when it was poured down his throat, but soon seemed to recover from his trance-like state.

'Jenny, my dear, how is Mildred?'

'I don't know. I came down to meet your guests.'

'Guests,' he said flatly, 'are they here then?'

'No, only the soloist and accompanist. But they will be here soon, so you must get ready. Go,' she gently chided him, as she would to one of her children, 'get ready and I will meet the guests and Matty will find out how Mildred is.'

Theo took hold of her hands and squeezed them tightly.

'How ever would I have managed without you to help, Jenny. You are very important to this family.'

Embarrassed by the fact that all the servants were listening, Jenny drew Theo out of the kitchen and shooed him upstairs.

Jenny hurried out of the kitchen and back to the large entrance hall. Just in time, as a maid was letting a couple in. With a relief, Jenny saw that it was Lord and Lady Martin.

'Lady Martin, Lord Martin, welcome to Mearly Hall. I am afraid that Lord Thievely and Lady Pennington have been detained. May I take you into the ballroom? I don't think that you have been here before, have you?'

'Jenny,' said Lady Martin, her half-sister, 'I didn't expect to see you here. Are you a friend of the family?'

'A fairly new friend, Morag, but confidentially, Lady Pennington has been taken ill, so I am helping Lord Thievely.'

Just at that moment, Theo came down the stairs, completely himself again.

'Good evening. I am Theo, Lord Thievely. Welcome to my home. I am sorry that I wasn't here to greet you.'

'Don't worry, my man,' said Lord Martin, 'we were ably greeted by your sister's friend.'

'I hope that I am considered her friend as well,' replied Theo, 'not just my sister's.'

Embarrassed by the sentiment, Jenny took hold of Morag's arm and led her away towards the other side of the room, leaving the men to get acquainted.

Morag laughed when they were out of earshot and imitated Theo's voice. 'Hope she is my friend as well,' she mimicked in a deep voice. 'You must tell me what is going on, Jenny. Do I detect a hint of romance?'

'No, you do not,' Jenny replied, just a shade too vehemently.

'Do not tell me, let me guess. You are just good friends,' teased Morag. Fortunately for Jenny the maid announcing the next guests interrupted them. The Jolleys and the Hastings had all arrived at the same time. Other guests arrived very closely afterwards and the soirée was soon in full swing.

The soloist was indeed, breathtaking. Her voice soared easily to the higher notes and it had a clarity and purity to it. Every word could be heard clearly and the accompanist was also excellent. He gave one or two of his own performances to give Sally's voice a rest between songs.

Theo insisted that Jenny sat next to him during the recital and the supper break and he managed to whisper that Mildred appeared to be slightly better, for which information Jenny was pleased.

Soon it was time for the guests to leave, but not before they had all praised the whole evening, both the entertainment and the supper. Theo graciously received all the compliments and wished them God Speed on their journeys.

Jenny was also asking for her coat but Theo asked her to stay a little while longer, so that she could go up and see Mildred.

'Surely Mildred will be asleep by now?' Jenny suggested.

'No, actually she is not. She is awake and asking to see you, as is Lord Pennington. Please stay.'

'Just for a few minutes then. I have no wish to tire Mildred and must get home myself.'

'Could you not stay the night?'

'No, Theo, I have children and a business to see to.'

'Couldn't the staff see to the children for once? Isn't that what you pay them for?'

'It is not. I pay them to help me function as a mother and a businesswoman. I couldn't manage without them and wouldn't miss going home at night to my children. They are very precious. They are all I have.'

Theo was silent at this outburst, so Jenny relented a little and said that she would stay for a while to see Mildred and her husband.

'We will go up to her room now, then,' said Theo. Jenny nodded and followed him up the main staircase. He knocked on the door, then opened it for Jenny and allowed her through first. Mildred and Richard her husband were holding hands together. Mildred was in bed, with Richard sitting by her side. He stood up as he saw Jenny and Theo.

'Have all the guests gone now, Jenny?' asked Mildred.

'Yes, and they all said that they had had a lovely evening, so you can rest about that. It all went off very well. Sally was marvellous.'

'I could hear her up here. I agree, she is marvellous. How am I ever going to thank you for all that you have done?'

'It was a pleasure to help you. Now what did the doctor say?'

'She is to stay in bed for some time,' answered Richard, 'and he doesn't advise that she moves from here until after the birth. You were right, Jenny, he is a good chap. I am sorry that I doubted you.

Looks like we will be here imposing on you for a long time, old chap,' he turned and said to Theo.

'It is no imposition,' replied Theo. 'You are welcome in my home at any time, think of it as your own.'

'How ever am I going to keep madam in bed for several weeks? Answer me that?' Richard laughed.

'With great difficulty, I should think,' laughed Theo in reply. 'I think that this is where our good friend Jenny might be able to help, don't you Mildred?'

'I will do everything that I possibly can to help, you know that Mildred, but obviously my time is limited,' offered Jenny.

'If you could only visit occasionally, that would keep her spirits up I am sure, and discourage her from getting out of bed,' said Theo.

'Certainly. But now I must get home to my children. Could you call my carriage for me, Theo.'

'Yes, did Roger bring you?'

'Yes, he did. Could I have my cloak as well, whilst you are ringing the bell?'

The maid soon returned with Jenny's cloak and told them that her carriage was waiting. Theo took the cloak from the maid and gently put it over Jenny's shoulders, seeming to take some little time to adjust the cloak to his satisfaction.

Theo walked down the stairs with Jenny after she had said her goodbyes to Mildred and Richard. He walked outside with Jenny and helped her into the carriage, lingering over her hand for as long as possible, until Jenny withdrew it, conscious that Roger was watching.

'Thank you so much my dear, for helping me out tonight. You were marvellous. You say that you weren't born to a life like this, but you looked perfectly at ease in being the hostess. You graced my home and it was a pleasure to watch you,' said Theo, to Jenny's embarrassment. She smiled and made no comment and asked Roger to set off. If Theo had his way, they would be still saying goodbye in another hour if she didn't stop him now.

Theo stayed on the doorstep for quite some time as Jenny was driven away from the house. Jenny couldn't resist turning around near to the end of the driveway, but he was still standing there, looking after her.

Her heart leapt inside her as she saw him and was glad when Roger drove around the bend and she could no longer see him. She pondered on all that he had said on the way home and thought about how he had been when she had found him in the stable. What a complex man he was. He appeared to be very charming at all times and a perfect gentleman, but he had been in a terrible state when she had found him in the stable.

It had been a tragic story about his mother she mused, but was surprised that he still reacted in this way so long afterwards. Why, Jemima must be ten years old by now and yet the thought of childbirth still had the power to grip him in fear and trembling.

She was glad that she had been able to comfort him in his need and felt strangely touched that he had responded to her care. All too soon, her thoughts were brought back to the present instead of dreaming, when they arrived home to Waddington Road. Roger said nothing to her as he handed her down from the carriage, but she could tell by the look on his face that he would have a lot to tell Maggie when Jenny had gone to bed. Well, let them talk. After all, there was nothing in it, was there? Or was there? Only time would tell, she told herself once more.

Chapter 20

During the following weeks, Jenny tried to visit Mildred as often as she could. Sometimes she took the children, but at other times she went alone. Mildred was certainly cheered up by her visits and Theo obviously enjoyed them.

But other duties also took her time. Three weeks later, Marian gave birth to a little girl whom she called Amanda Jenny. Marian was beside herself with joy, as were Will, George and Luke. She had lost a lot of blood during the birth, so the doctor advised that she stay in bed for four weeks instead of the usual two weeks, and eat lots of liver. Fortunately Marian liked liver, so it was an easy instruction, but the children began to get fed up of it and complained. Poor Katy ended up having to make two different meals each day, one for Marian and one for Will and the children, but she thrived on being busy.

Jenny went to visit Marian as soon as she could and was overjoyed to hold Marian's baby in her arms. She had felt a bond with Marian's firstborn, but there was a family bond there, as George was her half brother's child. But she felt the same bond again with Amanda. It was instant and special and Jenny was overwhelmed with the feelings that she encountered.

As soon as the baby was born, Catherine set to work to make a set of pretty baby girl dresses for Amanda, and Jenny took these with her when she visited. Jenny was thrilled to be asked to be Amanda's godmother and she readily agreed. The service wasn't to be for some time, as the doctor had advised that Marian didn't go out until she was fully recuperated.

Three weeks after Marian had her baby, Mildred's labour pains started and the doctor could not stop them this time, and simple rest did not work. Theo and Richard had gone to the races so missed the event. It was for the best as when they returned from York, the baby had been born. It was a boy, which delighted Richard and Theo, and both mother and baby were healthy, even though the baby was three weeks early.

When she heard the news about Mildred, Jenny went over to Mearly Hall as soon as she could, carrying a small gift for the baby. She was taken up to the bedroom where Mildred was delighted to see her. The two friends embraced.

'Go and take a look at my lovely son,' Mildred said. Jenny walked over to the crib and reached down to pick up the baby.

She cradled the little boy in her arms and felt an instant rapport, as she had done with Marian's baby three weeks before. She was so engrossed that she didn't hear Mildred asking her a question.

'Will you?' repeated Mildred.

'I am sorry, I didn't hear you. What did you say?' said Jenny replacing the baby into the cot.

'Will you be the baby's godmother?' Jenny was stunned. Mildred had mentioned it in an idle moment but Jenny hadn't taken her seriously.

'But I am not family. Surely there are others more worthy than me to be his godmother?'

'There are plenty who think that they are more worthy, but you have been so important to me these last few months, that I want to thank you in this way.'

'Then I would be honoured. Thank you. When will the christening take place?'

'We have them fairly early in our family. A throwback to our Catholic roots I think, or because the ancestors were frightened that the babies wouldn't survive,' Mildred laughed.

'And where will the christening be held?'

'Back in our family church in Tamworth. Our house is near to Tamworth and we have endowed the local parish church. We have a family box in it, so always have our services there.'

'How will I get there?'

'You could come with Theo. And your children of course.'

Jenny was relieved. She knew that finally the message had got thorough to this aristocratic family. Her children were more important to her than anything or anyone else.

'Thank you for inviting my children. I would have found it difficult to leave them behind.'

'I know Jenny. I think I understand a little of that now that I have given birth to the baby. It is a fierce feeling of pride and ownership all mixed up together, in the wonder of creation. It is hard to believe that because of your love, this little child has been created, isn't it?'

Jenny nodded. She was too full to answer. Eventually she managed to ask what they were going to call her godson.

'It's a Pennington family thing. The firstborn is always called Richard and then the grandparents' middle or other names. So he will be Richard Mathew John. Quite a mouthful, isn't it? But I think that we will add Theobold as well, as we are so grateful to him for letting us stay here and for all that he has done. Besides, he is the godfather.'

'It is quite a mouthful for such a little chap. Will you call him Richard?'

'I am not sure. I suppose that could get confusing. Although my Richard was called Richy until he attained the title after his father died, so I suppose that we will give him that name.'

As if he approved of the name, little Richy stirred in his sleep and began to cry. Jenny ran to the cot and picked him up. He was instantly quiet again and looked up, straight into Jenny's eyes and held the gaze for a long time. The feeling returned that she had experienced earlier. A mixture of yearning and wistfulness. Would this feeling of emotion when she held a baby ever go away? she wondered to herself. She carefully handed the baby back to Mildred who had decided to feed the baby herself rather than have a wet nurse.

'I will leave you to feed the baby now, Mildred. Until next time,' she said, stroking Richy's head before she left the room.

The next few weeks went quickly, with Jenny making many special visits to her two new godchildren. Soon, Mildred and her family returned to Tamworth, so that she could plan the christening. It was fixed for June 12th. It was arranged that Jenny would travel down with Theo, Jemima and Jenny's children and they would stay overnight at Mearly Hall before they set off, so that they could make an early start in the morning.

Before the christening, Jenny worked hard to get the workmen organised so that they could start all the alterations to the shop during the first two weeks of July. The workmen building the moving platform were all ready and were looking forward to carrying out the work. It was to be the first moving platform in Clitheroe.

For Richy's christening, there was already a family christening robe in the Pennington family, so Jenny had a beautiful carrying shawl made which was trimmed with down and a new set of quilted cot bedding for the ancient wooden family cot. Fortunately little Amanda's christening was not until the end of June, so Jenny had more time to decide on the present for Amanda.

On the 8th June, Jenny and family went over to Mearly Hall. The children were put upstairs in the family nursery with Jemima, whereas Jenny was given the lovely bedroom that Mildred had so recently vacated. As a concession to Jenny, Theo allowed the children to eat downstairs with the adults that evening and all the children were in very high spirits.

After the children had gone to bed, Jenny and Theo spent the rest of the evening quietly together, reading books. Jenny felt that she would like to talk a little, but Theo seemed disinclined to do so, so she remained quiet.

Next morning, after a hearty breakfast, the two families set off for the Pennington's house. It would take them two days to reach Tamworth, with several changes of horses. Theo's coaches were a lot older than Jenny's, and therefore bumpier. Jenny wished that she had offered her own coach for the journey but she had never thought of it. He and Jenny travelled in the first coach and the children all travelled with the servant in the second coach.

During the journey, Theo was a lot livelier than he had been in his house the night before. Perhaps he has moods, thought Jenny, but on reflection, she didn't think so. He didn't appear to be a moody person really, but he had definitely been distracted last night. But not today. They had long chats about everything under the sun, and slowly Jenny was coming to appreciate this man and his personality.

The overnight stay was in a very smart coaching house and was uneventful. By the end of the second day, however, tempers were frayed and all the children were tired and fractious. Eventually they arrived at the house. Jenny was shocked when she saw the size of it. The drive itself must have been over a mile long and ended in a large forecourt. The house was Elizabethan and very imposing, obviously having been extended over the years.

When the children got out of the coach, Ellen ran to Jenny and cried. 'Mummy, can we sleep in your room tonight? It is not nice being so far from you at night, please say yes.'

'Shush Ellen. I can't say where you will sleep. We are guests in this house. We will only stay for a few days, so I am sure that you will be alright. Besides, your brother and sister will be with you. At least you won't be on your own in the nursery like Jemima is.'

'But I want to be with you, mummy,' she continued whining.

'Ellen, do grow up. Mummy can't be with you all the time. Now go along, the maid is waiting to take you to the nursery.'

Ellen still refused to move. Then she saw a child on a pony riding through the grounds. Her face lit up.

'Will I be able to ride a pony?' asked Ellen eagerly, all traces of sullenness miraculously disappearing.

'You will have to ask Lady or Lord Pennington, but I am sure that you will be able to ride a pony whilst you are here. Now go upstairs, you are holding everyone else up.'

Ellen moved with great enthusiasm, to Jenny's relief. That had been difficult. It was probably the long journey that had unsettled Ellen. But a definite promise of a pony ride next morning averted the next crisis too, which was about the dining arrangements. The children were to be fed in the nursery and were not allowed downstairs to the dining hall.

After the meal, Jenny went straight up to the nursery to see the children, as she knew that they would be unhappy, but she found them all playing happily together with Jemima and her cousins.

The following day was the christening but Ellen managed to get someone to let her have a ride on a pony first thing in the morning. She was ecstatic. It was all she could talk about on the way to the church.

Young Richy behaved beautifully throughout the service and did not even mutter when the priest sprinkled the water on to his forehead. The baby was passed to her after the naming ceremony and she held him lovingly, gazing down on him for some time. When she looked up, it was to find Theo standing next to her, also gazing down lovingly, but it was at her and not the baby.

Jenny blushed and looked away, and handed Richy to the other female godparent, one of Richard's sisters, and engaged her in conversation about Richy. The ploy worked, for Theo went off to make conversation with someone else.

Going through the motions of speaking to people kept Jenny's mind off what had just happened, but in the carriage going back to the house, Jenny remembered the look that Theo had given her. It made her heart beat just a little faster and she was glad that the children were chattering noisily because she could think her own thoughts.

Eventually, they arrived back at the house and a large meal was enjoyed. Again, the children were made to eat upstairs and not join in the family festivities. Jenny reflected again how sad a system it was for the children of the gentry. Despite her austere upbringing in the workhouse, at least Jenny had the comfort of her friends there, whereas some of these children, like Jemima, had nobody but servants to talk to for long periods of the day.

As soon as they got back to the house, Ellen changed into her travelling clothes, which were the oldest that she had with her. She ran off outside towards the stables to see if she could have another turn on the pony. Jenny knew that when she got home, there would be a renewed campaign for Ellen to have a pony.

Rachel and Jemima had become inseparable during the stay with the Penningtons. Jenny was glad that perhaps Rachel was bringing some comfort into Jemima's life and hoped that the friendship would continue when they got home. Ben had been quite happy playing with one of the Pennington's nephews, who also had an interest in engineering. At least her children seemed to have the knack for befriending others and she was pleased about that. She determined that she would enjoy the rest of her stay in this beautiful house, with such lovely companions.

Chapter 21

For the return journey, they all set off soon after breakfast. Jenny and Theo again shared a carriage. As soon as they had set off, Theo started talking to Jenny, saying that he needed a serious talk to her before they got home. For a moment, Jenny worried that perhaps her children may have been rude or disobedient whilst at the Pennington's home, but he seemed to be talking about himself.

Theo seemed to be telling her his life story, she didn't know why, but at the end of it, he asked her to marry him. Jenny was stunned. She knew that he was becoming enamoured of her, but she didn't think that he would propose. The social divide was too large.

'Do I have to wait a long time for your answer?' Theo said eventually. 'If you want some time I will understand. I suppose that it is has come as a bit of a shock to you but I can't leave it any longer. When you were the hostess at my soirée, I kept thinking how right you looked in my house and how comfortable I felt with you by my side. And then at the church, when you held little Richy, I just wanted you to be my wife and hold our baby in your arms and look lovingly down on it.'

Jenny could hardly take it all in. Their relationship had taken a much more serious turn very suddenly. Did she want to marry him? It didn't take long for her heart to reply. Yes, she did.

Theo looked down when he had finished his discourse, unsure of himself and looking quite miserable. Jenny reached over and held his hand. He looked up at her, hopefully.

'Yes, I will marry you, Theo, but . . .'

'You will, you will marry me? Oh Jenny, you have made me the happiest man alive . . .'

'I said that there was a but,' Jenny interrupted.

'Yes?' said Theo expectantly, 'anything at all. What is your but?'

'It is several buts actually. I will still want to keep control of the shop.'

'Yes, I knew you would say that. What else?'

'And my other businesses.'

'Yes, anything else?'

'I would want my children to eat their meals with me in the evening, not be left in the nursery.'

'Is that all? Has your list of buts finished?'

'I think so for now, unless I think of any others,' replied Jenny laughing.

'You won't regret it, my dearest. We will live long and happy lives together, with our children beside us,' waxed Theo lyrically. Suddenly his facial expression changed. 'You will have more children, Jenny, won't you? I do need an heir if I possibly can.'

Jenny laughed again. 'Yes, I will have some children for you. I won't have much choice probably. I seem well able to bear children.'

'I know. That is part of your attraction,' Theo teased, 'your fecundity. And you have had one boy, which is even better.'

'Two.'

'Two what?' asked a bewildered Theo.

'Two boys. I lost one that I was carrying when Jonny died.'

'I am sorry. I didn't know about your other boy. There I go again reminding you of your loss. Do you remember, when we first met, I always seemed to be mentioning your loss in some way, even though it was inadvertently?'

'Don't worry. You weren't to know. Not many people did know about it.'

'Will we be able to tell everyone about our engagement when we get home? Shall we have an engagement party?'

'Not until I have told my children. I need to talk to them first. And no, I do not want an engagement party. I am not a young slip of a girl that wants parties.'

'We have a family heirloom engagement ring. Would you accept that or would you want to be a modern miss and go for something new?'

'No,' she said, looking down at Jonny's small engagement ring sadly, 'I will have the family ring. Best not to change traditions.'

'Good. That will save me some money. I have made no secret of the fact that I have not got a lot of money, so I do not bring riches to the marriage.'

'Neither do I. But I am comfortably off through the businesses.'

'Don't let us talk money. It is so depressing. I want to tell you how much I love you, not to see the state of your bank balance. And I do love you Jenny. Deeply and truly. I know that you don't love me as much yet, and I understand that. But I hope that you grow to love me more deeply as our marriage continues.'

'I too hope that our love grows. It is hard when I had such a happy marriage before. I never thought that I would remarry, but I am happy to marry you, Theo, and I am very, very fond of you.'

'Thank you my dear. You won't regret it. I want to spend the rest of my life loving you.'

'And you will let me tell the children before you tell anyone else?'

'Yes, if you wish. I will not tell anyone until you give me permission. Goodness, giving your orders already and you haven't even got the ring on your finger yet,' laughed Theo.

Jenny laughed too. She did hope her children would take the news well. They had seen so much change in their little lives. How could she bear it if they weren't happy with her remarriage? But she would tell them carefully, and she was sure that they would accept Theo as their stepfather. Ben especially seemed to be getting to know him quite well.

When they arrived back at Mearly Hall, Theo pressed them to stay a little longer, but Jenny wanted to get home with the children. She had things to tell them and she didn't want anyone else telling them. They thanked Theo for his hospitality and left. On arrival home, the children went straight to bed. Jenny decided that she would tell them the news tomorrow evening, after school.

The following evening Jenny waited until the tea had been finished and told the children that she wanted to talk to them all. She took them into the smaller lounge and sat them all down. Jenny stood by the fireplace and swallowed hard before she started speaking.

'What have we done wrong?' Rachel asked in a plaintive voice. 'We have all tried to think of anything that we have done wrong, but we can't remember anything.'

'You have done nothing wrong, children. Whatever made you think that?'

'You always tell us off,' said Rachel. 'What else could you be wanting to tell us?'

'Actually, it is not anything that you have done at all, it is something that I am going to do.'

'You are going to buy me a pony?' said Ellen excitedly.

'No, Ellen, I am not buying you a pony.' Oh dear thought Jenny. This is going to be harder than I thought. Ellen and her ponies. But then she had an idea.

'Well, it may end up that you have access to a pony, Ellen.'

'What do you mean?' asked Ellen.

'Lord Thievely has asked me to marry him.'

There was a stunned silence.

'Marry?' said Rachel horrified. 'I hope that you said no. How rude of him.'

'Er, no, I didn't refuse. I accepted.'

There was another stunned silence.

Ellen was the first to recover. 'What is all this to do with a pony?'

'Jemima has a pony.'

'Would we have to go and live there with Jemima?' asked Ben.

'Yes.'

'But what about this house?' said Rachel.

'I will keep it for now. I haven't thought about it really.'

'And will we have to eat our meals upstairs like Jemima does?'

'No. I have insisted that you have your meals together, with us.'

'But I don't want you to have a husband, mummy,' said Ben, 'I am your man of the house, you said so, after daddy died.'

'Sometimes I get lonely Ben. I liked being married and miss daddy too. But you will always be my special man.' Oh dear, thought Jenny, this is not the way I meant to tell them.

'Will I really get to ride Jemima's pony?' asked Ellen with starry eyes.

'Yes, I am sure you will be able to, Ellen,' replied Jenny.

'And will we be called Thievely if you marry him? I don't like that name. I like being Marshall,' whined Rachel.

'No, you will stay as Marshall, but I will change my name to Thievely after our marriage.'

'Well, I am glad mummy is marrying him, as he will let me ride the pony, I know he will,' said Ellen defensively.

'Shall we all go a walk by the riverside?' said Jenny, glad of a change to the conversation.

The children all agreed, and whilst they were walking together in the fresh air, they slowly came to accept the fact of the marriage although Rachel still had some reservations.

After they had gone to bed, Jenny sat in her favourite rocking chair and pondered the step that she had taken. She did hope that it worked out well. She would never forgive herself if the children were unhappy because of her marriage.

Eventually, Jenny managed to get to sleep, but had a broken night, constantly waking during the night and going over her decision in her mind.

Early next day in the shop, Janey announced that Jenny had a visitor. It was Theo. She took him to the tearooms and told him of the conversation that had taken place with the children, and of their fears.

Theo reassured Jenny that he would be a sensitive stepfather and that they would soon mould together as a family, with Jemima. Why, he reminded her, Rachel and Jemima were already becoming close friends. Jenny acquiesced, but was not as confident as Theo.

'Never mind that now. I have brought the engagement ring. I would like you to wear it, if you would.' He brought a box out of his inner pocket and opened it.

'Theo, could we go to my office, please,' said Jenny a little embarrassed, 'I would prefer a more private engagement ceremony than in the middle of my tearoom.' Theo laughed and followed Jenny up to her office.

As soon as they got through the door, Theo grasped Jenny in his arms and hugged her to him. Then taking her chin in his hands he gently and briefly kissed her and released her. As if he had regretted releasing her, he then took her back into his arms and kissed her thoroughly and deeply. Jenny looked at him with surprise, feeling the stirrings of desire. He had seemed such a controlled and respectable man, but now he was showing a spark of passion.

'Now I will give you your engagement ring, Jenny,' he said after he reluctantly released her. He picked the box up and drew out a large diamond cluster that looked like a daisy with about twenty diamonds in it. Jenny gasped. It was beautiful.

'Theo, it is beautiful. Thank you so much. I will treasure it always.'

'Not always, my dear,' Theo replied.

'Why not? I know that I will always treasure it.'

'You can only wear it until our son becomes engaged and then you must give it away to our son's fiancée.' Jenny blushed at the hint of intimacy.

'We have only been engaged for two minutes Theo. I can't think so far into the future at the moment.'

'But you will have my children, Jenny? You did say that you would.'

'Oh yes, I will have your children. I know how much you need an heir,' she laughed. 'I will be your brood mare.'

'I am sorry Jenny. I didn't mean to make it so obvious. Will you marry me soon? I don't think that I can wait much longer. I know it was remiss of me to kiss you like that, but I have wanted to do that ever since I met you, so I have been very patient, really. But now that I have kissed you, I want to kiss you a lot more. Please, marry me soon.'

'Yes, I think that I better had marry you soon after that kiss,' Jenny replied. 'What about November? Would that give you time to organise everything?'

'Jenny, it is you that will have to organise everything, won't it? Your trousseau and all that sort of feminine stuff.'

'I have a gown shop that specialises in weddings at my disposal. I am sure that I can be ready very quickly, Theo,' she laughed.

'Of course, and what will you wear?'

'It won't be a young bride's frilly gown, that is for sure. I am a mature matron, but then my friend Marian will not let me get married in a plain suit. She didn't last time. So it will be a wedding gown, but rather more sober. And that is all that you are going to hear. What she is to wear is a bride's secret,' teased Jenny.

'Please could you let Jemima be a flower girl? I will never hear the last of it if you say that she can't. She is desperate to be a flower girl.'

Flower girls. Of course, thought Jenny. That will appease the girls. They both enjoyed being flower girls before. This will help them come to terms with the marriage. And then she had another good idea. She would ask Ben to give her away, as he was her special man. Yes, that was another good idea.

'Yes, she can be a flower girl with my two girls,' replied Jenny.

'Can we get married on November 6th?'

'Why that date?' said Jenny, as it was the date when she had first received the letter about her inheritance back in 1883.

'You said that we could marry in November, and it is the first week of November, and I don't want to prolong it any further.'

'Yes, November the 6th it is then,' Jenny laughed. 'I had better go to see Marian tonight on the way home and get her to plan my trousseau.'

'Aren't you going to put the ring on?' said Theo quietly.

'Oh yes, I forgot,' replied Jenny. She took the ring out of its box and looked at it lovingly.

'Do you like the ring, Jenny?'

'Yes, it is beautiful. It is just that I have never taken my wedding ring and engagement ring off before. It will seem strange.'

'Well, leave your wedding ring on until our marriage and just wear my engagement ring. How does that sound?'

'Oh thank you Theo. That will make me feel better.' She slowly drew Jonny's engagement ring off her finger and tenderly placed it on her ring finger on her right hand.

Then she took Theo's ring and placed it next to her wedding ring. It completely overshadowed the narrow wedding band, and was far too large for her.

'It is too large,' said Jenny, 'we will have to have it made smaller I am afraid. Will that be satisfactory?'

'Yes, but we will have to tell our son to marry a girl with small fingers like his mother,' Theo replied gravely. Jenny laughed.

'I will take it off for now in case I lose it, and ask Mr Nettleton to alter it later today,' said Jenny.

'Why don't we go around to his shop now and then we can look at wedding rings as well?'

'I will go round and have it measured but I don't want to buy the wedding ring today. I have a lot of appointments. We will go another day.'

'Yes, my love. I will leave it to you then. But can I tell everyone that we are engaged now? I will have to put it in the Times.'

'The Clitheroe Advertiser and Times?'

'No, you goose, The Times, you know, London, court circular and all that. Have to let the old queen know what I am up to, being a peer of the realm.'

Jenny gulped. She had forgotten about that. Could she cope with being a Lady? Lady Jenny Thievely. Well, Theo seemed to think she could, so she would have to learn, very quickly. Although over the years, she had served many of them to know how they behaved.

'Yes, The Times,' she replied vaguely.

'And I will have to let Mildred know. She will be ecstatic. She has been on at me to marry for years, but will be so pleased that I have chosen you. She knows how I feel about you.'

'I am certainly looking forward to having Mildred as my sister-in-law.'

'Are we going to Nettleton's now?' said Theo changing the subject.

'Yes, we can do. I won't feel happy about it until the ring is made smaller.' The two of them went next door to the jewellers shop and the ring was measured for its alterations.

Theo then left Jenny and after he had gone, she slipped Jonny's small engagement ring back on her left hand with her wedding band. She would remove it when the new ring was repaired. That would be soon enough. For now, it was time to get back to her shop and carry on the day's business.

Chapter 22

On returning home in the evening, the children were quietly acquiescent about her forthcoming marriage. The two girls brightened considerably when Jenny told them that they were to be flower girls with Jemima. Even Ben looked proud when Jenny asked him to carry out the function of giving her away at the service.

'Where will the wedding be, mummy?' asked Ben.

'At our church in town, of course. You always get married at the ladies church, unless the husband has his own chapel in his house, and Theo hasn't.'

'When will you be getting married, mummy?' asked Ellen.

'Not until November.'

'What about Christmas?' asked Rachel.

'What about Christmas? asked Jenny in reply.

'We always have granny and grandfather and Aunty Marian and Aunty Susy and everyone on Christmas Day.'

'Then we can still have them all over to Mearly Hall for Christmas, I am sure. There will just be more of us this year. Now I think that it is time for bed, all of you.' The usual argument then broke out about who was oldest and why they shouldn't have to go to bed yet, but Jenny cut all the arguments short and packed them off to bed, promising to come upstairs soon and tuck them in.

When she had done that, she asked Roger if he could take her out on an errand. She went first to Susy's, then Marian's, and then her in-laws to tell them about her engagement. She didn't want them to hear from anyone else and was glad that she had told them herself. It was a relief when she had told them all as she felt that perhaps they would be cross with her for remarrying, but none of them were. They all understood that she was a young woman and had many years left to her.

Marian was the only one to immediately grasp that she would be a Lady and teased her about that, but Jenny just laughed it off. Marian said that she hoped that Jenny would still speak to her and Jenny reassured her, with laughter.

'Fancy, my Amanda, with a Lady for a godmother. Well, I never,' Marian said in an affected accent and Jenny laughed again. Oh it was good to laugh with Marian again. They had too little time together nowadays and she saw even less of Susy, though she was her sister-in-law. She promised herself that when she married Theo, she would not neglect her two closest friends.

It was soon time for Amanda's christening and all had a wonderful day. Jenny bought Amanda a sterling silver bowl and cutlery set. Marian was overwhelmed with the gift, but Jenny teased her to cover up her embarrassment.

'Well I could hardly have anything sewn for her, could I, without my most important seamstress knowing about it?'

'Thank you, Jenny. It is a beautiful set. Not that I will let her use it at all. It will stay on her shelf in her bedroom.'

'As long as I get plenty of cuddles from Amanda in return,' quipped Jenny.

'How are the arrangements coming on for the refurbishment of the shop?' asked Marian.

'The engineers are starting a week on Monday, so are you ready to go away? The house is now vacant in Blackpool.'

'Yes, we are all almost packed. It has been a busy time, getting ready for the christening as well. Young Katy is very excited. So is your Megan I believe?'

'She is. She can't wait. I think that she had her bags packed before the children's.'

'Do you want the children to sleep here overnight before we set off?'

'No, that is too much to ask you Marian. I will get Roger to bring them over first thing on Saturday morning. He is also taking Robert with a carriage to get you all over there, as you know.'

'And are Susy and Arthur coming to stay at all?'

'Not now. Susy is not very well with this confinement.'

'She does seem to be carrying very heavily, does she not?'

'I suppose she is. But then Jonny was a big baby.'

'Will you be coming to stay as well?'

'Yes, I will probably come for each weekend when I can. It will depend on the progress of the work, of course.'

'We will look forward to having you. You and Will can travel together on the third and fourth weekends, once he has gone back to work. It will be much safer for you.'

'What a good idea. I will do that. Thanks Marian, that will make my life easier. Until Saturday morning then.'

'Yes, Milady,' mocked Marian with a mock curtsey.

'Now stop teasing, Marian,' said Jenny, but she was laughing as she left the room.

Once all the children had left on the Saturday, Jenny went to the shop that was now empty. Mr Aggett was there, moving the mirrors from the top floor bedroom as promised. Jenny had to agree that they looked wonderful in the floor that was to be dedicated to wedding finery. Jenny left him to some of his preparatory work, which he had decided to do over the weekend and get a head start on the work before the engineers arrived on Monday.

Most of her stock had been moved out of the shop so that the dust didn't damage any of the fabrics. She had put it in a large storeroom at Low Moor mill, courtesy of Mr Duxbury. The staff had packed up all the stock the night before prior to going on their holidays.

Jenny was quite nervous about all her refurbishments. It was costing her a great deal of money, but she knew that it would make better use of her shop, especially the top floor. After making sure that Mr Aggett did not need her for anything else, Jenny set off to the coach station and got a coach over to Mearly Hall.

She had promised Theo that she would go to tea with him. It was something that Jenny was looking forward to. She had little enough time with Theo as it was, so she was making the most of her children being away at the seaside with Marian and Will.

Theo was waiting in the garden for her to arrive. He took her hand and was pleased when he noticed that she had her new engagement ring on.

'You have got your ring on, how lovely it looks. When did you get it?'

'Today. I thought you would like me to wear it tonight.'

'Tonight and forever, Jenny,' said Theo, with a loving look on his face. They had a pleasant evening together and then Theo took Jenny home in his carriage. He was quite prepared to come in and stay with her but Jenny would not allow him to, and told him to wait until they were married. He only said that he would go when Jenny promised that they could meet again for luncheon, after Jenny had been to church. It was only after he had gone that she realised that he had not offered to pay for the repair to her ring. Never mind, she could mention it another time.

Sunday was also a very special day for the two of them. They talked incessantly about each other and their plans for the future. Theo said that he would call into the shop or her house each day whilst the children were away and Jenny couldn't resist his idea. She would probably be quite lonely without the children and the staff anyway.

On Monday morning, Theo arrived about eleven of the clock, waving an envelope.

'Jenny, I have had an invitation to go and visit an old school friend this weekend. Please say that you will come with me. It is a perfect opportunity whilst the children are away.'

'Where does your friend live?'

'Over in the East Riding, beyond York. A small place called Pocklington. His estate is just outside, on the Wolds. Do say that you will come. I am longing to show you off to my friends.'

'I am not sure, I said that I would go and visit the children.'

'But you can go and visit them another weekend. Or during the week for that matter. I am sure that you are getting in the way of the workmen anyway,' he teased. 'The children have only been away for a few days and I know that you have spoken to them on the telephone. Oh please come with me.'

'Yes, alright, I will come with you. Is it just a weekend? I will need to be back early in the week to see Mr Aggett, my decorator.'

'We can go on Friday morning and return on Monday. How would that be for your business commitments?'

'That would be satisfactory. I could manage to stay away so long, but no longer.'

'Thank you, Jenny. You will like Percy and his house. It has a plain exterior, but inside there are many beautiful art treasures and furniture. It is a well-appointed house, and he is a good man, too. I can't wait for you to meet him. He will be my best man at the wedding, so I do want you two to like each other.'

'What kind of clothes will I need? You forget that I am not in the habit of attending these weekend house parties.'

'Oh, I do not know about such things. Ask your staff or some of your clients. You will need something for evenings and something for daytime. Does that help you?'

'Not at all,' replied Jenny. 'I will ask other people. It would be awful if I didn't have the right clothes with me. Not a good advertisement for my shop at all.'

'I suppose not, and there is no wife there to help you out or loan you something. Percy is a jolly bachelor. Married to his estate, really.'

'I will ask some of the clients. My staff are all on holiday whilst the children are away. And now I think that I had better get on with some work. Even though the shop is shut, there is a lot that I need to do.'

'Can I look at the moving platform? Is it installed yet?'

'They have made a start. It doesn't look like anything yet.'

'But your Ben has talked about it such a lot. He has made me quite interested. Perhaps we should have one at Mearly Hall as well, Jenny?'

'I think not. They are far too expensive for what they are, although I think that they will be a sound business investment for the shop.'

They walked together through the shop. Jenny showed Theo the new mirrors that were already installed on the wedding floor. Mr Aggett had been right. They did look magnificent in their new setting. Almost opulent. Brown and cream curtains had been hung by the side of each mirror, to make them more homelike. All that Jenny told him about her ideas and new features impressed Theo.

'Isn't it going to be very expensive, Jenny?'

'Very. But it will be worth it in the long run. You have to keep up-to-date with the latest fashions.'

They ambled slowly thorough the shop and then Jenny encouraged Theo to leave, so that she could get on with her work. He went reluctantly but promised to visit Jenny that evening for tea.

'In the meantime, I will write to Percy. No better still, I will telegraph him. He hasn't got a telephone installed yet. It is harder in the country as you know. That is why I haven't got one yet. I will go now and telegraph him. Until tonight.'

'Goodbye then,' said Jenny, glad that he was going and she could concentrate on her work. Theo has no telephone because he can't afford one, Jenny thought to herself, whether there are wires there or not, but she wouldn't have said anything to him. She didn't like to show off her own wealth, when he was short of money. Perhaps she could help him a little when she was married. She would certainly need a telephone, so that she could keep in contact with the shop.

Before she started on her work, Jenny rang the children at the holiday house in Blackpool. They were just about to go down to the beach, as it had been raining all morning and were keen to get going. They had little time to talk to their mother. She promised that she would come over and visit them on Wednesday, before she went away for the weekend.

Jenny was glad that they were happy at Blackpool. She could not have gone away if they had been unhappy. But they sounded to be having a wonderful time without her. It was quite a relief.

As Jenny started trying to work, the workmen suddenly made an awful noise and dust seemed to settle everywhere. The banging and vibrations were terrible and Jenny couldn't really concentrate on her work. In the end, she went home to work and came back at teatime before the workmen finished for the day. She checked with the chief engineer that all was going according to plan and was pleased with his reply. With Mr Aggett coming next week, she could not afford any delays.

That reminded her that she must contact Mr Aggett and tell him that she would be away for the weekend. She knew that he was going to work over the weekend again to make sure that the shop was finished on time.

Theo offered to come to Blackpool with Jenny but she refused. She wanted that time with the children on her own. He could have her undivided attention all weekend.

It was a lovely day spent at Blackpool. The children were happy and couldn't wait to tell her about their exploits. They seemed happy and carefree. Jenny was surprised however, that she was given a message that Roger wanted to see her before she left for the day.

The cottage that the staff were staying in was a few minutes walk from Ginn Square where Jenny had rented the large house. Maggie welcomed her in and made her a cup of tea.

'Is the cottage satisfactory, Maggie?' asked Jenny, wondering why they wanted to see her so urgently, that wouldn't wait until they were all back home.

'It is lovely, thank you,' but said no more. When Roger came in, he got straight to the point.

'Begging your pardon Jenny, but what is going to happen to us staff when you get wed? Will we lose our positions?'

Jenny was stunned. She had thought that the staff had been a little cooler towards her lately, but never thought that they were worried about their positions. How could she have been so thoughtless? She had been so tied up in the renovations at the shop and her own private life.

'I will make sure that none of you will be out of work, Roger. I am sorry; I never thought to say anything to you all. As you know, Lord Thievely doesn't have many staff and we will be a large increase to the establishment, so I thought that you would all like to come with me, or work in the shop or the delivery business. Or if you wanted a change, then you are welcome to move somewhere else. What is on your mind, Roger?'

'We would like to stay with you, Jenny. We really like working for you. Actually, we really like your house in Waddington Road. We love our little annexe at the back of the house.'

'I haven't decided what to do with Waddington Road yet. I might even rent it out to someone, in which case you could stay there and be the live-in staff, like you are for me. But I would hate to lose you to another family. I really appreciate you working for me.'

'As long as we have a job, preferably with you or at Waddington Road, we do not mind.'

'Were you all worried about your futures?'

'Yes,' replied Roger looking a little sheepish.

'I am sorry, it is my fault, and I should have realised. Will you tell all the others that they will remain in employment?'

'I will, thank you. That is a lot of worry off our minds, I don't mind telling you, Jenny.'

'Thank you for the tea, Maggie. I must go now or I will be late for the train. I will see you in a couple of weeks, after your holiday.'

'I believe that you are going away for the weekend?' asked Roger.

'Yes, to a house near to a village called Pocklington. By the way, Maggie, what do you think that I should take with me? We are only going for the weekend.' Maggie had previously been a maid to a very rich lady who went to house parties nearly every weekend.

'Take some evening gowns Jenny. If it is a weekend party, they will all dress up at the evening. And during the day as well,' Maggie laughed.

'Thanks for the advice,' laughed Jenny in return as she set out for the train station.

On the journey home, Jenny started planning her wardrobe for the weekend, but soon fell asleep, until she got to Blackburn station. From there, it was just a short journey back to Clitheroe and home again.

Thursday passed in a blur of packing and checking up on the workmen. The moving platform was installed and Jenny had a turn on it before she went away for the weekend, leaving the workmen with all the clearing up and final plastering. Jenny could hardly wait for the shop to reopen. It would be so exciting.

Chapter 23

The carriage rumbled along the bumpy, rutted road. Jenny was weary from the long journey and asked Theo how long they would be before they got to Pocklington.

'Another two hours probably. I just wish that I could afford a horseless carriage. We could have been there by now. Safe and sound, with a glass of something in our hands.'

'I am not so sure about safe and sound,' said Jenny. 'They look highly dangerous machines to me. They go so fast. I wouldn't like to go in one. I would be very frightened. But my son agrees with you. He can't wait to have a horseless carriage.'

'Do you think that we will be able to afford one when we are married, Jenny?'

'It is not a matter of money, Theo, it is more a matter of principal. I do not wish to own one.'

'But if I wanted one very badly, would you be inclined to buy one for me?' wheedled Theo hopefully.

'I might, but there are a lot more things that we would need to buy before a horseless carriage. Your house is in need of money spending on it first. Horseless carriages would have to wait.'

Theo said nothing else, but sulked into a corner.

Jenny looked out of the window and sighed. She could see that marriage to Theo was not going to be easy. Money would be an issue between them. Or rather, his lack of it, and her abundance. She would have to make sure that she sought advice from Joshua and set up some trusts for her children, so that her money would be safe. Although the Married Women's Act had made things safer for women, most men would assume that what monies a wife had were at the disposal of her husband.

The last time that Jenny had been to Theo's house, she had looked around it with different eyes. This was to be her home in the future, and she could see that there was a lot of maintenance that was needed to bring the house up to a decent standard, let alone improvements. And that was just the building; the furniture, furnishings and gardens were going to need some attention, too.

Jenny hadn't decided what to do about her own house. Some part of her wanted to keep the house that she and Jonny had lovingly bought and extended to accommodate a servants' small annexe in the grounds. And yet, it would bring some valuable income into the marriage if she either sold it or rented it. There was plenty of time to make a decision. The marriage wasn't for several months yet. She would discuss it with Joshua as soon as she got home from this weekend visit. Her thoughts turned to her children. She hoped that they would come to be happier about Theo. He didn't seem to mind that she was bringing three children to the marriage: indeed, he said that it increased her value in his eyes as she had a track record for producing boys.

These thoughts reminded her of Lord Jeremy and his ceaseless desire for an heir. She shivered inadvertently.

'Cold, my dear?' Theo asked. 'Here, take this blanket and keep yourself warm.'

'Thank you,' said Jenny, not revealing the thoughts that had made her shiver. Did she want more children? Because children would be required of her, that was a surety, especially boys. Theo would want his own heir, rather than the title and house to pass to another nephew, as it had passed to him.

Jenny closed her eyes, more to avoid talking than for any desire to sleep, but eventually she drifted off. A jolting of the carriage, and the voices of the groom speaking to the horses awakened her.

'Whoa, there, whoa.' The horse whinnied and drew slowly to a stop. Jenny sat up and looked around her. They were at the side entrance of a large house, which had a plain exterior. The butler hurried to welcome them to the house, followed very closely by the owner.

'Theo, good to see you. Did you have a good journey? What time did you set off from home? Has the weather remained fine? And is this your lovely fiancée? I can see now why you have decided to marry at last,' he laughed raucously. 'Do come inside my dear,' he said politely to Jenny, not having waited for an answer to any of his questions.

'Jenny, this is my good friend Percy Tattersall. Percy, my fiancée, Mrs Jenny Marshall.' The two of them shook hands formally and then he guided them both inside. Percy was small, rotund and nearly bald, for such a young man.

'I am sure that you would like to have a warm drink, but first my housekeeper will show you to your room. I know that you will wish to freshen up first. Ah, Spencer, here is Mrs Marshall, Lord Theo's fiancée.'

A tall thin lady of indeterminate age smiled gently at Jenny.

'Come this way, if you please, Mrs Marshall. I will see that your case is unpacked for you.' Jenny followed the housekeeper.

'Thank you Mrs Spencer, that is most kind of you,' replied Jenny smiling. Mrs Spencer looked at her in a surprised manner but said nothing and merely led the way.

After climbing two flights of stairs, Jenny was shown into a beautiful large front bedroom, overlooking the garden. The neat formal rose gardens were laid out under her window, with a small grass terrace. At the end of the terrace, Jenny saw that the garden fell away to a larger lawned area, with several paths leading into a wooded area.

'This is a lovely room, and such a view. Thank you Mrs Spencer. I am sure that it was your choice that I was put in here.'

'It was Mrs Marshall. As there is no lady living here, such duties befall to me. I am pleased that you approve my choice.'

'It is very peaceful here, isn't it?' said Jenny still looking out of the window.

'Yes, I love the peace in this house and this view, too. I feel very fortunate to be an employee here. Lord Tattersall is a very good employer. I want for nothing.'

'Except your own home?' Mrs Spencer turned her head sharply to look at Jenny.

'I have known no home but this one. And I am sure that when I am too old to give service, his Lordship will find me an estate cottage. That is his usual reward for loyal service.'

'Known no other home?' said Jenny aghast.

'No. I was born here to a maid who was married to a gardener. My mother died in childbed and my father died after a cut turned nasty that he sustained in the garden. They were both quite young. Oh, listen to me, Mrs Marshall. Telling you my life story. As if you would want to know such trivia.'

'I assure you that I am very interested, Mrs Spencer. I have not always been a lady of means. I lived in a workhouse until I was twelve years of age, and then I was a scullery maid in a house like this until I was eighteen years of age.'

Mrs Spencer was speechless for a while. On recovering her voice, Mrs Spencer asked Jenny what happened to change her circumstances.

'When I was eighteen years of age, I inherited a shop. I worked very hard at first to make it a success, and now it is very successful.'

'That is pleasing to hear such a story. Were you married or is yours a courtesy title like mine?' Mrs Spencer gasped at her own audacity. 'Oh Mrs Marshall, I do apologise. It is no business of mine.'

Jenny laughed. 'I don't mind you asking, Mrs Spencer. I am glad to tell you my story. I was married but my husband was killed in an accident. He saved the life of a child from being trampled by a horse, but got trampled himself. The doctor said that he would have felt no pain.'

'And did you have children?'

'Yes. I had three. I was to have had a fourth, but I lost him after the accident.'

'I am sorry. You have had a tragic life for one so young, Mrs Marshall.'

'Oh do call me Jenny.'

'I could not indeed, Mrs Marshall. Whatever would his Lordship say?'

'Will his Lordship know?'

'He would be most put out if he heard me calling you by your first name. Most put out.'

'Then it will have to be just in private, then. What is your given name?'

'Denise.'

'And mine is Jenny, in case you had forgotten. We servants must look after each other,' Jenny laughed.

'Let me show you around the bedroom or the kitchen will all be in a tizzy if I am not there to supervise. We have a new Cook and although she is very competent, she worries when his Lordship has visitors.'

'I can understand that. The Lord must be kept happy at all times, mustn't he?' remarked Jenny, knowing only too well how the tenor of the house reflected the mood of the Lord. 'Could you tell me where the bathing room is?'

'Of course, it is two doors away, on the left. Also there is a commode in your dressing room for your convenience in the night. I will send a maid up to prepare your bed and unpack your clothes. Have you decided which gown you will be wearing tonight? If so, I can get that out now, to see how well it has travelled.'

'Oh, not really. Is it to be a formal gathering?'

'They are all formal here. Even though his Lordship is alone most nights, he still dresses up for dinner and expects full service from us. I would recommend a formal gown, if I might make so bold.'

'Thank you for the advice, Denise. I would not have worn an evening gown tonight, but stayed more informal. I can see that you are going to be a mine of helpful information during my stay here. Now let me see, I will wear the lemon one, I think. It still feels strange wearing light colours. I seem to have been in mourning for so long.'

'How long is it since your husband passed away?'

'Three years. But with having a business, I tended to stay in mourning longer, so that I didn't offend anybody.'

'A wise move, Mrs Marshall.'

'Jenny.' Mrs Spencer looked over her shoulder, as if to check that no one was listening, then replied 'Jenny,' very quietly.

'There, it is easy when you try,' laughed Jenny.

Mrs Spencer smiled but then said that she really must be off to the kitchen and bustled out through the door.

Jenny remained where she was, by the window, gazing out over the park, wondering what the children were doing at this very moment. Having a lovely time and not thinking about me, I'll be bound, thought Jenny.

Soon, a young maid came into the room and asked Jenny if she would like to go down one flight of stairs to the library, where a cup of tea would be served. Jenny agreed.

'Come this way, madam and I will show you where it is,' said the young maid.

'Thank you,' said Jenny and followed her down the stairs.

She was not prepared for the sight that met her eyes when she walked into the library. The ceiling was the first thing that she saw. It was a beautiful many-arched ceiling. It had panels that were reminiscent of Wedgwood's Blue Jasper pottery; the contrasting blue and white flowers set off by yellow centres. It was exquisite and brought tears to her eyes. Never had she seen such a ceiling anywhere, let alone in a library. Most libraries seemed to be gloomy, dark and on the ground floor, with wall upon wall of high bookcases and hardly any windows, but this one was bright and airy and on the first floor. It was more like a long gallery than a library.

'Do come in Mrs Marshall. You are stood as if rooted to the spot. Is there something amiss?'

'No, Lord Tattersall. I was admiring your ceiling. It is so beautiful. I have not seen its like before.'

'Ah yes, it was put in by my great great grandfather, the first Lord Tattersall. It is similar to one at Sledmere House, a few miles away from here. Done by the same architect. Look, there is a Wilton carpet to match the ceiling, specially woven at Driffield.'

'It is truly beautiful. I could sit in here for ever.'

'Ha, ha, I don't think Theo will approve of that idea, what? I think that he would much rather have you sat in his own home for ever, don't you?'

Jenny laughed in return. 'I suppose you could be right. But I do hope that Theo and I are able to visit here frequently. I love this room.'

'You are welcome to come and visit any time you like, my dear. Never mind about Theo. You would be a welcome addition to my table at any time. You must consider it an open invitation to my house.'

'Well thank you, Lord Tattersall. That is most kind. Most kind indeed.'

'My pleasure. Remember, any time.'

'Any time what? What are you two planning behind my back?' Theo said laughingly as he entered the room.

'Your fiancée said that she would like to sit in my library forever. I told her that she was most welcome. Pity you came in when you did, Theo. I might have persuaded her to marry me, instead of you.'

'Sorry old chap. She is mine. Find your own woman,' Theo laughed.

'May she pour the tea, or will you think that I am presuming too much, Theo?'

'She may pour the tea, but remember; I will be watching you all the time we are here. Friend or not, I don't intend to lose Jenny to anyone. She is mine.'

'No I am not,' replied Jenny sharply, 'I am my own person. I do not belong and will not belong to anyone else.'

'I think that the law would say otherwise, my dear,' said Theo ingratiatingly.

'I don't care about the law,' replied Jenny no less sharply. 'Enough of this talk. I will pour the tea and please change the topic of conversation.'

Jenny began to fuss with the tea service and poured them all a cup. She deliberately offered the first cup to Lord Tattersall. Theo had annoyed her and she would make him wait. She didn't like the proprietal way he had of talking about her, but she supposed that may be because they were newly engaged and he was feeling pleased with himself. It would be better if she had a word with him in private later in the evening, if they got chance to be alone. She would make her position quite clear to him.

After the cup of tea had been drunk, Lord Tattersall suggested a stroll around the garden. Jenny eagerly agreed, but Theo decided that he would rather catch up on the day's news, and asked Lord Tattersall for a newspaper. Lord Tattersall showed him the rack of papers at the side of the fireplace, and they left him to a quiet read.

Offering Jenny his arm, he led her out into the garden. They walked for some time around the formal rose garden, which Jenny had seen from her bedroom window, and then he took her into a lovely walled garden at the side of the house. Throughout their walk, Lord Tattersall kept up a stream of light chatter and Jenny found him to be a very comfortable companion.

On returning to the house, Jenny made her way to her bedroom and changed her shoes for indoor ones. Soon it was time for her to start getting dressed for the evening dinner. When Denise came in, Jenny asked her how many people there would be for dinner that evening.

'Only yourselves, madam and some neighbours. We are expecting some other guests tomorrow evening, though.'

'How many will there be tomorrow?'

'Just a small party. About twenty altogether. Mainly local families from the neighbourhood.'

'A small party? Twenty?' asked Jenny.

'A small party, compared with our usual ones. We can sit forty people around the table when needed.'

'I suppose that I will have to get used to holding dinner parties of all sizes,' sighed Jenny. 'I don't suppose that you want a change of position? I couldn't persuade you to come and live with me when I marry?'

Denise laughed. 'I am afraid not, Mrs Marshall. As I said, I am very happy staying with Lord Tattersall.'

'I can tell you that I find the prospect of running a large house daunting. But it doesn't appear that Lord Theo does a lot of entertaining. He doesn't seem to have made many friends in

Lancashire yet. Although he does go to the occasional ball or social evening.'

'Is that where you met, at a ball?'

'No. My children were asked to perform at his house last New Year's Evening. They have the same music teacher as Theo's younger sister. And then soon after, his sister, Lady Mildred came to my shop. She spent a lot of money, although I am not complaining about that of course,' Jenny laughed.

'I believe that Lady Mildred was expecting a baby?'

'Yes, that is right. It was born in late April, a little boy, Richard, like his father. She asked me to be godmother to her child. It was a great honour, as we are not even related fully yet. That is why she was buying so much at my shop. She needed a new wardrobe of clothes, which she could wear for the next few months. Lady Mildred is quite a modern young woman and doesn't really believe in locking yourself away whilst awaiting the baby. She even bought ball gowns, which were loose fitting so that she could still go to balls. It is the first time that we have ever made a ball gown for a lady who is so far advanced in her condition. But is has certainly been talked about in Clitheroe. I think that many more matrons in an interesting condition will venture out now.'

'It makes sense, doesn't it? Everyone knows what is going on, so why does the lady have to hide away?'

'I don't know Denise. I never did. I carried on working as long as I could. My friend Marian just made me new gowns that were looser fitting. And I went back to work soon afterwards as well. I had to. I had a shop to oversee. Not that my husband was very keen. It became a problem between us at times.'

'I must go. I could stay and talk to you all day, but nothing will get done. I do hope that you will be frequent visitors here. It has been a pleasure to meet you, Mrs Marshall. Oh yes, I am sorry, I mean Jenny.'

'And you, Denise. I have enjoyed meeting you.'

'I'll send young Martha up to help you dress for dinner. She is a little slow, but very keen to help.'

'I can manage myself, you know,' Jenny said with a laugh.

'I know, but his Lordship wouldn't allow it,' replied Denise as she left the room.

Shortly afterwards, a young girl knocked on the door and came gently into the room.

'Begging your pardon, Missus, I am here to help you. Martha's my name, Missus.' Martha curtsied as she said this little speech.

'Thank you, Martha. My good friend who lives in Burnley is called Martha, too. It is a nice name.' Young Martha beamed.

'Thanks Missus,' she grinned. 'I like my name too. Are you ready for me to help you on with your gown?'

'Yes, thank you.'

Martha slipped the lemon gown over Jenny's head and smoothed it down over her body, standing back to admire the result.

'Yes, that looks alright. Now turn around and I will fasten you up at the back, Missus,' which she proceeded to do. 'Now I will get your shoes and things. Do you want me to do your hair?'

'No, I prefer to do my own hair, Martha. It is very difficult to do. I can finish off getting ready if you want to go.'

'Thank you, Missus. Cook wants me to finish stirring the custard so I had better go if you don't need me now.' Young Martha hurried importantly out of the room and back down to the kitchen.

Jenny waited until she was long gone and then started laughing. What an unusual girl she was. Nothing like her friend Martha who bore the same name.

As soon as she was ready, Jenny went down into the peaceful library and looked at a magazine until Theo came to find her.

'Jenny my dear, there you are. I thought you were still dressing. You look ravishing, by the way. That colour suits you.'

'Oh Theo, you are such a flatterer. You say that about every colour that I wear.' But secretly, Jenny was pleased. It was so long since any man had complimented her that she soaked it up like a sponge nowadays.

The dinner gong sounded and Jenny and Theo made their way downstairs to the dining room. Jenny had been placed next to her host and an elderly gentleman who, it turned out, lived across the fields in the nearest large house to this one.

Theo was much further down the table and was sat between two genteel ladies of middle years, the Misses Schofield, Judith and Grace. Most of the dinner guests were older than Jenny and Theo but they had a pleasant time together and conversation flowed freely.

After the five-course meal, the ladies were taken to the drawing room where tea and coffee were served. The men repaired to the billiards room for brandy and a smoke. As the oldest ladies in the room, the Misses Schofield led the conversation and Jenny was relieved at that. It would be soon enough to be in charge of functions like this when she was married, she decided. But she watched what happened and remembered the format for when she was Mistress at Mearly Hall. Jenny shuddered. Less than six months to the wedding.

A maid handing her a cup of tea interrupted her thoughts. She quickly thanked the maid and tried to recapture the conversation. Fortunately she quickly rejoined the trivial discourse, because the conversation soon turned to her wedding.

Yes, she answered, she was getting married at the church in Clitheroe. No, it was to be a quiet wedding, with her being a widow. And yes, she wasn't wearing the traditional white, as unsuitable for an older bride.

'Have you any children, Mrs Marshall?' asked the younger, livelier Miss Judith Schofield.

'Yes, I have three. Two girls and a boy.'

'How nice,' replied her sister, Grace.

'How old are they?' asked Judith.

Jenny gave the children's ages and then got the inevitable question about Ben going away to boarding school. She could feel the air of disapproval as she repeated her often-stated belief that she didn't want her children to go away to school.

What was the matter with these upper classes, Jenny thought to herself. They have children, then give them to the nannies to be looked after, and then send them to school when they are seven or eight years old. She couldn't see the point in having children. She was glad that she wasn't upper class.

And then the awful realisation dawned that if she and Theo had children, he would expect them to be cared for totally by the nanny and go to boarding school. A cold chill of fear for her as yet unborn children gripped Jenny's heart. She must talk to Theo about it in the morning. Jenny tried to make light conversation with the other ladies, but her thoughts kept returning to the new worry that she had.

Eventually the men returned and the elderly gentleman's wife entertained them with songs whilst playing on the piano. The recital was very good, and Theo leaned over to Jenny and whispered that she was a little better than his sister and her children. This set Jenny giggling and she struggled to keep her face straight afterwards.

Throughout the rest of the evening, Theo was very attentive to Jenny, looking at her tenderly all evening and her worries subsided for a time. She felt loved and that love would conquer everything.

As the company left, Jenny went up early to bed. She was very tired, probably because she had been on her best behaviour all evening. What it would be like tomorrow night when there was a larger company, she could only imagine. As she drifted off to sleep, thoughts of Theo's tenderness gave her a warm feeling all over. It would be nice to be made love to by a man again. She had missed it, even though there had always been the worry of another child starting. But tonight, the eventualities of love were not thought of. Only the feeling of being cherished and adored. Jenny was soon asleep.

Chapter 24

The following day, Jenny hardly saw Theo or any of the men for that matter. They had been out hunting very early in the morning and had then gone into York for a new gun for Lord Tattersall.

Jenny had dined alone at both breakfast and light luncheon. There seemed to be no other guests actually staying at the house, although Denise said that most of the guests that were dining tonight would be staying for a few days, in honour of her and Theo's visit. She had taken the time to write letters to her children. It certainly whiled away some of the time that she was alone.

In her room, there was a lovely fire screen, which turned out to be a writing desk when it was unfolded. Jenny was very taken by this and decided that she would like a similar one for a wedding gift. Jenny had also enjoyed the fact that the writing paper had the family crest and the name of the house written on the top of the paper. It was something that she would look forward to having in her own home when she lived at Mearley Hall.

Later in the day, Jenny asked Denise if this had been a normal day in this sort of household.

'What do you mean, a normal day?' asked Denise perplexed.

'Well, all the men have been off on their own pursuits and I have been alone.'

Denise laughed. 'Oh yes, that is quite normal. They expect the ladies to occupy themselves during the day, but be sparkling and amusing at evening dinner for their entertainment. Actually, most ladies don't get up as early as you do. And they certainly don't go out for walks in a morning. Or spend as much time in the library as you have done.'

'I suppose that it will be better when some more ladies are staying here. I would find it quite boring spending every day alone. I am not used to being idle. I am used to having every minute of every day taken up with either the business, the house or the children. I don't have much free time to myself anymore.'

'After your marriage, you will have more time to yourself, I suppose. You won't be going to the shop anymore, will you?'

'Not as frequently, but I have insisted that I continue to oversee the shop as it will be an added income for us. When Theo inherited the house and title, there was very little money left, so we will have to be careful.'

'The postman will be coming at four of the clock. Do you have any letters to post?' said Denise suddenly; a little embarrassed at the private information that Jenny was giving to her.

'Yes, I have written to my children. Could you take the letters for me please, Denise?'

'Certainly. I will put them with the other letters immediately. Thank you.' Denise took the letters from Jenny and left the room. Jenny was left to her own amusement again for several hours, relieved only by maids arriving to ask her if she would like some refreshments. Goodness, thought Jenny. I will be much heavier if I stay here for long. I will have to be careful or I will never get in my wedding dress that Marian will be so carefully making.

Her thoughts kept straying to the children, wondering what they would be doing at that moment. Oh, how she had missed them and they had only been away for one week.

It was soon time to get ready for that evening's dinner. Denise advised Jenny to wear a ball gown, as there was to be a dance after the meal. She was glad that Maggie had persuaded her to take a few of her fancier clothes away as now she would be prepared for every type of entertainment. She shivered as she slipped the peach ball gown over her head, aided by young Martha. She did enjoy wearing these fine clothes, even though in her usual life she hardly got any chance to wear them.

On arriving in the drawing room, there were about forty people stood around, with small glasses in their hands. Theo came straight to her and introduced her to many of the people. He seemed to know them all very well and Jenny hoped that she would remember all their names.

It was obvious that many of the party, especially the women, were taking a close look at Jenny. News of their engagement had obviously got around. Young women came up to Jenny and congratulated her on her betrothal and admired the family ring, which Theo had given her. There seemed to be quite a lot of interest amongst the men as well as Jenny was fussed and feted over.

The meal started and seemed to go on for hours. Jenny was again seated next to Lord Tattersall but had a younger man on her left. Theo was farther down the table, but he was visible to her. The lady across from Jenny was asking a lot of questions about the wedding and quite a lot of the other guests were interested.

Jenny answered the questions as best she could but tried to change the subject at every opportunity. She didn't want to go through the discussion about boarding school again.

Eventually the meal ended and the ladies went into the drawing room, whilst the men went into the billiards room. The talk again returned to Jenny's forthcoming wedding.

Miss Judith Schofield was the first to mention it. 'Do tell us about your wedding finery, Jenny. We all love talking about weddings. Where will you be having your gown made?'

'At my shop, of course. I couldn't go anywhere else. My friend Marian would be mortally offended.'

'Your shop?' asked one of the other ladies aghast.

'Yes, isn't it exciting,' replied Judith, 'Jenny owns a ladies gown shop in Clitheroe. It is quite a romantic story. Do tell them Jenny,' Judith continued.

Quite embarrassed, Jenny merely replied that she had inherited the shop from a relative who she didn't know. Some of the ladies appeared to be looking down their noses at Jenny and she wished that Judith hadn't mentioned anything. Jenny desperately tried to think of a topic of conversation to steer things away from her.

Miss Grace Schofield, who started talking about fashions in London, saved her. Jenny wondered how soon she could leave the party and then remembered that there was to be a ball. She had never felt less like dancing. Feeling hot and bothered by all the conversation, Jenny excused herself and left the room. She decided to go into the garden to cool down a little and then hopefully the ball would be starting and she could talk to Theo.

Jenny walked outside, turning to the right of the building and going towards the formal gardens at the right hand side of the house. She enjoyed a short walk around the gardens and then feeling a little chilled, walked back towards the house.

As she passed the outside of the billiards room, she heard a lot of raucous laughter. Slowing down to listen to the hilarity, Jenny heard Lord Bremner teasing Theo.

'Quite a surprise you gave us Theo. Marrying at last. Thought you were going to be the eternal bachelor. The anguish of every mother of marriageable girls in the Lancashire and Yorkshire area. As bad as old Percy, almost.'

Lord Scanlon replied for Theo. 'Do you blame him? She is a lovely woman. And a proven track record, as she is able to have children.

Soon have an heir, eh Theo?' Jenny blushed to hear their coarse talk and was moving away, until she heard Theo's reply.

'Yes, I was attracted by her fertility, but it wasn't her only attraction. You know how it is when you inherit a place with no money with it? You just need to marry money, even if you have to marry trade. Her background is somewhat suspect.'

'But she is a rich little widow, though?' asked one of the men.

'Yes,' replied Theo.

'But not for long,' laughed Lord Bremner. 'Not with all the repairs that need doing to your place, and not to mention your debts, either. You will soon get rid of her wealth for her.'

'It will be a relief,' said Theo. 'I was getting worried about money until I met her. My sister befriended her, made it quite easy really. She hurried things along,' Theo laughed.

Jenny froze to the ground, unable to move even if she had wanted to. She couldn't believe what she had just heard. Theo was only marrying her for her money and didn't love her at all. And to make it worse, he was laughing about it with his friends. Oh the embarrassment of it all.

Jenny felt as if her heart would break in two. Slowly the tears ran down her face and she felt for a handkerchief, but in her hurry, she had left her little evening bag behind in the drawing room. Brushing the tears away, Jenny galvanised herself into action. She would soon tell Theo what she thought of him and she didn't care who heard.

Going back into the house, Jenny managed to get upstairs to her room before anyone saw her. She paced up and down the floor, going over in her mind what she would say to Theo. She was going down now, and would tell him in front of all his friends. Suspect trade background, indeed. She would tell him that she was as much a Lord's daughter as he was. More so, because his own father had only been an Honourable. Theo had only inherited his title by an accident of birth.

Jenny was just about to go downstairs when there was a knock at the door. It was Denise.

'Is there anything I can get you? I noticed that you had come back to your room.'

Jenny sniffed before replying. 'Yes Denise, there are several things you can get me. First I would like to see Theo in the library if you could ask him to go in there. Then I would like to see Lord Tattersall. Then I would like a carriage as I am going home.'

'Home? Tonight?' gasped Denise.

'Yes, my engagement is cancelled, although I haven't told Theo yet. But I am about to do so. Please come back and wait in my room whilst I tell him, Denise, I will need you afterwards.'

'What on earth has happened?'

'I have just heard Theo telling his friends that he is marrying me for my money only, even though he is having to marry trade.'

'I am so sorry for you. That is terrible. Can I get you a drink of anything?'

'No, I am fine; just get Theo into the library for me. No, on second thoughts, it is such a beautiful place that I don't want to sully it with what I am going to say. Where do you suggest?'

'The small dining room. It has been closed off for the evening. No one will disturb you there.'

'Thank you. I will go there immediately and await Theo.'

Jenny went down the stairway without seeing anyone and went into the small dining room. She stood by the marble mantelpiece, trying to compose herself before this ordeal. Theo soon joined her. He was laughing as he came in the room

'Now Jenny, what is this all about? Why must you see me straightaway? I was having a good time in the billiards room and was winning the game. What do you want?' Jenny fumed but tried to keep her speech calm.

'Yes, I know you were having a good time in the billiards room. I heard you. I was too warm and went out into the garden to cool down. On my way back, I heard you discussing me. Telling your friends that you were only marrying me for my money. Well, the engagement is off as from now.' Jenny removed the ring from her finger and gave it back to Theo. His laughing face soon turned to dismay.

'Don't be foolish, Jenny,' he blustered, trying to force the ring back into her hand, 'I was only teasing. I didn't mean anything I said. It is just how men talk when they are together.'

'So you didn't mean that it was a shame that I was trade, but I was rich so I was good enough to marry, so that you could get your hands on my money?'

Theo had paled considerably. 'Jenny, I am sorry. Don't be so hasty. We can talk about this tomorrow. Your ancestry isn't important to me.'

'No, I understand that now, only my money. Well let me tell you, I am not 'only trade' as you say. My father was a Lord, which is more than you can say about your father,' Jenny shouted, and then felt quite shocked about what she had just said.

'But I thought that you didn't know who you were when you inherited the shop?'

'I didn't, but I found out later, and I was so ashamed that I have never told anyone. And I would thank you not to tell anyone either. But after all, I am cancelling our engagement.'

'No Jenny, don't be so rash,' pleaded Theo desperately.

'It is too late. I will be leaving tonight.'

'Tonight? But everyone will know.'

'That is your problem. No doubt you will find some story to explain my absence.'

'But I will look such a fool.'

'That too, is your problem, Theo,' Jenny said coldly and walked slowly out of the room. As soon as she shut the door behind her, Jenny ran up the stairs into her room and was grateful to find Denise waiting there for her. As soon as she got in the room, she burst into tears.

The kindly Denise held her close and hugged her, passing a handkerchief to her. It was several minutes before Jenny's sobs started to subside. Denise sat her down and gave her a drink of brandy. The spirit caught in the back of Jenny's throat, but Denise encouraged her to drink it all up.

As Jenny finished the drink, there was a knock at the door. Jenny desperately scrubbed her face, telling Denise not to let Theo in. She couldn't stand to see him again so soon. It was not Theo. It was Lord Tattersall. Denise stood back to let him in.

'Mrs Marshall, I am so sorry about what has happened. I am appalled at the way things have turned out. I wasn't in the room when most of the conversation took place, but the other men have told me. I am so embarrassed for you. Theo doesn't deserve you. Now I believe that you want to go home? Yes, I will get my coachman out immediately. Have you packed your belongings yet? Will you be alright travelling on your own? No of course not, I will organise someone to travel with you. Now let me see,' Lord Tattersall paused for a moment.

'If you will pardon me Lord Tattersall, I would gladly travel home with Mrs Marshall, if you could spare me,' said Denise.

'That is highly irregular to let you go, but I suppose we have done Mrs Marshall a great wrong, so yes, that will be satisfactory. That is, if you would wish it too, Mrs Marshall?'

'Yes, I would find it helpful.'

'Good, then we will get everything ready for you. I will make sure that you can set off as soon as possible.'

'Thank you Lord Tattersall. You have been most kind. I was enjoying my stay at your lovely house.'

'Come any time, my dear. Bring your children. They would love it here, I am sure.'

'That is most generous of you, but I think not. It would be too painful.'

'Hum, I suppose so, but if ever you feel that you can come back, you have only to ask. I must be honest; I have enjoyed having you here. You have been a refreshing change from many of the young ladies here about.'

'Why, thank you. Now I will get ready, if you don't mind.'

'Of course, of course. I will leave you two ladies to get prepared. My apologies again, dear Jenny.' As he left the room, Denise followed him, explaining that she would get some things together for the journey.

An hour later, Jenny and Denise were ready to go. By Jenny's request, they went down the back stairs and out of the back door to get into the waiting carriage. As they were leaving, Lord Tattersall came and pressed a small bouquet of roses into Jenny's hand. This kind act was Jenny's undoing, but she managed to thank him and the coach driver drew away before she burst into tears again.

Her life in tatters, Jenny wept for a long time, with Denise trying to cheer her up. Eventually, through sheer exhaustion, Jenny slept. They travelled throughout the night and after several stops at coaching houses to refresh the horses and themselves, they arrived home the following evening. The house was in darkness.

'Where are your staff, Jenny?'

'They are on holiday. I sent them all away, saying that I would manage without them, whilst the children were away.'

Jenny let them both into the house, showing the coachman where to stable the horses at the back of the house. She insisted that they stay the night rather than trying to get home again straight away. Between them they managed to get some hot food and then they all settled down for the night: the coachman in Cook's room and Denise in one of the children's rooms.

Following a hearty breakfast cooked by Denise, the two servants left Jenny alone in the house. She was truly alone, but was able to give vent to her feelings, alternating between rages and feeling sorry for herself. After two days of hardly eating anything, she became more used to the idea of her betrayal by Theo and could start to think about the future again. No more would men feature in her life. She would just concentrate on her children and her businesses. Suddenly, she felt as if she needed her children near her. Rather than spoil their holiday, she went over to Blackpool to surprise them, taking little presents with her.

They were delighted to see her, and it gave Jenny the opportunity to tell Marian what had happened. In the presence of her children, Jenny started feeling better, and she quietly told the children about her cancelled engagement. The children were mixed in their reaction; first shocked, then relieved. Ellen of course, was more bothered about not having a pony to ride on, but all considered, the children reacted favourably, which was a great relief to Jenny.

After a day or two, she decided to go back to Clitheroe. She knew that immersing herself in the shop work would help in the healing process. Once back in her office, completely alone in the shop apart from Mr Aggett and his workmen, Jenny became so busy that she managed to put the awful ordeal behind her for large parts of the day and concentrate on the future.

Chapter 25

The grand re-opening of the shop took place the following Tuesday, in time for the weekly market day. All the staff had returned from their holiday on the Monday and had worked until late in the evening, getting the shop ready. The children had come home from Blackpool for the reopening.

The cleaning ladies had been into the shop on the Sunday, saying that they hoped God would forgive them for working on the Sabbath, but Jenny reassured them that she and Marian had worked a few Sundays when the shop had first opened to prepare some stock.

Jenny had taken the children to the shop on Sunday after church, to appease Ben's pleadings. He was longing to have a ride on the moving platform. They also came straight to the shop in the late afternoon on Monday, to help with the preparations. Maggie brought a picnic for tea and the children and Roger and Maggie helped with the preparations.

Ben met the new boy, Charlie, who was to work the moving platform. Jenny had got Charlie from the workhouse and provided him with a smart suit in brown, trimmed with cream braid, with a small hat to match. He was a similar age to Ben. It was obvious that Ben was very envious of Charlie, and it was all Jenny could do to get Ben to go back to Blackpool the day after next. Only after promising that Ben could help Charlie at the weekends did he willingly return to the holiday house on the Wednesday afternoon.

Early on Tuesday morning, Jenny walked around her newly refurbished shop. Inevitably, it had cost much more than the original estimates, but it had all been worth it. The shop looked magnificent. There was a much more obvious structure to the departments, and it was far easier for the customers to find their way around. The moving platform would be a great enhancement for her more elderly customers and would encourage all of them to go upstairs.

Jenny was very pleased with the results and walked round with a smile on her face. It was to be hoped that the customers would like the new shop and would spend lots of money. There was an urgent need to replenish the coffers after all the expensive changes that had taken place.

Before the shop opened, Jenny provided a breakfast for all the staff and thanked them for their hard work. Eventually, it was time to open the doors. Jenny had advertised that there would be free drinks and cakes for all their customers on the first day, in a hope to entice a few customers through her doors.

There had been no need to advertise or make promises of free refreshments. By ten of the clock, the shop was full and the staff in the new top floor tearoom had to ask ladies to wait their turn. Jenny circulated through the shop for most of the day, speaking to customers old and new. The customers continued to come to the shop all day and up until the early evening.

By two in the afternoon, the cook had run out of cakes and had to ask the kitchen maid to run down to Crabtree's bakery to buy some more. Even Mrs Marshall, Jenny's mother in law had been called in to help on this special day.

Eventually, at seven of the clock, all the customers had gone home and the staff started tidying up. They were all exhausted. Jenny thanked them all for their hard work and they slowly drifted to their own homes. Ben had helped Charlie work the moving platform and had a wonderful time. Rachel and Ellen had helped their grandmother in the tearoom and were tired but happy.

On the way home, Ellen told her mum that perhaps now she wouldn't look after horses or paint when she was grown up, but would like to help in the shop.

'I am going to run the shop when I am older,' snapped Rachel. 'Tell her, mummy, the shop is going to be mine, isn't it?'

'No it is not, Rachel. You will all share the shop, but not for a long time yet,' replied Jenny equally sharply. She was too tired to get involved in their petty squabbles tonight but Rachel needed correcting about her assumption to sole right to everything, due to being the eldest. Why, if it had been an inheritance or peerage that had been at stake and not a shop, it would be Ben that would inherit as the oldest boy.

Thoughts of male inheritance reminded her of Theo and her heart contracted with pain. But not for long. The pain soon turned to anger again, but at least she was getting on with her life and needed to have nothing more to do with Theo. Irritated by her own thoughts, she snapped at the children who were still squabbling.

From then on, the walk home was carried out in silence, but it didn't last for long at home and their usual boisterous behaviour returned. Jenny was glad to tuck them all up in bed that night and fell asleep immediately herself. It had been an exhausting week and she was glad that it had been, as it had kept her thoughts away from Theo.

Gradually, the shop fell back into a routine and the number of customers reverted to the usual level. After the flurry of the new reopening, sales had been greatly increased, but they had flattened out since then and for a while the shop was showing less profit than previously, but Jenny was not unduly worried. She was used to peaks and troughs in her sales sheets. There was always a dip during the summer months whilst families were taking their holidays.

Jenny took the opportunity with Sarah to plan for the winter stock. With the extra storerooms that they now had, Jenny was able to get much of the winter stock in early so that at the first hint of cold weather, they could start displaying the winter weight clothes.

One of the new features that they had stocked had been divided skirts for cycling. They had sold in hundreds. Will, Marian's husband, had managed to find a reasonably priced supplier for this new fashion item, until they could start making them. Sarah had made a display in the shop showing a lady wearing the new skirts on a bicycle. She had borrowed the bicycle from the local shop, Cunningham's, that sold them.

The cycling mania was growing and women from all walks of life wanted to buy the divided skirts. Many of the mill girls were starting to come into Mitchell's Modes. At first they came for the divided skirts, but often bought small items that they could afford. Some of the better-paid weavers who ran several looms were now coming into the shop on regular occasions. This pleased Jenny and she asked Sarah and Will to develop a range of cheaper clothes that were ready made. Or customise cheaper clothes into original garments that would look more expensive.

Slowly, a whole new range of customers were coming to the shop and recommending it to their friends. Ever since Jenny had planned Robert and Emily's wedding, she had felt challenged by the fact that most brides could not afford anything new for their wedding.

A new range of ready-made wedding clothes was introduced. If a bride chose an outfit, Jenny allowed them to pay a little each week until the trousseau was paid for. Sarah reported that some brides-to-be still felt that the cost of wedding finery was too much when other important things had to be bought for the marital house.

This resulted in Jenny deciding to hire some wedding gowns. Mitchell Modes became more and more popular for all the local brides, from the most meagre wedding to the most sumptuous. After a gown had been hired, the gown was altered in some definable way for the next bride, so that each bride felt that her gown was unique, which it was.

The bridesmaid's gowns were usually the kind that a working girl would wear for Sunday best, but if they couldn't afford to buy the bridesmaid's gown, they were available for hire as well.

One bride told another and soon girls were coming from far and wide to buy their wedding finery at Mitchell Modes, or their cycling skirts. The divided skirts were very popular with the girls Jenny met at the Suffragist movement meetings, and new customers came through that contact, too.

Many of the Suffragists were local mill girls and were some of the best-paid women in the town, so had available money to spend, which their mothers had never had. Some of them were beginning to go to meetings and speak in public, so needed smart clothes to wear. Fairly plain, long, straight skirts in dark colours became very fashionable, and wide ranges of different coloured blouses were stocked to complement them. The most popular colours were still white and cream, but some young women were getting more daring in their use of colours and the blouses ranged from plain styles, to ones that had lots of frills and flounces; plain material to floral patterns. The customers were changing, as the new century was getting nearer.

And yet, despite the influx of many working girls as customers, Jenny did not loose her richer middle and upper class customers. They continued to patronise the shop and came to meet their friends and visit the tearoom on the top floor, whilst buying some items from the shop.

One of her regular customers was Lady Bethany Hastings, the first bride whose wedding Jenny had planned. Bethany had been the local daughter of a mill owner who was a wealthy self-made man. Jenny had since made her some special clothes to wear during her pregnancies and a beautiful christening robe and shawl for her first baby.

Lady Bethany had regularly bought her ball gowns from Jenny, and had introduced her new found friends and relatives to the shop. Many of Jenny's original customers were still coming to the shop and their friends with them.

All in all, the shop seemed to be going from strength to strength, even though she had needed to invest so much of her capital into the refurbishments. Jenny would need to be careful until she recouped the losses from her expenditure, but as soon as she could, she would start refurbishing the shop in Blackburn and also another shop that she had bought in Burnley. But for now they would have to wait.

First she had to go through her outstanding accounts, as these were still a problem that she had encountered since first inheriting the shop. The young mill girls were much prompter in paying than the gentry, Jenny mused. But then, from talking to other business people in the town, it was a common occurrence. Eventually they paid, but often it was a long wait.

With a big sigh, Jenny got down to some work, not feeling in the mood for it today. She had a great urge to buy herself a bicycle and go out for a spin. She laughed to herself, reflecting that she must be feeling better if she felt a trifle frivolous.

Chapter 26

Later in the day, Janey brought Jenny her mail into the office, left it on the desk, and was preparing to leave when Jenny called her back.

'Janey, could you come in and do some letters for me later. I need to get up to date with some accounts that are overdue.'

'Certainly, Jenny. Just call me when you are ready for me.'

'I will just sort out these letters to see if anyone has decided to pay their overdue account after all, then I will not need to send a strongly worded letter.'

'I will be ready,' repeated Janey and left the room. Jenny started opening the letters and placing them in piles according to their urgency or need. She got to the last letter and noted that the envelope was one of quality. Inside she found a letter with a solicitor's heading on it. Thinking that it would be about a client's account, Jenny quickly read the letter but soon reread it, as she couldn't believe her eyes. The letter was headed

Marshall versus Thievely
Breach of Promise settlement

Jenny read the letter several times, but still could not make sense of it. It appeared that Theo was going to sue her for breach of promise, because she had broken off their engagement. What nonsense, thought Jenny. He can't do that. I had just cause to break off the engagement. He made it plain that he was only after my money, in front of many witnesses. She reached for the telephone and waited for the person on the telephone exchange to answer.

'Could you put me through to Mr Briggs the solicitor, please.'

'Putting you through, madam,' replied the exchange clerk and a little later, Jenny was connected to Joshua's clerk.

'Good morning, Cookson. Mrs Marshall here. Is Mr Briggs available to speak to me?'

'I am afraid not, Mrs Marshall. He is out on a visit. May I ask him to call you on his return?'

'Yes please, it is a very urgent matter. In fact, I would be grateful if you could ask him to call on me at his earliest convenience.'

'Of course, Mrs Marshall. I will give him the message as soon as I see him, although I am not expecting him back until this afternoon.'

'Thank you, Cookson. Good morning to you.' Jenny put the telephone receiver down and walked about her office in a ferment. What could this letter mean? Could he sue her, or was he just trying to get even with her for causing him some humiliation? Well, it served him right, she thought.

Lunchtime passed by and Jenny refused all offers of food from Janey, saying that she had a particular problem that she needed to solve and she did not want to be disturbed, except by Mr Briggs when he came later in the afternoon.

It was three of the clock before Joshua appeared. By this time, Jenny was very agitated and almost threw herself at him when he arrived in her office.

'Jenny, what is the matter, you seem very upset?'

For answer, Jenny thrust the solicitor's letter into his hands and watched his face keenly. She was not reassured. Joshua remained silent for several minutes, and then slowly looked up at her.

'Jenny, I am so sorry. I never thought he would stoop so low as this. You did right to break your engagement, as he has shown his true colours now. A breach of promise like this is very unusual from a gentleman to a lady It is usually the other way around when a young lady sues her former fiancé if he cancels the engagement.'

'But can he do it?'

'Oh yes, I am afraid he can. An engagement is binding. My dear, I am so sorry. I have never heard of a case like this before in Clitheroe.'

'But what will happen?'

'I don't know. I will contact his solicitors and ask how much they want for a settlement.'

'And will I have to pay?'

'Probably, yes. You broke the engagement.'

'But he was just wanting to get his hands on my money. Surely if you told the solicitor that, he would understand?'

'I am afraid most upper class marriages are about money and it would not be thought unusual that as a man he would want control of your money. That is still quite an expected arrangement.' Jenny sat in silence, too stunned to answer for a while. Eventually she spoke to Joshua, in a very small voice.

'How much will I have to pay?'

'I don't know until I have spoken to his solicitor. I will deal with this as an urgent matter and let you know as soon as I hear anything. I am sorry Jenny, but there may be nothing that I can do.'

'Thank you Joshua. I know that I can expect your best efforts for me. I will have to be patient until I hear from you.'

'Yes, I am afraid so. Goodbye my dear. I am sorry that I couldn't be any more hopeful but this is a serious matter and I wouldn't want to raise your hopes unnecessarily.'

Jenny watched Joshua leave the room and then collapsed in her chair, leaning on the desk, and broke into racking sobs. She couldn't believe what was happening to her. How could Theo have taken me in, she asked herself?

Eventually, the sobs subsided and she went to the bathroom to wash her face. It was on her way back when she saw Janey.

'Jenny, whatever is the matter? Have you had an accident?'

'No, I am alright, Janey, just a little upset. I would be grateful if you could bring me a cup of tea.'

'Yes, right away,' replied Janey and hurried out of the room. Jenny was glad that she was on her own for a few minutes, so that she could regain her composure.

When Janey returned, Jenny was indeed calmer and Janey was somewhat reassured.

'I have brought you a sandwich as well. I don't remember that you had any lunch.'

'Thank you Janey. You are so kind.'

'You are sure that you are alright? Is there anything else that you need?'

'No. No thank you Janey. I will be alright. I will get on with my work now.' Janey stared at Jenny for a further moment, then walked out of the office.

Jenny sagged against the desk and put her head into her hands. She tried to concentrate on her work, but her mind was too distressed. After a vain attempt at planning a wedding, Jenny put her quill pen back into its stand and gave up. Wedding planning was not her favourite topic at the moment. She went into Janey's outer office.

'I am going home, Janey. I have developed a headache.'

'Shall I ring Robert or Roger to give you a ride home?'

'No, I prefer to walk. It will clear my head. I will see you tomorrow.'

'Good night, Jenny. I hope that you are soon feeling better. I am sure the walk home in the fresh air will do you good.'

Jenny smiled tritely and left the shop. If only she could just take a walk in the fresh air to solve her problems, she thought on her way home. It would take a lot more than fresh air. By the time she got home though, her head was indeed clearer, and she was able to smile when her children arrived home from school and listen to their usual chatter.

The next few days dragged slowly by, waiting for a word from Joshua. Eventually he arrived at her office, late one morning. She was in the middle of a stock planning session with Sarah, but asked her to leave when Joshua was announced.

'I will catch up with you later today, Sarah,' and waited until she had left. She immediately asked for Joshua to be shown in.

'Joshua. How good of you to come. Please tell me if there is any news?'

'There is news, Jenny, but not the news that you will want to hear.' Jenny's heart was beating erratically as she waited for his news. 'He will not retract his case and has suggested a figure of ten thousand guineas.'

'Ten thousand guineas?' gasped Jenny in horror. 'Why, that is more than I have. How can he ask for all this money?' With that, she burst into tears. Joshua was beside her in seconds.

'I am so sorry Jenny. I wish that I could have taken this away from you, but he is adamant that he has been distressed by your actions and wants recompense. He claims that you have made a fool of him in front of the whole county. But I must say that the figure is far in excess of any claim that I have ever heard about.'

Jenny was silent for a while, still with Joshua holding her hands.

'Upset because he can't get my money is a more likely story,' said Jenny bitterly. Joshua patted her hand, sympathetically. 'And how long have I got to find this money?'

'There was no set date. At your earliest convenience, the letter said.'

'My earliest convenience would be well into the next century,' said Jenny bitterly.

'I don't think that he would wait so long, Jenny.'

'I know. I think that I wish to be alone now and think about this. I need to work it all out in my mind. Do you mind, Joshua?'

'No, I understand. I will call again in the morning, if you wish.'

'Yes, I would be grateful for that. Thank you Joshua.' She watched as he left the room and sat slumped in her chair despondently. She remained like that for several minutes, her mind numbed by the news that Joshua had brought. Jenny realised that Joshua had sorted out many of her troubles, both small and large since she had inherited the shop. It was almost as if he could sort out any of her problems, but not this time.

After a while, Jenny went to the cupboard where she kept all her balance books and bank accounts. She would look at everything at home this evening. In this way, she could work out her assets without the staff being aware of what she was doing.

With a heavy heart, she collected her belongings together and made her way home. After spending time with the children, Jenny then went into the office and tried to work out if she could reach this exorbitant, unfair figure.

She could not. She did not have so much spare money at her disposal as a lot had been spent on the refurbishments. Jenny decided that she would lay all her accounts before Joshua and ask his advice. Jenny looked at the time. It was after ten of the clock. Too late to ring Joshua tonight. But first thing in the morning, she would ring him and ask if she could see him in his office, rather than at hers.

Jenny made her way up to bed but did not sleep, her mind racing around in circles, trying to think of a way out of this predicament. Eventually, Jenny fell asleep and slept fitfully until morning. She woke unrefreshed, with the beginning of a headache already, by the time that she had seen the children off to school. After ringing Joshua at his office, she arranged to go in and see him, and then rang Janey to explain why she would be late.

Later in Joshua's office, Jenny showed him all her accounts from her three businesses. There appeared to be a healthy amount of money, but it was all tied up in capital, buildings and stock. Her several bank accounts did not add up to much in the way of available money.

'What is this account with £1000 in Jenny?' asked Joshua.

'That is my *never to be touched* fund. If you remember I inherited the £1000 with the shop. As soon as I could, I replaced that amount in a separate account so that if ever I fell on hard times, I would always have this emergency money to fall back on. So that I would never have to go back to the workhouse again,' said Jenny with a small voice.

Joshua stared at her with sympathy. 'That has always been a driving force throughout your life, hasn't it, Jenny? Your fear of the workhouse has made you into a successful businesswoman, and one of the best employers in town.'

'Yes. That is why I have always tried to employ girls and boys from the workhouse, as I know how hopeless it feels to be in there, with no chance of getting out,' said Jenny sadly. 'And now I may be going back there, all because of this man. How could I ever think that I loved him?' At this, Jenny burst into tears.

Joshua remained at his desk, but reached across with a handkerchief. He yearned to hold her and comfort her, but held back as he knew that it would only make him wish for things that could never be. Already he had been tormenting himself with thoughts of 'if only'. If only Jenny had consented to marry him, he thought, this would not have happened.

But realistically, he knew that Jenny didn't love him and wouldn't have been happy. She was the sort of woman who loved totally and couldn't pretend. It would have been easier if she hadn't loved Thievely and then she wouldn't be hurting as much now. Joshua suspected that Jenny was also feeling that she had been stupid to believe Thievely's lies, so was cross with herself as well as worrying about the money.

'Let me get you a cup of tea, Jenny. I know it won't solve anything, but we can start to plan what we are going to do.'

'Thank you, yes. I would like a cup of tea,' Jenny sniffed appreciatively. 'What would I do without you, Joshua? You are such a help to me and I don't deserve it. I have treated you shabbily, and then come to you with my troubles.'

'Nonsense, Jenny. I thought you agreed that we were friends?'

'We did, but it seems to be a one-sided friendship. I seem to take and you give.'

'No Jenny, you have given me a lot of time and joy in being with your family on special occasions. I value that. You have also sent a lot of business to me as well. Don't forget that.'

Jenny sniffed again, then smiled as Cookson came into the office with a tray of tea. The smile faded as he left the room.

'What can I do then, Joshua? Where can I start to try and pay this enormous amount of money?'

'There are several ways you can make some money. First, the most sensible plan would be to sell the interest in your buildings down Bawdlands. You could sell them to another landlord. That would release a considerable amount of capital.'

'No,' said Jenny aghast, 'I can't sell the houses. What if they got a nasty landlord who wouldn't be fair to them? They might increase their rents and not do repairs to the houses and the poor people would be back in trouble again. No, don't ask me to get rid of my houses, Joshua. I couldn't bear it.' Jenny's eyes filled up again, so Joshua tried to change the subject.

'You could always sell the delivery business instead,' Joshua suggested.

'No, I couldn't sell the delivery business. What would my poor father-in-law do for work? He loves going to work in the office. It gives him esteem and dignity. Besides, there is young Robert as well. He has only just got married and he needs a job.'

Joshua sighed. This was going to be harder than he thought. Jenny was rejecting all his ideas out of hand.

'Jenny my dear, you can't live other people's lives for them. You aren't responsible for them all.'

'I am for my father-in-law,' replied Jenny stubbornly.

'Yes, I suppose you are, but you have to raise this money, so you are going to have to do something fairly drastic.'

Jenny sat silently for a while.

'What about if I sell my shops in Burnley and Blackburn?'

'What shops in Burnley and Blackburn?'

Jenny had the grace to blush. 'I thought that I might expand into other towns, on similar lines to my shop here in Clitheroe.'

'But you never told me about it. I haven't dealt with the property sales,' said Joshua a little puzzled.

'I used local solicitors in the towns, rather than you. I thought of keeping my other businesses totally separate. I was going to set them up and put managers in, but oversee them from a distance. I am sorry Joshua; I wasn't trying to keep you out of my business. It was just that when I was negotiating with the land agents, I thought that it would be easier to have a solicitor in the town rather than some miles away.'

'Actually, that is quite sensible Jenny. Don't worry, I am not offended, you have every right to use another solicitor, but you have always asked my advice before on business issues.'

'Yes, and I will continue to do so in the future, but this was a bit of an impulse when I was visiting Burnley and Blackburn.'

'Are the shops in trading now?'

'No, I was going to refurbish them first and I was waiting a little longer, as I spent more than I intended to on the refurbishment at Clitheroe.'

'So are they solely your properties?'

'Yes, both of them.'

'Where are they?'

'St James Street in Burnley, and King Street in Blackburn. Both prestigious addresses.'

'How much do you think that they are worth?'

'I don't know. I paid over £200 for each of them.'

'Could you bear to sell them?' Joshua asked gingerly, following the reactions she had had to his other comments about selling her properties.

'Yes, I am not attached to them and I do not have any staff as yet, so it will not be so much of a blow.'

'Well, that would raise some capital. Would you like me to arrange to sell them for you, Jenny?'

'How can I when I didn't use you to buy them. Don't make me feel any more guilty, Joshua.'

'It doesn't matter; I can sell them for you. Just give me the name of your solicitor in both Burnley and Blackburn and I will contact them both and arrange for them to be sold. But that only raises a fraction of the money that you need. Have you any more ideas?'

Jenny shook her head sadly.

'No other little hidden properties that I don't know about?' he teased gently.

Jenny smiled a very weak smile. 'No, these two are the only ventures that I have made without you.'

'What made you buy them anyway?'

'Do you remember that I went to find the daughter of Bruce at Blackburn workhouse?'

'Yes, you went by train, if I remember.'

'I missed the train back and went for a walk around the town until the next train was available. I saw a shop for sale and thought that it would be a good idea to expand. I found the land agent and asked to see the shop and bought it straightaway. I told you that it was on impulse. It was a very similar sized shop to mine when I first inherited it, before I expanded into the two shops on each side.'

'That was an impulse buy. But what about Burnley? You didn't then rush over to Burnley and do the same there, did you?'

Jenny laughed. 'No, not so rashly. I went on a visit to see my friend Martha from Burnley and we went for tea in the local tearoom. It was when I was about to take Martha home that I saw the notice in the shop window. I took Martha with me to view the shop and she thought that my sort of shop would be very much welcomed in Burnley by the local ladies. To be perfectly honest, I thought of setting Martha up as the manageress, but I didn't mention the idea to her. I am glad of that now, as I would have been too upset to sell the shop.'

'Trying to sort the world out, as usual, I see.'

'Yes, I suppose I was. In my mind, I thought that I could set Bruce's daughter up in the Blackburn shop, but that plan went wrong as well.'

'Why did you want to help her? I would have thought that Bruce was the last person that you would want to help.'

'But it wasn't Bruce. It was her daughter. She got left in the workhouse by Bruce through no fault of her own, and I thought I could rescue her.'

'But you didn't?'

'No, Miss Bruce didn't need rescuing, thank you very much. She had made her own career.'

'You sound resentful?'

'Oh no, I have made a good friend there. But I would have been happy for her to manage my Blackburn shop. Anything to get her out of the workhouse.'

'Did she need getting out of the workhouse?'

'Yes and no. She is still in a workhouse but it is by choice. She has got a job in a workhouse as the matron. The one on the outskirts of Preston. It is a very large one and she is very happy there. She has made a lot of improvements since she became matron.'

'So you definitely have no attachment to the shops, then?' said Joshua, trying to turn the conversation back to the issue in hand.

'No. I could easily sell them. Is there anything else that I could do?'

'If you are unhappy selling your other businesses, then you could use all your savings, including your emergency account, but that would leave you with virtually nothing in the bank, which is very risky business practice. The only other alternative would be to raise a loan on either your shop or your house.'

'I would not be happy doing that, Joshua.'

'You may have no option, Jenny. Think it over tonight and call on me tomorrow and we shall see if anything else has occurred to me or to you.'

'Thank you so much Joshua. I will never be able to repay you for all your kindnesses. I feel stronger now, even though I still have no idea how I am going to pay that odious man.'

'At least you realised what he was like before you had actually married him. It might have been too late by then. He could have lost you everything.'

Jenny gave a tight smile and said goodbye to Joshua, leaving his office with a heavy heart, wondering again how she could have been so silly as to contemplate marrying into the gentry. She walked back to the shop with slow steps, but put on a cheerful face as she approached the shop.

Chapter 27

The evening meal that day went from bad to worse. The children were fractious, Jenny had yet another headache, and Cook was unhappy because the children had played a trick on her. In the end Jenny snapped at both Cook and children.

Cook took the huff and the children went up to their bedrooms in a sulk. Jenny sat in her rocking chair in the lounge and eventually burst into tears. Where or where was she going to get ten thousand guineas from, without putting her children's lives at risk? Or all her staff at the shop as well?

Eventually she calmed down, and then felt guilty for all the upset that had happened during the evening. Her children were probably crying themselves to sleep at this moment, and Cook writing her notice. Why on earth did she have to get cross with them? It wasn't their fault that she had a breach of promise settlement hanging over her head, and yet she had taken out her feelings on them all. She must make amends immediately.

Jenny went upstairs to see the children, and found Ben and Rachel playing a game happily together. Ellen was sat in their bedroom, singing to her dolls. So much for them being upset about her outburst. They all looked up and smiled at Jenny when she came in. It made her feel even guiltier that she had shouted.

'Children, I am sorry that I shouted at you. I have a headache, but I shouldn't have shouted at you.'

'Oh, it's all right, mummy, we are used to you shouting at us,' replied Rachel coolly.

Such cheek, thought Jenny, always shouting at them indeed, but she was so relieved that they were not upset by her outburst that she simply nodded and left the room.

Next, Jenny went up to Cook's room on the top floor. She knocked on the door and waited. Cook actually came to the door and opened it and stood looking at Jenny without speaking.

'Cook, I am sorry that I was sharp with you earlier and also that the children were naughty. Please forgive us all. I have told the children off about their prank and they will come and apologise to you tomorrow.' Cook sniffed and looked away, still silent.

'If there is any way I can make it up to you, I will try,' pleaded Jenny.

'Apology accepted then, Jenny. Children will be children, I suppose,' replied Cook with another large sniff.

'Thank you, Cook. That is so kind of you,' said Jenny, mightily relieved that Cook wasn't going to leave her in the lurch. That would have only added to her current problems. And then Jenny felt guilty as she was walking back downstairs to the drawing room. How selfish she had become. Only concerned about Cook being a problem if it affected her own life. She would try and make it up to Cook tomorrow and would get those children to apologise first thing in the morning.

As it was Maggie and Roger's evening off and Cook was upstairs, Jenny went into the kitchen and made herself a hot drink and took it into the drawing room.

Sat in the rocking chair, Jenny went over and over the facts about the money. She could find no tenable solution without losing some of her business interests. Tomorrow, she would see if Joshua had come up with any good ideas.

For tonight, she must try and get some sleep, or she would not be able to make any decisions about her life. Jenny climbed the stairs with her candle and lit the gas mantle in her bedroom, blowing the candle out. Picking up the latest book which she had bought, Jenny tried reading to make herself tired, but found that the words were going round and round in her mind, without her taking any of the story in. Eventually, she gave up and turned out the lights.

Next morning the children made a sweet procession to the kitchen and asked forgiveness for their misbehaviour. They were quickly forgiven, and all hugged by Cook, who smiled across at Jenny. Jenny breathed a sigh of relief. At least two of her problems were over. If only the other problem was as easy to solve.

Joshua called at the office at ten of the clock. Janey brought them both a cup of tea, and then Joshua got some papers out, but kept them shut on the desk.

'I have looked at your predicament from every angle and can see no way out without selling any of your businesses.'

Jenny visibly drooped.

'Except there is one solution that came to me last night,' Joshua said expectantly.

'Yes,' said Jenny hopefully.

'I don't want to offend you but it would be one way out of all this trouble.'

'Yes, do go on,' replied Jenny. 'I will consider anything except marrying Theo, of course.'

'If you married me, I could pay off these debts as your husband. I know you don't love me, but I know that you are quite fond of me,' said Joshua all in a rush, 'and I know you have refused before, but in the circumstances, you may wish to reconsider.'

Jenny was appalled.

'Joshua, that is so kind of you, but I couldn't possibly just marry you because I am in debt. But that is so kind of you to offer.' Jenny realised then how much it must have hurt Joshua when she turned him down. But she could not marry him just to get her money problems sorted out. Poor Joshua.

'It is hard to watch you suffering like this and not being able to help. Would you consider a loan from me to help you out of these difficult circumstances?'

'No, Joshua. I must find my own solution to this problem, but thank you for all your offers. I will be eternally grateful to you for your kindness. I can never thank you enough.'

'There is one other option, Jenny.'

'Another option?' Jenny said tentatively.

'You could arrange a mortgage on one or all of your properties. The bank would then forward you the money that you would need.'

'Yes, I suppose my brother-in-law would be able to help me there. He is the local bank manager, as you know.'

'But the interest will be very high from the bank.'

'Yes, I know, but I would rather borrow form the bank than from friends.'

'What about loans from friends where you give them a share of the business? In that way, you could pay them back and regain the full control of your business gradually.'

'I will have to think about these things. I think that I will go and have a word with my brother-in-law. Joshua, thank you for all your help. I feel much better now. I feel as if there are several options I might try, or a combination of more than one option. That is far more acceptable to me than selling my businesses.'

'Let me know how you get on with your brother-in-law then, Jenny.'

'I will. And you must come for tea soon.'

'I will look forward to that. Goodbye.' Joshua left the office. Jenny called for Janey and told her that she was going out to the bank. No time like the present, she told herself.

'Is there any money to go to the bank today, Janey? I might as well take it whilst I am going.'

'Yes, it is all here in the bag.'

'Thanks; I will go to the bank, then. I might be a while.'

Jenny walked out of the shop and into the town. Going down the hill to the bank, she met several townspeople and bade them good day as she went, smiling as was her usual self and hiding her real feelings of panic, which kept emerging.

On arrival at the bank, she asked if she could see Arthur. The clerk was reluctant, saying that he had important clients to see.

'I am an important client,' Jenny snapped at the man, 'so please ask him if he will see me.'

Without speaking in reply, the man went into the back of the bank. Really, thought Jenny as she waited, I am getting very crotchety these days. Very soon, the man returned and asked Jenny to follow him to a small room. It was not Arthur. It was his deputy, Mr Johnson.

'Good morning Mrs Marshall. How can we help you?'

'I would prefer to see Mr Butler.'

'Is your matter urgent? Mr Butler has gone over to Leeds for two days to head office.'

'Oh of course, I had forgotten. Well, it is rather urgent. Perhaps you can set things in motion for me in his absence. I would like to apply for a mortgage on my properties, see how much capital I could raise and how much the repayments would be.'

There was a long silence.

'I am sorry Mrs Marshall. We are not accustomed to lending money to ladies.'

'But I am a very valuable customer at this bank,' Jenny exploded.

'Nevertheless, loans can only be made in the husband's name.'

'But I am a widow. And anyway, all these properties are mine. They never were my husband's.'

'I am sorry, Mrs Marshall. I can only tell you our rules. I cannot process a loan for you.'

Jenny jumped up suddenly. 'I have never heard such silly rules in all my life. Thank you and good-bye.' Without giving him a chance to respond, Jenny stalked out of the office and out of the bank. She walked down Wellgate towards Shawbridge to calm down before she could go back to the shop. What an insult. They were glad enough to take her money every week, but now she wanted some back, they didn't want to know. Jenny looked over the bridge and watched the stream flowing past, allowing the action to soothe her.

When she had recovered her equilibrium, she walked slowly back to the shop. She would wait until she could speak to Arthur himself, he would be able to advise her. But it truly was a man's world. No wonder the women's Suffragists were gaining in popularity, especially in the local area. There were so many women trying to make a life for themselves, only to be held back by the men. Perhaps she ought to be more active in the local Suffragist movement. In the past she had made generous donations to their cause, but as she was now virtually penniless, all she had to give would be her time.

On arrival back at the shop, she was soon immersed in the daily running of the business and her money worries had to wait for the time being.

It was two days before Arthur contacted her. He called at the shop, just after lunch.

'Arthur, what a relief to see you, do come in. I will get Janey to make us a cup of tea.'

'Well, Jenny. You certainly upset my deputy manager. He was most put out by your visit.'

'I am sorry Arthur, but I was in such a state. All I need is a loan to help me over some financial difficulties. Now what are your terms and how long will I be paying back?'

There was an embarrassed silence.

'Jenny, my deputy manager was actually right. I cannot lend money to you as a woman.'

'Arthur, not you as well? It is so insane. I make a lot of money and pay my taxes like all you men, so why can't I have a loan? I have now decided to become an active member of the Suffragists movement because of this.'

'Jenny, Jenny, calm down, get off your hobbyhorse. This is the way of the business world I'm afraid. And anyway, what on earth do you need a loan for? Surely your business is not in trouble? You have always made such good profits. Are you hoping to expand?'

Now it was Jenny's turn for silence.

'I just need some money, that is all, Arthur,' she said stubbornly.

'That would not be sufficient information to grant you a loan, even if you were a man. There would have to be a specific reason or necessity for it. This is not like you, Jenny.'

Jenny thought for a while and decided that she would have to take Arthur into her confidence.

'I trust that what I tell you will go no further, Arthur?'

'Of course,' said Arthur, obviously mystified by Jenny's request and behaviour.

'You know that I have broken my engagement to Theo?'

'Why yes, I was sorry to hear about it. But what has this to do with your money problems?'

'He has sued me for breach of promise.'

'No, the cad! I can't believe that. Jenny I am so sorry, Susy didn't tell me.'

'Susy doesn't know,' Jenny replied through gritted teeth.

'She doesn't know?' said Arthur with surprise, 'but you two tell each other everything. I am surprised that you haven't told her.'

'I was too embarrassed. I have told no one. Except Joshua Briggs, my solicitor.'

'And what did he advise?'

'Selling some of my businesses.'

'And are you going to do?'

'I can't Arthur; people rely on me through those businesses. How can I let them down?'

There was another long silence.

'How much Jenny? How much did he ask for?'

'Ten thousand guineas,' said Jenny miserably.

'Ten thousand guineas!' exploded Arthur. 'Jenny, that is terrible, most excessive. No wonder you are upset. But I am afraid that I wouldn't be able to let you have a loan even so.'

Jenny burst into tears, sobbing loud and long.

Arthur was horribly embarrassed, fiddling with his collar and wishing the earth would swallow him up, but not knowing what to say or do to comfort Jenny. He passed her a handkerchief, which Jenny used gratefully. Eventually, the torrent of tears subsided.

'I am sorry Arthur. I just do not know where to turn. I don't want to sell my businesses, as that is how I make my money which will help pay off my loan.'

Arthur thought for a while. 'There is one way around this. A way that would get you a loan.'

'Yes?' said Jenny hopefully.

'I could borrow a loan in my name, and then give the money to you.'

'Could you? Oh, would you Arthur?'

'I would for you Jenny. It is through you that Susy and I met. Nothing that I can do for you would repay you for that. I would gladly lend you the money. But it will have to be between us and no one else. I could be in serious trouble with my bosses if they knew what I had done. I will need a reason for the loan, even so. We will have to think up a credible scheme.'

'What about if you pretend to buy my delivery business, and then I will "buy it back" afterwards, when I have the money again?'

'That will be fine.' Arthur started laughing.

'What is so funny? I don't feel like laughing.'

'If I borrow the money for you, you will get the loan at the staff rate of interest, so it won't cost as much.'

Jenny joined in the laughter.

'That pleases me, to cock a snook at the people who make rules that exclude women. Thank you Arthur, that has really cheered me up. Shall we work out how much we can make the business worth?'

'Yes, I am sure that you will make it a very expensive business, just to make sure that I get a very large loan.'

'Of course. Let's work out some prices.'

The two of them worked amicably, preparing a bill of sale for the delivery business and drafting a contract for Joshua to see. Jenny insisted on this, although Arthur said that it was unnecessary. Jenny wanted to make sure that he would be able to get his money back at any time, and also she would always retain real control of the business.

'I can't thank you enough Arthur. Please don't tell Susy if you can manage it, but if you have to, then that is alright. I wouldn't want to cause a problem between the two of you.'

'I don't often discuss work with Susy. We talk more about our son than anything else nowadays.'

Going home that night, Jenny felt better than she had for many days and it was with a lighter heart that she welcomed her children as they ran to her at the front door.

Chapter 28

Within twelve weeks, Jenny was able to raise enough money to pay the breach of promise settlement to Theo's solicitor. It left her in dire straights. She had sold both of her new shops in Burnley and Blackburn through Joshua, had borrowed a large amount of money from Arthur, emptied her emergency £1000 bank account, and almost emptied her business account. She would have to live very carefully until she could pay off the loan.

As a final piece of revenge, she knocked the price of having the engagement ring altered off the bill, as Theo had never offered reimbursement for it. She included a duplicate copy of the receipt from Nettleton's to show that she had paid the bill herself. It was only a tiny amount, but it made Jenny feel better about the rest of the money. Theo's solicitor made no qualms about it. Theo was probably too embarrassed about it to argue.

The following week, Mary Bruce came to stay. The original date for her holiday with Jenny had had to be delayed as her replacement was taken ill and the holiday had to wait.

The two women had a delightful time and Jenny took a few days off from the shop to be with Mary. She introduced her to Susy and Marian and their children and they all had enjoyable times together; Mary seeming to fit into the close knit friendship that already existed between the other three. When Marian commented on this, Jenny laughingly said that it was because they were all brought up in the workhouse: it led to a bond of kinship.

On one of the days, they all went down Waddington Road to Brungerley Bridge for a picnic with the children. They had an hilarious time: the children splashing and running about in the River Ribble.

During her stay, Mary was introduced to Joshua. After he had gone, Jenny was subjected to a barrage of questions about Joshua from Mary. And the day after, at a business meeting, she received the same barrage of questions from Joshua.

Surprisingly, Joshua became a regular visitor to Jenny's house that week. There was always some trivial reason: a book for Ben on engineering or an invitation for them all to his house for tea. This last excuse for a visit really made Jenny laugh to herself. They had never been in the habit of going to Joshua's house: rather he had always come to their house, as it was more convenient for Jenny.

But visit they did and a good time was had by all. At the end of Mary's stay, Jenny had arranged for Robert to take her home again, but she declined the offer, saying that Joshua had offered to take her instead. Jenny pretended to be surprised, but Mary had some story ready about Joshua having to go to Preston on business. Jenny nodded and said that would be very convenient, but privately thought to herself that in all the years she had known Joshua, he had never gone to Preston on business. But she kept her own counsel.

After Mary had gone, all the family missed her. She had been good fun and the children had adored her. But Jenny promised that she would come again to stay and they were happy with that. It had been a good break for Jenny as well. It had taken her mind off her recent experiences and given her some happy times again.

Following the short break that Mary had caused to Jenny's routine, it was back to a hard grind. Jenny had to make a success of her business, even though she was in financial difficulties. She learnt to make small savings in the way she did business.

One ray of light in the gloom was when she went for her regular monthly visit to Arthur, to repay his loan. Jenny was told that he wasn't available. Jenny panicked. How would she repay this money if Arthur weren't available? She asked the clerk where he was and was told that Arthur had gone home on private family business. Light dawned on Jenny. It must be the baby, coming early. She thanked the clerk and hurried round to Susy's house. Sure enough, Susy was having labour pains.

Arthur was glad to see Jenny. The baby was early by four weeks and Arthur was worried. Jenny did her best to reassure him, but was worried herself. There were soon cries heard from upstairs, and Arthur rushed to the stairs. The midwife was coming downstairs towards them, a big smile on her face.

'You can come up now if you like Mr Butler.'

'How is she? What is it? Is it alive?' blurted out Arthur.

'Goodness, what a lot of questions,' said the midwife, revealing nothing.

Arthur and Jenny followed the midwife into the bedroom and there was Susy propped up on her pillow, with a tiny baby in each arm.

'Twins!' shouted Jenny, the first to recover from the shock. 'Just like me. Are there one of each?'

'No. Both girls and alike as two peas in a pod,' replied the midwife. 'They have beaten the doctor here as well. They weren't waiting for anyone, weren't these two. That is why you went into labour early, Mrs Butler, because of the twins. They often come early.'

'Yes, my twins came early, too,' replied Jenny.

'More twins? You didn't tell me that there were twins in the family, my dear. It wouldn't have been such a shock to me,' replied the midwife.

'The doctor might have known,' replied Susy, 'but as you say, the babies weren't waiting for him.' Susy laughed weakly. Just at that point, the doctor arrived.

'Well, looks like I am too late here,' he joined in the laughter. 'I should have known to get here soon. You were very quick with your first baby if I remember rightly. If you will all leave the room, I will just examine our new mother and then you can come back in.' He chuckled. 'I had a feeling that it was twins, but I thought I had better not say so, in case I was wrong. Have you got names for them yet?'

Both Arthur and Susy laughed. Arthur explained. 'We couldn't decide between Hannah and Lydia if it was a girl, and now we don't need to decide. We got both,' chuckled Arthur.

'Hannah and Lydia it is, then,' said the doctor. 'Now away you go. I need to look at the patient and her two new babies.'

'Does your mother know that you were having pains, Susy?'

'No. It all happened so quickly again. Could you go round and tell her?'

'It would be a pleasure.' Jenny peeped down at her two new nieces and her heart sang for joy. She hurried off to her father and mother-in-law's and told them the good news.

On her way home to tell her children, Jenny was glad for Arthur and Susy and hoped that the children would thrive well, despite their early start. The children were ecstatic to hear that they had not one but two new nieces and pestered Jenny to take them to see Hannah and Lydia as soon as possible.

But only a week after the happy news about the twins, sadness again came to the family. As Jenny was tidying her desk at the end of the day, Robert came rushing into the office.

'Jenny, Jenny, come quickly, Mr Marshall doesn't look well.'

Jenny followed Robert into the back of the shop and down the yard to where the delivery business was situated.

Old Ben Marshall was half lying down on the seat of a carriage. He was clutching his chest and his lips were blue. Mrs Marshall came running in after Jenny and ran to Ben, cradling him in her arms and rocking him like a child.

Ben was trying to speak to his wife, but he couldn't get his breath. Just odd words came out, 'love . . . glad . . .' and then he collapsed.

The doctor arrived within minutes: Robert having sent young Jack to summon him, but it was too late. Ben Marshall had died in his wife's arms, quite peacefully. Mrs Marshall was crying and still rocking him, but the doctor gently moved her away, whilst he made certain that old Ben was dead.

'I think that his heart just gave out,' the doctor said sadly. 'I don't think his body ever got over the effect of living in the workhouse and not getting the proper treatment for his injuries.'

'At least I had these last few years with him,' reflected Mrs Marshall sadly. 'I thought he was dead long since, but he came back to me. I'm grateful for that. Grateful to you as well, Jenny, because you found him for me.' Jenny smiled at her mother-in-law, too choked to say anything.

The doctor arranged for Ben to be taken away and Jenny took Mrs Marshall home with her, after arranging for Robert to go and tell Arthur at the bank, who could go home and tell Susy.

Jenny would tell the children later. For now, her attention must all be focused on Mrs Marshall. She rang Marian, and then her own house, and asked Roger to take the children round to Marian's for the evening. She would collect the children later and tell them at bedtime.

Mrs Marshall was numbed by grief, but glad that she had arrived in time to see him alive. Her tears kept brimming over and reminded Jenny of when she had lost Jonny. Suddenly, Jonny's name was being spoken, and it brought Jenny out of her painful reverie.

'Can he? Can he go in with Jonny in the churchyard?'

'Of course, I would like that. Together again.'

'I think that Ben would have liked that. He often used to go and sit on Jonny's grave you know and tell him what a fine lass you were.'

'I know. I think that you are right. He would like to be with Jonny again.'

The funeral was soon arranged and the whole family felt a mixture of grief that old Ben had died, with a sense of gratefulness that they had had the unexpected bonus of spending the last few years together again. Jenny felt extra grief when Jonny's grave was opened up again to receive her father-in-law, but she tried to be strong for the children, who had only fairly recently come to know their grandfather.

Old Mrs Marshall didn't seem to pick up after the funeral, but slipped more and more into herself, as she had done in the workhouse after little Martin's death, Jonny and Susy's younger brother.

Susy and Jenny met regularly to talk about what could be done. Mrs Marshall was neglecting herself and her house, which she had been so proud of previously. Both Jenny and Susy would gladly have taken her into their homes, but she was stubborn and didn't want any help from her daughter and daughter-in-law. Eventually Susy had an idea. She told her mother that she was having difficulty coping with the twins and little Jonny, who was still only a toddler. Susy asked her mother if she could possibly come and live with them to help her.

The ploy worked. Mrs Marshall came to live with Susy and although she did very little in the house, she felt that she was helping Susy. It also meant that Susy could keep an eye on her mother, without seeming to. It was an ideal solution all round. However, Mrs Marshall never really recovered from her husband's death, and six months later, in the beginning of 1897, she joined him in the family grave.

Susy felt bereft, as she now had no living relatives apart from her own children and her nieces and nephews, and Jenny supported her through the first few difficult months.

In the early months of the New Year, Jenny had two weddings to plan. One that gave her great joy and one that gave her a sense of unease.

The first one was between Joshua and Mary Bruce. This wedding delighted Jenny as she had introduced them. It also made her feel less guilty that she had refused Joshua earlier. Seeing the couple together, it was obvious that they were made for each other.

Jenny was delighted to make the wedding plan for them as her wedding present to the happy couple. The wedding took place at Fulwood church, near to Sharoe Green workhouse in Preston. Jenny's two daughters were again called upon to be flower girls, which delighted them both. Even Ben had a role to play. He guided all the guests to their seats in the church.

After the wedding, the couple spent two weeks down in Hereford, visiting Joshua's relatives. After their honeymoon, the happy couple returned to Sabden where Joshua lived. Mary Briggs seemed to have become more beautiful since her marriage and Jenny was delighted for them both.

Jenny was not delighted about the next wedding that she was asked to plan, but couldn't refuse an old customer. Lady Jolley had been one of Jenny's first gentry customers when she opened the shop. She had four young daughters; two sets of twins. Within one year between 1894 and 1895, Jenny had planned weddings for the first three of her daughters, Rebecca, Charlotte and Rachel. All three girls had then presented their husbands with a boy within the first year of their marriage. Lady Jolley seemed to be a regular customer for many months for either wedding outfits or christening outfits. But Jessica had not married: because she was too choosy, her mother said.

Now Jessica was betrothed, and Lady Jolley wanted yet another wedding to be planned. Jenny was happy for her until she heard the name of the bridegroom. It was Lord Jeremy Ormerod, her half brother who had treated his first wife so cruelly, and was hardly out of mourning.

Jenny managed to keep her face from registering any shock when Lady Jolley told her the name of the groom and continued planning the wedding. Eventually, Jenny's half-sister, Morag came to request an outfit for her brother's wedding.

During the fitting, Morag started to talk about the bride-to-be.

'Jessica is such a lively girl. I have never seen Jeremy so enamoured of anyone. He is completely besotted. It is quite funny to see him following her around the room, like a faithful retriever dog,' said Morag laughing.

Jenny smiled, but made no comment.   Morag looked at her, obviously expecting a comment.

'What is the matter Jenny? Do you not approve of this marriage?'

'It is not for me to approve or disapprove,' replied Jenny stiffly.

'So you do not approve? I can tell by your voice.'

'I remember Lady Hortense.'

'Yes, I suppose you do. But Jessica is a different girl. Hortense was weak and allowed herself to be bullied by Jeremy. He needs a woman to stand up to him. Jessica will do that, I can tell. She orders him around already and he just does what she says.'

'I hope she does, then' said Jenny, not convinced by this, but keeping her own counsel. Time would tell and she would reserve judgement.

'I think that he is attracted by the fact that her sisters all produced boys within a year of their marriage. He is so desperate for an heir.'

'Yes,' replied Jenny abstractedly, remembering that Jeremy had arranged for Marian's little boy to be snatched by a ruffian, just because he wanted an heir. But she didn't mention that to Morag.

Lady Morag left soon afterwards, but the knowledge of the wedding hung heavily on Jenny's mind for some time. She almost felt like telling Lady Jolley what Lord Jeremy was capable of, but it would be difficult without revealing her source of knowledge, and would be betraying the confidence that was inherent when working for a family.

Jenny soon had nicer events to take over her thoughts. It was the old Queen Victoria's diamond jubilee celebrations in June. The town was having parties and putting trimmings up and the parish council were looking for ways to celebrate this special occasion. Jenny decided that she would do a display in the shop.

A competition was held amongst the staff to design a window dressing in commemoration of the jubilee. On the day itself, Jenny trimmed the whole shop up and the staff wore bright red, white and blue sashes. Jenny provided free drinks and biscuits for all their customers on that day, and a happy carefree atmosphere prevailed all day. The shop closed early so that the staff could attend other celebrations that were taking place in the town.

The winner of the competition was young Josephine. In her years with the shop, she had developed immensely. She showed a talent for design and an eye for detail. Josephine was allowed to set up the window and following this, she was promoted to work with the team led by Catherine, Marian's chief designer and seamstress.

Josephine was delighted by this upturn in her career and worked even harder to achieve her goal to open a shop and design her own clothes eventually. Jenny was glad that she had rescued Josephine from the workhouse and continued to use girls from there as her main source of staff.

It was particularly pleasing therefore, to get a letter from the workhouse shortly after the jubilee. It requested the pleasure of Mrs Jenny Marshall to join the Board of Governors at Clitheroe Workhouse. Jenny was ecstatic. She rang Joshua immediately, assuming that he had arranged it for her. But she was pleasantly surprised.

'No, my dear, nothing to do with me. It was Captain Parker that recommended you. Although I did vote for you,' Joshua chuckled. 'By the way, my dear lady wife is coming into your shop today. Are you available for her?'

'I certainly am. I am available for Mary anytime. Is she requiring anything in particular?'

'Do not ask me, a mere man. I am sure there will be some frippery that she urgently needs. Although I must say, she is not in the least extravagant.'

'That is the workhouse training for you. None of us had urgent needs; they were never met anyway,' laughed Jenny. 'When is the next meeting of the Board of Governors?'

'Not until next month. They will send you the notice about two weeks before. May I pick you up and escort you to your first meeting?'

'Oh yes please. I would really appreciate that. It would give me more confidence if you were with me.'

Joshua laughed. 'You! More confidence? I think that you have quite enough confidence to do all that you do.'

'It will help me, nevertheless. Thank you, Joshua.'

Only a short while later, Janey knocked on Jenny's door to say that Mrs Briggs was here and could she see you. Jenny went down into the shop to welcome Mary and they went to the tearoom for hot chocolate.

Mary confided to Jenny the real reason for her visit. She had been to the doctors and he had confirmed that she was expecting her first baby.

'I am so pleased for you,' said Jenny. 'I have just been talking to Joshua and he never mentioned it.'

'He doesn't know. I didn't want to tell him until I was absolutely sure. I have been to the doctor this morning and he has just confirmed it. I am so excited I had to tell someone. Don't tell Joshua that I told you first, though.'

'Of course not. But I know that he will be pleased. He will make a lovely father.'

'Yes, he will, but I will probably not be allowed out of the house until it is safely born, if I know him,' laughed Mary.

'Just tell him that I ran a shop whilst I was having all my children and never came to any harm,' suggested Jenny.

'I will try, but you tell him as well, so that I can get out now and then. Now perhaps I should be looking around your department for ladies who are to be confined?'

'Not yet. Tell Joshua first and then come another day. That will be your excuse to get out of the house,' replied Jenny laughingly.

'I think that I will go to his office now. Perhaps he will take me out for lunch and I can tell him then.'

'Good idea. Why don't you telephone him from here?'

'Oh thank you.' Jenny passed the telephone to Mary and soon she was out of the office going to meet Joshua. Jenny watched her go out of the office and was pleased for her friend. Another christening robe to be made, she thought, but not for a little while yet.

Chapter 29

Over the next two years, Jenny slowly paid off her debts by sheer hard work and painful economies. There were times when she got fed up of all the pressure to make money, but the need to be without debt drove her on. As she had fairly recently refurbished her shop and bought all new uniforms for the staff, she was able to spend virtually nothing on buildings, repairs and staff uniforms for some time.

Thankfully, she did not see Theo during this time. She avoided going to any balls, dinners or any other venue where she would be liable to see him. One of her customers told her that he was engaged to be married and there was to be the briefest of engagements before the nuptials. His money must be running out again, thought Jenny cynically, he must have spent my money already. The lady in question was a rich heiress from Derbyshire, so she would come highly recommended to Theo, thought Jenny.

The only sadness from that episode in her life was that she never saw her godson, Richy. Jenny and Mildred did keep in touch, but it was brief and superficial contact, after the closeness that they had shared whilst Mildred lived in the Clitheroe area.

The children were often frustrated by Jenny's economies during those years, but although they didn't understand the full necessity for it, they learned to live without the luxuries they were used to.

Each month, it gave her great pleasure to personally take the repayment to Arthur, usually going to his home rather than his bank. Eventually, the great day came when she had paid the last instalment and Arthur tore up the agreement that said that he was the owner of her delivery business.

Now she could start to rebuild the emergency £1000 fund that would make her feel more secure and less likely to end up back in the workhouse, whatever happened. On the day that she finally achieved her £1000, she took treats home for the children and ordered a sumptuous tea from Cook. Now that she was more financially secure, she might even buy Ellen a pony at long last. Although the children all seemed to be more interested in their bicycles than ponies nowadays.

The following Sunday, she arranged a tea for Susy and Arthur and Joshua and Mary Briggs, as a thank you for all their hard work in helping her overcome her problems from the breach of promise settlement. Never again would she be caught up in a situation like that. She would never remarry.

The party was a riotous success: the house alive with children. Joshua and Mary now had two small children. A toddler called Henry, named after Mr Shoesmith, Joshua's former partner, and a new baby girl called Cynthia. As well as Jonny, Hannah and Lydia, Susy and Arthur now had another little boy called Geoffrey. With her own three children, it was a noisy affair, but Jenny revelled in spending time with these precious friends and relatives.

Ben was telling them about his new school He had recently commenced at the Grammar School in York Street in Clitheroe and was enjoying it, although he found some of the work a little hard. Rachel was envious of her brother as there was no equivalent school for the girls. She had made an increased campaign to leave school when Ben went to the Grammar School, as she was beyond the usual school leaving age for most children. But Jenny had insisted that she stay on for a few more years.

A few weeks later, Ben brought a letter home from school, requesting that Jenny attend a meeting at the school, to discuss Ben's progress. Jenny was instantly suspicious and asked Ben if he had been in any mischief. He vehemently denied it, so Jenny had to wait for the meeting.

The meeting was at five of the clock, so Jenny went straight from the shop. She gave her name in to the school administrator and he asked Jenny to sit in the foyer and wait for Mr Taggart, the head of the English department. For some reason, Jenny expected a head of department to be a crusty old man, so she got a surprise when a lively young man bounced into the foyer.

'Mrs Marshall? Philip Taggart at your service. Thank you for coming in to see me. Do come this way. The headmaster has given me permission to use his office – a rare honour I must say. Mrs Marshall? Are you unwell?'

Jenny pulled herself together and stood up. 'No I am fine, Mr Taggart,' she said with as calm a voice as she could muster. She followed him down the corridor to the headmaster's office, glad of the respite from looking at this young man. Besides his piercing blue eyes, he had floppy fair hair and an engaging grin that lit up his whole face. He was just above medium height, but held himself very well, giving an impression of being taller than he was.

'Do sit down. I have been ordered to give you tea. I trust that is acceptable?'

Jenny nodded, unable to think coherently. She was mesmerised by this man and she had only just met him. She accepted the cup of tea from him and tried to concentrate on what he was saying.

Apparently Ben was doing very well in all his subjects, especially maths, drawing and physics, which would make him an excellent engineer, but he was not doing very well with his English. This would hamper him in the event of his going to university later.

'Do you understand me, Mrs Marshall?'

'Er, yes, but he often reads books. Surely that will help his English?'

'With all due respect, Mrs Marshall, what kind of books is he reading?'

Jenny thought for a moment. 'I suppose that he only reads books about engineering,' she replied lamely, 'that is all I can get him interested in.'

'Precisely. That is the problem. I can't get him to realise that he needs to have a wider knowledge of basic literature if he is to go to university. That is where the future is for engineering; a university based education that concentrates on sciences instead of languages and the classics. But the professors still demand a great knowledge of the classics for university entrance.'

'What would you suggest, then?'

'I would recommend some extra coaching lessons. I know it is some years before he goes to university, but he needs to work hard from now on to get up to standard.'

'Would you be available to coach him?' Jenny found herself asking.

'That may be possible, but I would have to ask the headmaster first. I would have to make it all above board.'

'Of course,' replied Jenny, 'I wouldn't want to compromise you.'

'I will ask the headmaster tomorrow and see if he is agreeable.'

'Thank you. That would be most satisfactory,' replied Jenny.

'Well, that would be a satisfactory solution as I am his form leader this year, so I can supervise him more closely at school as well. I will contact you as soon as I have a decision.' Mr Taggart jumped up, grasped Jenny's hand and shook it with a firm grip, leaving Jenny a little breathless.

'Thank you for taking an interest in Ben. I appreciate that,' said Jenny, remembering her manners.

'It is my pleasure. Ben seems to like talking to me.' No wonder, thought Jenny to herself. I quite like talking to you, but for different reasons than Ben. Finding herself blushing at her thoughts, Jenny quickly got up and walked away from Mr Taggart.

'I will look forward to hearing the headmaster's decision,' she managed to say as he helped her through the door. On the street outside the school, Jenny took a deep breath. What a lovely man. He seemed to have such energy and made you feel he was interested in everything that you had said.

Jenny shook herself. What was the matter with her tonight? She had no intention of getting interested in any man, especially after the fiasco with Theo. Besides, Mr Taggart was probably married with six children, she chided herself. No, if he helped Ben with his work, then she would be grateful, but that is as far as it would go.

As it happened, Jenny's thoughts were taken away from Ben and his schoolteacher by unwelcome news from afar. Her deputy, Sarah, had a letter from her fiancé. He had been hurt in a skirmish in the Boer country and had lost an arm. He was being invalided out of the army and coming home. Sarah was beside herself with worry and Jenny promised her that she could have some time off with him when he came home.

The more welcome news came a few days later. Mr Taggart had permission to give extra lessons to Ben, if Jenny was agreeable. Oh yes, I am agreeable, thought Jenny privately to herself, but merely wrote a polite acceptance to Mr Taggart, inviting him to tea the following week, to discuss the programme.

That afternoon, Jenny left the shop early and changed out of her work clothes, putting on a day dress that was just a trifle more elegant than she would usually wear for tea. She just hoped her children wouldn't make comments and embarrass her. Fortunately, they behaved for once.

Ben was fairly subdued with his teacher being there, anyway. Jenny sent the children out to play whilst she talked with Mr Taggart and drew up a plan of work. Ben was then invited back in again so that he could see what was planned. Jenny was amazed how he responded to Mr Taggart when they were on their own. It was obvious that Ben had great respect for this man.

Jenny suggested that the lessons took place at her house so that Ben would not have to walk home on his own. Mr Taggart readily agreed. His lodgings were not conducive to coaching pupils and his landlady would not be too keen on the idea, he said.

Jenny's heart lifted. Lodgings. Landlady. No wife then, not that she was interested, she tried to tell herself. But as the weeks passed, Jenny came to admire this man more and more. Eventually one evening, when they had got to know each other a little better, he asked her about Jonny.

'Ben told me his father was killed some years ago. Does it offend you if I ask you about him?'

'No, it doesn't offend me at all. Jonny was a good man. A good husband and father.'

'How did he die?'

'He was run over by a horse,' said Jenny flatly.

'That was awful. What happened?'

'A child ran out in front of a horse and he was passing, so went and dragged the child to safety.'

'Did the child survive?'

'Yes.'

'But not your husband?'

'No.'

'It must have been awful. How did you some to terms with such a tragic occurrence?'

'It was hard. I just curled up in bed and wanted to die myself. Even the children couldn't bring me out of myself. My mother-in-law and sister-in-law looked after the children and the shop, even though they were grieving themselves.'

'So what made you come out of yourself?'

'I started thinking about the little girl. How she had lived because Jonny had died. Then it made me think about the lessons we learnt at church. That we only live because Jesus died for us. That made me able to go on. That my Jonny had given his life for the little girl, like Jesus. It made me feel better. I asked to see the little girl and after that, I started living again.' Jenny dropped her head into her hands, fighting back the tears.

'I know how you feel.'

'Do you? Why? How can you know what I went through?'

'Because I went through a similar experience.'

'You did? What happened?'

'I was engaged to be married. We were very happy. We knew that we would never be rich, with me being a schoolteacher, but she was a pupil teacher and our dream was to start our own school for poor children. I say a dream because we would never have had any money.' He seemed to be desperately trying to keep hold of his feelings.

Jenny sat silently, feeling for this man, who had also suffered like her. Eventually, he recovered himself and told her that his fiancée had developed consumption and died quite quickly.

'I am sorry. It is hard to love and then lose them, isn't it?'

'Yes, it makes you never want to love again, in case you get hurt.' Jenny nodded in agreement.

'I am sorry Mrs Marshall; I have been a little morbid tonight. Not my usual jovial self.'

'I understand. And my name is Jenny. You don't have to be jovial here. You are amongst friends. Tell me about your family.'

'Only if you promise to call me Philip,' he teased, completely recovered again.

'Philip it is then,' Jenny replied.

'I am the youngest of four sons. That is why I will never have any money. We have followed the traditional route for families. My eldest brother, Alexander is the heir to my father's estate. He is a gentleman farmer. Then there is Gregory, who has gone into the army. Then there is Thomas who has gone into the church, and then me. The one who has to earn his living in another way.'

'So that is why you teach?'

'No. I would have taught anyway. I just love taking young minds and introducing them to knowledge.'

'What made you come to Clitheroe? Where do you come from?'

'From Durham. I came to this new position after Amelia died. I wanted to get away from the area where we lived and worked.'

'I can understand that. I couldn't get away. My only livelihood was in the shop, so I had to stay.'

'What about your family? Do they live locally?'

'I have no family really. Just a few half brothers and sisters that I don't acknowledge.'

'Why ever not?'

'They would not recognise me. I am a child born out of wedlock, from a maid and her master.'

'A common story. How did you get the shop then?'

'My mother's protector bought her a shop and I inherited it three years after his death.'

'Why three years?'

'I don't know, I suppose it was so that no one would connect him with the inheritance. The only man who knew anything about it was his solicitor, who died without revealing any information to me.'

'At least he must have looked after your mother, to buy her a shop?'

'Yes, I think that he really loved her.'

'You sound resentful?'

'He took me to work for him in his house. Rescued me from the workhouse where I had been left after my mother died. He even made me look after his ailing wife. And all that time, he never gave me even a hint that he was my father.'

'You have had a sad life, Jenny, but you have obviously made up for it.'

'Yes, I have had great sadness, but I have also had great joy, like you.'

'Thank you for sharing your story, Jenny. If ever I feel down, I will remember that you have also suffered and I will feel better for remembering my friend.'

Jenny smiled. Something had happened here tonight. A deep bond had formed between them, even though neither had said anything to the other. She thought about Philip and his story for a long time that night and decided that she would try and help him as much as she could.

And when he was ready to start a school in Clitheroe, she would have a ready-made pupil teacher for him. Marian's boy, Luke. He too, desperately wanted to be a teacher and would soon be old enough to start work. She could see Luke and Philip working well together. They were two of a kind. A way with children and people, and a thirst to pass on their knowledge.

The next day, Jenny got a message from Sarah. Her fiancé Andrew had arrived home to his mother's house in Whalley, a nearby village. Sarah wanted to go immediately to see him and Jenny gave her a week's holiday.

'You can have longer, if you need it,' she shouted as Sarah rushed out of the office, 'and if there is anything I can do to help ....,' but Sarah had gone.

It was two weeks later that Sarah returned to the shop. She asked Jenny for an appointment.

'Now what is it Sarah?'

'I am getting married to Andrew. As soon as we can arrange it. But I would like to keep my job if I may, because Andrew won't be able to work. Not for a while anyway. Or ever, possibly.'

'How badly affected is he?'

'The wound is healed, but he is very low in spirit. He feels useless. The army has been his life and now he feels that he won't be able to support me.'

'Sarah, the manager of the delivery business has just left. Do you remember, the one that I took on after my father-in-law died?' Sarah nodded. 'Robert hates doing the business side of the work. Could Andrew do that, do you think?'

'Easily,' replied Sarah, 'he was in a cavalry division and his job was responsibility for horses and getting equipment moved around. It would be ideal, and it would give him a chance to feel useful again. That would be perfect. A real wedding present to both of us.'

'That is settled then. It makes it easier for me as well. I don't need to look out for a new manager. Robert will be delighted. Tell Andrew to come and see me as soon as he can. Now before we get down to planning your wedding, there is another thing that I wish to discuss with you. We need to come up with a good idea for New Years Eve. It is such an important time, going into a new century. We need to make the start of the twentieth century memorable for all our staff and the town. What can we do?'

'That will take a lot of thought. Why not ask the staff in the shop again? It worked for the jubilee celebrations.'

'That is a good idea. I will put up a notice in the staff room. It will be very exciting, won't it? The twentieth century, it sounds so different. So much is happening to our world, so many changes, who knows what will happen in this next century.'

'I agree, now what about my wedding? That is the most exciting thing for me before this twentieth century starts.'

Jenny laughed and got out her planning books. An hour later, Jenny was left on her own again as a bright eyed Sarah went off to Whalley to tell Andrew the good news.

Reflections of the way her life had changed began to invade Jenny's mind. New babies in the family; new godchildren; proposals of marriage; the breach of promise settlement; death of her in-laws;

new friends; marriages; the moving platform at the shop. So much in so few years.

The world itself was changing too. England was at war; she had an old Queen, who surely could not live much longer. Her son would be a very different monarch and bring England into a new era. And there were so many new inventions nowadays. It was hard to keep up with all the new fangled machinery that was being invented. Who would have thought that horseless carriages would ever be popular, and yet they seemed to be taking over the roads, to the detriment of the horse and carriage.

The New Year and the dawn of the new century kept returning to Jenny's thoughts. What changes would happen to her in this new century? So many changes had happened to her in the last few years.

And what changes would occur with her children? And her shop? To Clitheroe and the world around her? And more importantly, what changes would occur between her and Philip? Their relationship was growing deeper and deeper and yet there was no hurry. They had been frightened to love deeply again, but it had happened without their consent, as they had been slowly but inexorably drawn closer together.

This love was new and different from the love that she had had for Jonny. It was slower but stronger from having been born of previous pain.

Yes, Jenny was looking forward to the new century with expectation and joy and a great deal of hope. And she knew that whatever changes came her way, she would take up the challenge as she always had. Changes? Why, she positively thrived on them!